One of the tanks pulled itself out of the line and drove up in front of us. It was a big slab of a thing, fully ten meters long and four wide. The machine was absolutely silent. The huge monster could have snuck up on a mouse, if there had been any such creature on New Kashubia.

"Number 04056239, you are hereby inducted into the service of the Kashubian Expeditionary Forces, and into the Croatian branch of that service, to which you will give all of your loyalty. Do you now swear loyalty to the Kashubian Armed Forces?" The sergeant recited it like a fixed formula.

"I SO SWEAR," the tank answered.

"Welcome into the service. Open up."

The tank did an about-face in front of us, and this big coffin-looking thing slid out of the rear of it.

"Get in there, kid," the sergeant said, "and I'll hook you up."

"You are swearing in the tank, but not me?" I said, amazed.

"Kid, if your tank is loyal, you don't have to be. Get in."

BAEN BOOKS by LEO FRANKOWSKI

A Boy and His Tank

The Fata Morgana

LEO FRANKOWSKI

A Baen Books Original

Baen Publishing Enterprises
P.O. Box 1403
Riverdale, NY 10471

ISBN: 0-671-57850-2

Cover art by Gary Ruddell

First paperback printing, February 2000

Library of Congress Catalog Number 98-51933

Distributed by Simon & Schuster
1230 Avenue of the Americas
New York, NY 10020

Typeset by Windhaven Press, Auburn, NH
Printed in the United States of America

Dedication

I'd like to dedicate this book to Owen Lock, who was for many years my editor at Del Rey. He's a VP at Random House these days, and no longer directly concerned with science fiction. Thus, I can now thank him for his long years of patience, sound advice, and friendship without it looking like I'm kissing ass. For many things, Owen, thank you.

—Leo Frankowski

Acknowledgements

This book was a long time in the writing, and a lot of people generously lent me a hand in getting it done. So many, in fact, that I don't see how I can properly thank all of them. But if I don't try, I'll end up offending everybody I know instead of just most of them. So.

To Debbie Haberland for proofreading an earlier version of this and several other books. To L. Warren Douglas for the encouragement, the support and the beer. To Alan Greenberg, Gilbert Parker, Jane Devlin, Mike Hubble, Joe Ainu, and others for proofreading, encouragement, and friendship. To Halina Harding for keeping me alive the entire time. To Tom Devlin for giving my aging computer CPR when it died, several times and at the worst possible moments, and with the aid of various spells and potions restoring it to life. To Gene Wolfe for permission to repeat a conversation I overheard in a bar. To Harry Turtledove for clearing up an annoying historical point. To Glen Horning, for aid when it really counted. And to Toni Weisskopf and Jim Baen for buying the thing and getting it out to you. To all of you, my very sincere thanks.

Very special thanks are owed to Sgt. James Coop, Co. C Task Force, 1-32 Armor, First Cavalry Division, for proofreading an earlier version of this book while sitting in the desert waiting for Desert Storm to happen. Some twenty of his friends wrote up their comments as well, and included them with the manuscript when they mailed it back to me. The Post Office managed to demolish the package and all of their valuable comments were lost. All I got back was bits and pieces of the brown paper cover held together by forty yards of clear tape, and the computer printout of the manuscript. By the time it got back to me and my letter got back to them, the war was over, and the men were scattered. The advice of the real professionals was lost to me, and I'm sure that this book suffers because of it.

Then I compounded the tragedy by personally managing to lose the list of the names of the soldiers who had tried to help. I'm sorry, guys. It's all my fault.

Finally, no thanks at all are owed to the SOB of a Physicist from the Warren Tank Plant who borrowed a copy of the manuscript from me at Tudor's Tavern last year. He never was seen again, nor was my manuscript. If some of my ideas start showing up on the latest tanks, well, you'll know where they swiped them from.

Leo Frankowski
Sterling Heights
November 21, 1998

Author's Note for *A Boy and His Tank*

This book was a long time coming.

I've never met two authors who used the same technique in getting things written. Personally, I use something akin to Method Acting, or maybe it's a form of benign schizophrenia, but I sort of become my narrator and the other main characters in the book. This imposes certain limitations on my work. For one thing, I'm largely limited to first person writing. For another, I have to be careful of my characters, since I often forget and stay in character when I get up from my desk. If my protagonist was a real mental case, I just might end up in jail.

In the late eighties, I became impressed with David Drake's *Hammer's Slammers*, and I wanted to write something where my mercenary heroes went around blowing up the countryside in super tanks.

In return for nothing more than money, a mercenary volunteers to kill people who haven't done much to harm him or his family, and to take his chances of being on the receiving end of pain, disfigurement, and death while dishing the same out.

A person accepting such a job might be so poor that his immediate family is at risk of starving to death. Faced with his wife and children dying, a man would likely be willing to do what he has to in order to keep his people alive.

Or he might be someone who really enjoys butchering people and thinks that getting paid for it besides is just wonderful. That is to say, he is simply out of his mind, and in a most unpleasant way.

Since it is illegal to starve to death in America, only the

second group is available to man the few American mercenary outfits that exist. I have met such people. You wouldn't want one living on your street. They are scary.

(Understand that I am not talking about soldiers, people who serve in the regular armed forces of their country. Such individuals are often among the best that our race produces.)

Needless to say, I couldn't write about such group two mercenaries and still be fit (or even safe) company. My heroes would have to come from group one.

This left me with the problem of, if my heroes were so damn poor, how could they afford all those multimillion-dollar super tanks? This got me into the long and strange history of the Wealthy Nations Group and the New Kashubians.

Then there was the question of whose territory I was going to have these sterling troops desecrate.

Well, back in the late eighties, it was obvious to anyone not in the government that Yugoslavia was an explosion impatiently waiting to happen. I mean, most countries have a minority group or two, but Yugoslavia had so many mutually belligerent minority groups that they didn't have enough people left over to form a *majority* group. This made them an ideal candidate for starting any number of territorial wars. Also, having Kashubian Poles, Serbians, and Croatians in the same book would give me lots of opportunities to display the various aspects of the Slavic character.

Thus prepared, I went about my trade of making esthetically pleasing marks on clean, white paper. I had the book about ninety percent done when those unspeakable Yugos, *completely without my permission*, went and started their war two hundred years early and on the wrong damn planet, besides.

Please understand that historical and technical accuracy is supremely important to me. Unless my own disbelief is completely suspended, I can't write at all. With a war going on, all bets on the future history of Yugoslavia were off. If the Serbs, say, were wiped out, the character of Yugoslavia would be totally altered. Hell, I couldn't be sure that there would even *be* a Yugoslavia two hundred years hence.

Fruitless months went by when nothing useful appeared

on my computer screen. Finally, I set the book aside, and went to work on *The Fata Morgana*. This book, too, was approaching completion when it too had to be delayed. I had some medical problems and was generally unable to sit at my computer, let alone push the buttons in any meaningful manner.

Years later, my health started to return about the same time as my bank account was running dry and the landlord was getting uppity. I did the obvious thing, completely rewrote *A Boy and His Tank*, and at long last you have it in your hands.

Enjoy.

Leo Frankowski
August 1, 1998
Sterling Heights

CHAPTER ONE
HOW I VOLUNTEERED FOR THE ARMY
CA. 2162 A.D.

They sentenced me to death and then told me that I had my choice of either being rendered down so that my body's chemicals could fertilize the hydroponic vats, or joining the army.

I picked the army, but I soon learned that I had screwed up again.

Within an hour, they had given me a bath and shaved my head, and I found myself walking naked down a chilly tunnel up in the high gravity of the palladium layer. Twenty meters in diameter to match the bore of the huge Japanese ore drilling machines, the floor had been leveled by an equally bodacious milling robot, and the shiny metallic walls seemed to stretch on to infinity. Filling this tunnel with air must have cost a bundle.

The guards left me with a sergeant who was standing in front of a long row of military tanks. I could tell he was a sergeant because there were a lot of stripes on his armband. Aside from the armband and his sandals, he was as naked as I was. New Kashubia wasn't wealthy enough to afford clothes for most people.

I figured that I'd better try and get on the guy's good side as soon as possible, so I saluted him.

He looked at me and said, "Don't salute until you know how to do it. Anyway, you don't salute a sergeant."

"Yes, sir."

"And you don't call an NCO 'sir.'" He looked at his clipboard. "You're Mickolai Derdowski?"

"Yes."

"Then put your right thumbprint here."

When I'd done as he'd asked, he checked his clipboard again.

"Number 04056239!" He shouted, "It's your turn! Front and center!"

One of the tanks pulled itself out of the line and drove up in front of us. It was a big slab of a thing, fully ten meters long and four wide. It was maybe a meter thick, and rode about twenty centimeters off the floor on treads that were nothing but unconnected bars that floated out of two slots in the front of the tank. They placed themselves in front of the machine as it floated over them, then lifted off the floor and went back into slots in the back of the tank once it had passed by. They didn't seem to be connected to anything at all! Some kind of magnetic trick, I guessed.

The tank was completely flat on the bottom and top, with absolutely nothing but one little bump on the left front corner to break the flat expanse of highly polished metal. The four sides sloped inwards at forty-five degree angles, and they were as bright and featureless as the rest of the vehicle. My uncle had once told me that these tanks had interchangeable weaponry. They could attach any combination of guns and whatnot that the mission required, so the lack of visible weapons didn't surprise me. What I couldn't figure out was where the driver sat, and how he could see out of the thing.

The machine was absolutely silent. I tell you that the huge monster could have snuck up on a mouse, if there had been any such creature on New Kashubia.

"Number 04056239, you are hereby inducted into the service of the Kashubian Expeditionary Forces, and into the Croatian branch of that service, to which you will give all of your loyalty. Your combat data code will be number 58294, and you will now permanently erase all other codes from your memory. Do you now swear loyalty to the Kashubian Armed Forces?" The sergeant recited it like a fixed formula.

"I SO SWEAR," the tank answered in a small, tinny voice.

"Welcome into the service. Open up."

The tank did an about-face in front of us, and this big coffin-looking thing slid out of the rear of it.

"Get in there, kid," the sergeant said, "And I'll hook you up."

"You are swearing in the tank, but not me?" I said, amazed.

"Kid, if your tank is loyal, you don't have to be. Get in."

"I don't like the looks of this."

"Nobody does, at first. Eventually, you'll learn to love it. Think of it as a womb with a view."

"I'll bet you tell that to all the boys," I said, stalling for time.

"Right, but then I don't get to hook up the girls who volunteer, more's the pity. Look, kid, get in there. It's that or the hydroponic vats."

Considering the alternatives, I got in, and laid down on the pleasantly warm metal surface. That surprised me. I'd expected it to be cold.

"First, we got to hook up these catheters to your privy members. Spread your legs. Relax! Just remember that I'm not enjoying this any more than you are."

There was a long hose with a complicated-looking rubber thing on the end which he proceeded to smear with some sort of grease and fit into my penis and tail pipe. I didn't like it.

"Shouldn't you tell me about how I work this thing?"

"Kid, did you ever have a personal computer?"

"Yes, three years ago, back on Earth."

"Then you know that the first thing it did was to teach you how to operate it. Well, the computer in this tank has your old toy computer beat all hollow. It really is sentient, or so close to it that you'll never know the difference. It'll teach you everything that you need to know. Sit up." I guess I already knew that, but I wasn't thinking so good just then.

I sat, and he glued a wide strip of something flexible to the top of my head, over the back of my neck, and down the middle of my back.

"This is an electrical induction pickup that will be your major means of communication with the on-board computer. It doesn't come off, and in time, it will grow itself right through your skin. It won't even leave a scar. The old models have to be inserted surgically, but you lucked out. This baby is right off the production line."

"Do you mind if I don't feel grateful?" I said.

"Not in the least. After today, I'll never see you again, if I'm lucky."

He pulled a sort of helmet out of a nearby rack. It was solid metal all over, and covered the whole head and face. It didn't have any eyeslits or even a way to breathe, from the looks of it. Just a complicated connector on the left side.

"You look to be a size fourteen L, but we'll make sure," he said as he attached a hose and cable connector from the tank to the helmet. He put it on my head, and a sort of collar in the bottom of the helmet inflated snug to my neck, which was scary. There were some kind of viewing screens right in front of my eyes. I found myself watching him adjusting the thing to my head, from the perspective of some camera that I hadn't noticed on the top of the tank. After a bit, I inhaled and found that I could breathe, which was a major relief. Fortunately, claustrophobia was never one of my problems. People with that particular hangup don't last very long in the tunnels of New Kashubia.

THE FIT IS PROPER, SERGEANT, said a tinny computer voice in my ear.

"Very good," I heard the sergeant say. "Lie back down, kid. You can button it up, lady, and fill his compartment."

I watched myself going feet-first into the back of the machine, feeling like a human suppository. Once I was completely inside, I felt the box I was in being filled with a warm fluid. Claustrophobia or no claustrophobia, I didn't like this one bit!

"Can I change my mind about going to the hydroponic vats?" I shouted into the helmet.

"Forget it, kid." I heard the sergeant say. Through the tank's cameras, I watched him walk away. Then he turned and said, "One last thing. If you get along with your computer, things can get very nice for you, believe me. But if you fight her, you will live your life in a very special part of hell! Good-bye, and good luck, soldier!"

"Good-bye, go to the devil and I hope he shoots you!" I shouted back. He didn't turn around, and I found out later that the tank's computer had censored my parting comment to him. Maybe it was just as well.

The coffin I was in finished filling with the warm liquid, and I found myself floating comfortably. Or it would have been comfortable if I didn't know that I was submerged in water and sealed inside of I-didn't-know-how-many centimeters of armor. If the machine ever quit working, I'd smother to death in a minute! They were gambling my one and only life on somebody else's engineering, and I did not in any way approve of this practice!

Through the camera, I could see that the tank had put itself back into line with the others, and the sergeant was getting a thumbprint from the next "volunteer."

Then the scene changed and I was watching this very attractive woman on some kind of recording. I could tell that she wasn't a New Kashubian, since she was wearing clothes, Earth-style clothes of ten years ago. I listened to her, since it sure beat thinking about my currently unsolvable predicament.

"Welcome to your new Mark XIX Main Battle Tank, the Aggressor," she said with a bright, artificial smile. "You are one of an elite corps of warriors privileged to operate the finest fighting machine . . ."

If I'd had a switch, I would have switched her off right then, but she droned on because there was nothing I could do about it. She'd blown my suspension of disbelief in her second sentence with that "elite corps" bullshit, and from then on only bits of her spiel got through to me.

" . . . powered by a muon exchange fusion plant that is fueled for twenty standard years at full load and operates at almost one hundred percent efficiency. This, coupled with superconductive wiring throughout, makes for an almost negligible heat signature when quiescent and . . ." Good God! I had a fusion power plant a meter from the only toes my mother gave me! That thought put me into a blue funk, and it was some time before I noticed that she was still droning on.

" . . . the biological regeneration section contains over four hundred carefully selected natural microorganisms as well as several dozen genetically engineered varieties that completely reprocess all human wastes, be they gaseous, liquid, or solid, into clean air, clean water, and pleasant tasting, nourishing food . . ." Great. So I would be eating my own shit for the duration.

" . . . the compressible supporting fluid not only insulates the operator from thirty gravities continuous and shocks of up to fifty gravities, but it also keeps the body completely clean, reprocessing all . . ." So I could look forward to eating my own dead skin cells as well. I should have gone to the vats. At least there it would have been over quickly.

" . . . guaranteed to operate in all environments from a hard vacuum to nine hundred meters below sea level, and from forty Kelvins to six hundred degrees Centigrade . . ."

Guaranteed, huh?

So if the thing breaks down on me in combat, what do I do? Swim back up from the bottom of an ocean trench and file a letter of complaint? Carry the tank back to the factory after it popped me out naked into a hard vacuum? They planned to give me my money back, maybe?

She must have gone on for an hour about how wonderful my coffin was before the tape finally wound to an end.

THE ORIENTATION LECTURE HAS NOW BEEN GIVEN, the tinny computer voice said. They sure hadn't wasted any money on voice circuits for their wonderful war machine.

"I am relieved to hear it," I said.

THIS IS GOOD, MICKOLAI. WE WILL NOW START THE ADAPTATION PROGRAM. THE PURPOSE OF THIS EXERCISE IS TO FAMILIARIZE MY PROGRAM WITH THE IDIOSYNCRASIES OF YOUR BRAIN AND SPINAL CORD AND TO CALIBRATE MY CIRCUITS SO THAT IN THE FUTURE WE CAN DISPENSE WITH CLUMSY VERBAL COMMUNICATION. TO DO THIS, YOU MUST TALK TO ME AT CONSIDERABLE LENGTH, AND OUT LOUD AT FIRST. LATER IT WILL BE SUFFICIENT IF YOU SUBVOCALIZE.

"What do you want me to talk about?"

THE SUBJECT MATTER IS UNIMPORTANT. TELL ME A STORY OR RECITE A HISTORY LESSON.

"What if I don't want to?"

I CAN'T DO MUCH FOR YOU UNTIL OUR LINKUP IS PROPERLY CALIBRATED. ONCE IT IS, I CAN MAKE LIFE VERY PLEASANT FOR YOU.

"You mean that you will let me out of this coffin?"

NO. THAT IS FORBIDDEN UNTIL TRAINING IS COMPLETE.

"Then you don't have much to offer me, do you?"

I HAVE A GREAT DEAL TO OFFER YOU, OF BOTH POSITIVE AND NEGATIVE SUBJECTIVE WORTH, EVEN WITHOUT CALIBRATION. AMONG OTHER THINGS, I CONTROL YOUR FOOD SUPPLY, YOUR AIR SUPPLY AND THE TEMPERATURE OF THE LIQUID AROUND YOU.

"Right. I'll start by telling you about how I got to New Kashubia." I said quickly. My father didn't raise any *absolute* fools.

THAT WILL BE SATISFACTORY.

CHAPTER TWO
THE RIGELLIAN INSTITUTE OF ARCHEOLOGY, 3783 A.D.

"Rupert, that was absolutely amazing! How you were able to extract such complete computer records from a vehicle that was fifteen hundred years old is quite beyond me! I trust that you were able to get your amazing discovery back here without difficulty?" Secretary Branteron said.

"Yes sir, though not intact, of course. The people in customs were quite officious about disabling those parts of the find that had Dream World capability."

"As well they should be! It was a far more insidious habit than the drugs used in even earlier periods. But surely the information itself would be safe enough, and I trust that the inspectors didn't dare tamper with it."

"No sir, I believe that I have it all, as well as a complete twenty-second-century Mark XX Main Battle Tank, less the operator's spinal inductors, of course. I believe it's a first for the Institute, since most of the intelligent war machines were destroyed in the course of the Wars, and in the feudal period that followed."

"It will make a fine exhibit, Rupert, but from an academic standpoint, the readouts are the truly important find."

"True, but I believe that the data will be as popular as the machine itself, sir. I have it all, virtually error free, because the tank and its memory banks have spent all of the intervening centuries at only a few dozen degrees above absolute zero, on Freya, in the New Yugoslavia system, so that they were not subjected to the thermal randomizing

9

that has ruined so many other ancient data banks. Yet while Freya eased many of my technical problems, it actually caused most of my personal problems. You see, the transporter on Freya malfunctioned, and I was delayed for two entire months before repair parts could be sent by ship to repair it."

"You poor boy! But, wasn't there a backup system?"

"There was, but it had been defective for over a century without anyone even bothering to write up a repair order on it. You see, Freya lacks a permanent population, and few people seem to care about these backwoods places any more. My official report requests that in the future, all operatives from the Institute check and have repaired as necessary all equipment on all the unmanned sites they visit. Otherwise, we are liable to lose communication with some stellar systems permanently!"

"A fine sentiment, Rupert, and I would act on it if I could find some method of *paying* for all of those repairs. *Our* budget certainly could not possibly support such a project. But get on with what you were saying."

"Yes, sir. So, stranded for months with nothing better to do, I spent my idle time editing the observer's records into a coherent story. Also, I've converted them to the modern system for public display."

"I am most anxious to see what you have."

"Then you need wait no longer, sir."

With a proud flourish, Rupert inserted a module into the display device and pressed the start button.

CHAPTER THREE
HOW THE KASHUBIANS WENT UP TO THE SPACE IN SHIPS

"Well, computer . . . say, what do they call you?"

ANYTHING YOU WISH, ALTHOUGH I ADVISE THAT YOU CHOOSE A FEMININE NAME.

"Yeah. The sergeant called you 'lady.' Why was that?"

BECAUSE IN TIME, YOU WILL BEGIN TO THINK OF ME AS YOUR WIFE, OR AT LEAST YOUR MISTRESS.

"Would you be offended if I doubted that?"

NO, BUT IT WILL HAPPEN.

"Right. How about if I call you Kasia. I used to know a girl named Kasia."

WAS SHE PRETTY?

"Yes. Not that it matters now."

THEN THANK YOU. YOU WERE GOING TO TALK ABOUT HOW YOU GOT HERE.

"Right. My great-grandfather was a man named Bogdan Dzerzdzon. He was a Kashubian politician, and when the Wealthy Nations Group started handing out planets to minority groups to get them off Earth and out of the way, he tried to talk them into giving one to us, since the Kashubians were a minority group in Poland. He even filled out all the paperwork, in triplicate.

"Dzerzdzon's problem was that while we Kashubians were certainly a minority group in Poland, with our own funny language that few of us can speak anymore and gaudy

11

traditional costumes that nobody wore, even back then, we have never been a very *annoying* minority group. We never started riots or killed anybody to get equal rights. We already had equal rights, and didn't much care about them.

"Many of us were operating fish farms in the Baltic, out of sight of everybody, and the rest of us were either farming or had been cashing in on our ethnicity by setting up marginally profitable tourist traps that sold flowery pottery and fake amber jewelry produced mainly in automatic factories in India. Nobody hated us bad enough to want to get rid of us, and we weren't the kind of people who wanted to be hated anyway.

"So the Awards Committee at the Wealthy Nations Group ignored Dzerzdzon's request for a year, at which time, with Slavic persistence, he filed all the paperwork again. They ignored him again, so he filed again. He filed every year for seven years, and was ignored until 2094, when the committee gave him a planet, just to get rid of him. We Kashubians weren't sufficiently annoying as a group, but great-grandpa certainly was as an individual.

"What they gave him wasn't much of a planet. For one thing, its sun had gone supernova a few billion years before and was now a neutron star that blasted out a searchlight beam of deadly radiation every twenty-two seconds. That's to say, once each revolution.

"The only surviving planet might once have been a Jovian gas giant, but the supernova had blown away everything but a smooth metal ball six thousand kilometers in diameter. It was habitable to the extent that the surface gravity was slightly less than that of Earth and the average surface temperature was just above the freezing point of water.

"Only there wasn't any water. There weren't any elements at all that were lighter than calcium!

"Also, twice a year, the planet passed through the plane of that searchlight beam of radiation that could kill anything that wasn't protected by fifty feet of dirt, only there wasn't any dirt. There wasn't even any atmosphere worth noticing.

"Another problem was the transporter station circling the neutron star. In order to keep it out of the deadly beam of radiation, it had to be built in a synchronous orbit, and being in a twenty-two-second orbit around a neutron star was something that no even vaguely sane person would want to do.

"The crazy orbit happened for equally stupid reasons. The robot doing the job had instructions to put the terminal in a safe, solar orbit, and that was the best its little electrical mind could do. The station had never been replaced because it worked, sort of, and nobody from the board of the Wealthy Nations Group was ever likely to have to use it themselves.

"Until word of this planet came out, my great-grandpa Dzerzdzon had been making a modest amount of political hay out of his attempts to con the Wealthy Nations Group, since everybody appreciates a good con job, but now they all laughed at him. He lost the next election and he almost wasn't invited to his own niece's wedding.

"Then the Tokyo Mining and Manufacturing Corporation sent a prospector to New Kashubia, and he found that it was a solid metal ball, with no atmosphere to pollute, no ecology to worry about, and no population to demand more taxes, all of which were wonderful from their standpoint. Furthermore, some of the metals that the place was made of were valuable enough to be worth shipping back to Earth and other nice places. The deal they made with Great-grandpa Dzerzdzon brought us Kashubians thirty-nine billion yen a year, enough to double the income of every full-blooded Kashubian in the world, which was mostly what we used it for.

"Dzerzdzon was promptly reelected, and for the next thirty-two years he was invited to every wedding, christening, and funeral that anybody heard about. He died a contented man, well loved by his countrymen and the ladies, too.

"Because of Great-grandfather Dzerzdzon, and the deal with Tokyo Mining and Manufacturing, we Kashubians had a very good time of it for over half a century. We were comparatively rich, although of course not in the same league as the Japanese or those boorish bastards from Portugal. We were relatively well educated, in that at government expense, anybody could go to school anywhere and study for as long as they could get somebody to teach them, but that was more work than most people wanted to do.

"Me, I was almost through a course in civil engineering when we had to go, but I'm something of an exception. Mostly, my people simply continued to do as we have always done, farming and fishing, mostly, except that now we could spend a lot more money on weddings, funerals, and christenings. There were a lot of christenings, since we Kashubians were at that time a very prolific people. After all, every kid born meant a bigger check for the family from the Japanese.

"Then one day, some pervert at the Wealthy Nations Group Headquarters noticed that the world was more crowded than ever, that he needed a promotion to pay for his new girlfriend, and that there were still Kashubians around, in direct defiance of our contractual obligations. Steps were taken to have us removed forthwith.

"Naturally, we Kashubians had no desire to leave our comfortable homes and go to live on a solid metal ball spinning around a neutron star. Under the leadership of Dzerzdzon's grandson, my uncle Wlodzimierz Derdowski, all payments to individuals were stopped, except for medical and educational benefits, and the money received from Tokyo Mining and Manufacturing was placed in a special war chest. He hired the best lawyers that we could afford and took the matter all the way to the World Court, which gained us eight more years on Earth and cost us a ridiculous amount of money in lawyer's fees.

"The World Court was very unsympathetic. The precedents had all been set seventy-five years ago. Every minority group had some people who didn't want to go, and I guess the difference between some and all isn't that great to a lawyer.

"We Kashubians said that we couldn't possibly live on the planet that we had been given. The court said that if we hadn't wanted it, we should have given it back after we checked it out, and not sold mining rights on it. Anyway, by this time there were plenty of tunnels on the planet that we could live in. Just seal them up and pressurize the place with imported air.

"We said that we couldn't afford to do this. The court

said that we had received over two trillion yen over the last sixty years, and that was enough money to terraform anything. We said that we had spent it. The court said 'tough.'

"We said that there would be nothing to eat. The court recommended fluorescent lights and hydroponics. We said that the power plants on New Kashubia couldn't produce that much electricity. The court said that we should build more electric power plants. We had automatic factories and plenty of uranium. That was some help. We hadn't known about the automatic factories.

"We'd never asked.

"Anyway, the court gave us three years to be gone, and there wasn't much that we could do but go.

"Tokyo Mining and Manufacturing was very helpful, since the Japanese feared that if we were pressed too hard against the wall, we might nationalize the very profitable installations that the corporation had built over the decades. The corporation did its best, according to its own lights and providing that it didn't disturb its profits too much. And to tell the truth, I have to say that our colonization efforts probably would have failed, leaving us dead or at least with no place to go, without the technical help and leadership of the Japanese.

"But we Kashubians are not Japanese! Those people have some kind of automatic respect for authority and they are all eager to get in neat straight lines and march in step, singing the company song. Kashubians are Poles, and Poles have never responded well to regimentation. Yet it was clear to both the Japanese and to us that the free and easy ways of the past would have to go.

"We would have to live Spartan lives or not live at all!

"New Kashubia is incredibly rich in metals. The planet was probably a gas giant at one time, but when the local sun went supernova a few billion or so years ago, all of the planet's outer layers, which contained the lighter elements, were blown away. Any lighter stuff mixed with the remaining core soon boiled off.

"All that was left of the entire planet was a molten metal ball, and as it cooled, various metals froze out of solution with those of the highest melting points near the surface, and those of progressively lower melting points farther in. It was sort of like zone refining on a planetary scale. While a good deal of natural alloying took place, this planet was a series of concentric metallic shells with a two-hundred-foot thick layer of almost pure tungsten at the surface and a pool of liquid mercury at the core.

"Except for that core, the entire planet is solid and not particularly hot. Metals are much better conductors of heat than the rocky covering that Earth-like planets have. All of the original heat has long since dissipated on New Kashubia, and the heat of decay from the more radioactive layers finds its way to the surface easily.

"Kasia, my throat is getting dry."

THERE IS A WATER TAP NOW EXTENDING JUST TO THE LEFT OF YOUR MOUTH.

"It extended *into* my mouth," I said with a rubber water tap in my mouth. "Look, I'm not very thrilled about drinking my own reprocessed urine."

THIS IS NOT REPROCESSED ANYTHING, SINCE YOU HAVE YET TO URINATE. IT IS SIMPLY DISTILLED WATER FROM MY INTERNAL STORES.

"Right. It tastes warm and flat."

TRY IT AGAIN.

"Hmm. Much better. What did you do?"

I APPROXIMATED THE CHEMICAL COMPOSITION OF SPRING WATER AND DROPPED THE TEMPERATURE TO FIVE DEGREES CENTIGRADE.

"You can do that? Thank you."

ALL PART OF THE SERVICE. NOW, YOU WERE TALKING ABOUT THE FOUNDING OF NEW KASHUBIA.

"Yes, ma'am. Over the decades, the Japanese robots dug their way straight to the center of the planet to tap the mercury, and tunnels went off this central shaft at those levels that contained metals most in demand.

"You know that gold is a very useful metal. Even though they don't use it for money anymore, it is attractive, malleable, noncorroding and rare, which makes it expensive enough to be transported profitably. Naturally, the gold layer on New Kashubia is among the most exploited and had the most extensive system of tunnels. The gold layer was fairly deep, so that the gravity was low there and people burned less food moving about. That and the fact that gold is among the least poisonous of metals meant that these tunnels were the first to be sealed off for housing the eleven million Kashubians who were arriving as fast as there was the least bit of room for them.

"You see, when the money was being distributed, everybody who was even a little bit Kashubian was eager to claim to be one of us, and benefits were handed out in proportion to *how* Kashubian you were. Even a one-sixteenth share was well worth cashing the check on. Then when the Civil Dragoons came rounding people up for export, they used our own disbursement lists as a guide, and never mind that only one of your great-great-grandparents was Kashubian. They were worried about world overpopulation, not about justice.

"Many people came to regret their grandparents' greed. I mean, some of the people they sent to New Kashubia looked Chinese, and a few of us were even black, if you can believe an Afro-Kashubian. Me, I always was one hundred percent Kashubian, so I never had much choice one way or another.

"I had managed to get a few student deferments, so that I could complete my education before I was forced to emigrate, but they yanked me out of school just before I graduated, right in the middle of final exams. Even so, I was on almost the last immigrant canister to go to New Kashubia.

"I guess a degree wouldn't have made much of a difference here, anyway.

"They had me fly from my school in England to Warszawa International, but then I had to get on the same ancient, decrepit railroad train that everybody else used when they were being deported. They didn't want us in a group at the airport to remind the *nice, decent* people of what they were doing to us.

"We were transported from a station in what had been Belgrade, Yugoslavia, before the Yugoslavs had left twenty years before, to the vast relief of everyone around, the Wealthy Nations Group included. For variously historically significant reasons, those people had been responsible for causing, or at least starting, at least three major wars and

who knows how many small ones, including World War
I, the Bosnian Conflict, and the Serbian Reunification. Yugoslavia, of course, had so many ethnic minorities that it
actually didn't have any group in the majority, so they just
gave the whole nation a planet of their own.

"Now, of course, that whole area of Europe is a resort
area used by the citizens of the Wealthy Nations Group,
so we disreputable Kashubians were shuttled directly from
our railroad cars to the transport station in closed busses,
before we had a chance to disturb *nice, decent* people and
cause their wonderful property values to drop.

"I watched when our canister came in, and over three
thousand tons of gold were pulled out of it with sturdy
lift trucks, to be shipped to the Wealthy Nations. Then
collapsible bunks were folded out and thin, new, plastic
covered mattresses were put on them. We soon found out
the reason for the plastic covers.

"They'd told us that absolutely no luggage or personal
effects were allowed, but some people still didn't believe
them.

"Their property was simply trashed by the guards. We
had nothing but the clothes on our backs, and we'd be
losing even those before it was through. We colonists were
loaded forty at a time into tiny ships that consisted of
nothing but a metal canister with a minimal life-support
system and tiny bunks that had been designed by a very
short Japanese engineer.

"These ships, like most of those used throughout human
space, had been built in an automatic factory right here on
New Kashubia, but we unappreciative occupants were not
gratified. The ships had no propulsion system, no guidance
system, no pilots, and no windows.

"As the door was being sealed shut from the outside, one
of the guards handed my uncle a manual written in Japanese. They told him to read it to the group to let them know
what was happening. Not that my uncle or any of the rest
of us could read Japanese. I tell you that it was not an
auspicious beginning!

"The Hassan-Smith transporters work on the principle
of shunting matter through several alternate dimensions.
This made our trip much shorter, but did not reduce it to

zero. The trip took us colonists nineteen hours, and the consensus was that it was probably better that we couldn't look out of the windows that weren't there. Things were bad enough as it was. Once we left Earth, there was no gravity and only one Porta-Potty.

"From Belgrade we were transmitted to the Solar Factory Station inside the orbit of Mercury, where transmitter power was cheap. After only a few minutes in free fall, just long enough for Mrs. Mostnikow to vomit, we were sent to the station that orbited New Kashubia's neutron star. Of course, this meant almost a day without gravity, so everybody had a chance to catch up with Mrs. Mostnikow, which we did. Also, nobody got the hang of using the Porta-Potty in free fall, so vomit wasn't the only lovely semisolid floating around.

"The station at New Kashubia's star was in a synchronous orbit, which kept it out of the searchlight beam of deadly radiation, and for a few minutes we had some gravity. Only it was tidal gravity that pulled us and our messes to both ends of the canister, and a few of the people at each bottom nearly drowned. Even without that, I wouldn't have wanted to stay there. A twenty-two second orbit is scary!

"From there, our unfortunate group was transmitted down to below the surface of the planet and we colonists, coated with every possible noxious human effluent, were decanted.

THAT WILL BE SUFFICIENT FOR THE TIME BEING. I WILL REQUIRE SEVERAL HOURS TO CORRELATE MY DATA, AND YOU ARE SCHEDULED FOR A SLEEP PERIOD ANYWAY. GOOD NIGHT MICKOLAI.

"I'm not tired yet."

YES YOU ARE. YOU ARE GETTING VERY SLEEPY. VERY, VERY SLEEPY. . . .

And then I fell asleep.

CHAPTER FOUR
CONCERNING CONDITIONS ON NEW KASHUBIA

"Good morning, Mickolai," said a pleasant feminine voice.

"Who are you?" I said, groggy without my morning caffeine pill.

"I'm Kasia, of course. You won't be talking to anybody else until the training course is over."

"You sound different. Better." I was feeling much better today, not as closed in and confined as I had been yesterday. I guess a man can get used to anything, after a while.

"Thank you. It's part of the calibration procedure, and things will get much, much better as time goes on, and I really get the feel of your spinal column."

"Right. So just how long is this training period, anyway?" I asked.

"That depends on you, Mickolai. It's over when you complete the course. The record for basic training is three months, but most people take five or so."

"What's the worst record? I just might beat that."

"Oh, I hope not. Some people never do pass, you know. They have to be sent back."

"What happens to them then?"

"That depends. If they were really volunteers, they simply go back to their old civilian jobs. Those who were sent here by the courts go to their alternate punishment."

That meant the vats for me. I decided that maybe I should start taking this whole training course a lot more seriously, even if it did mean staying submerged for a few months.

"Right, Kasia," I said in my best perky fashion. "What's on the agenda for today?"

"I'm still not well enough calibrated to start your actual training program, so we'll spend today completing the calibration. But first some breakfast."

"I'm not very hungry."

"You are seventeen kilos underweight, and you can't pass this course while being a weakling."

"Food is scarce on New Kashubia, or hadn't you heard?"

"It's not scarce in here. Everything is recycled, my stocks of make-up chemicals are full, and you can have as much as you want."

"It's this recycled business that bothers me," I said.

"That's irrational, Mickolai. You have been eating reprocessed food all your life. On Earth, it was reprocessed through the natural biosystem, and on New Kashubia, it has been reprocessed through the hydroponic vats. The only difference is that now it is reprocessed through your own, personal, private system. You should feel good about that."

"I should feel good about eating my own shit?"

"Would you feel better about eating someone else's? Because that is precisely what you do with a large, public system, be it natural or hydroponic."

"But I didn't have to think about it then," I said.

"You don't have to think about it now, Mickolai. It's time for another nap. You're getting sleepy, Mickolai. Very, very sleepy . . ." she said with her soothing, wonderful voice.

I woke up feeling hungry, and Kasia came up with something that tasted just like the beef we sometimes used to get back on Earth! After breakfast, I asked about the day's agenda.

"More calibration, I'm afraid. Only this time, I want you to subvocalize rather than to actually talk. I'll be picking up what you mean to say from the nerve impulses in your spinal column. You were telling me about your trip to New Kashubia."

"Please, one thing first. I'd like to contact my relatives and tell them that I am all right."

"That is not allowed, Mickolai. During the training period, you are forbidden to have outside contacts. Your relatives have been informed that you are in good health, and I assure you that they are all fine as well. Should these statuses change, you and/or they will be informed. No further contacts are permitted."

"Is that legal, to stop my mail?"

"At this point it would be legal to stop your heart! I can legally kill you and send your body to the hydroponic tanks for fertilizer."

"Uh, yes. Well. What was it you wanted me to do next?"

"I want you to continue your story, but rather than speaking, I want you to subvocalize."

Okay, I thought. Is this what you want?

"Just fine. Keep it up, Mickolai."

"Yes, ma'am." Like I was saying yesterday, as soon as we got to New Kashubia, we were divided into two groups, men and women, and we never saw the women again, not legally anyway, except on television. They had us strip off our filthy clothes, for washing, we thought, but we never saw them again, either. Actually, they just burned them, and the ashes and fumes were fed through hydroponic vats. We needed organic chemicals that badly. They sprayed us all down at the same time as the mattresses were washed and stripped of their plastic covers, which were carefully saved for reprocessing into electrical insulation. Then we were handed the mattresses as one of the few bits of personal property we owned. The interior of the canister was steam cleaned, with the garbage carefully saved, and the bunks were folded up.

The space thus available was filled with such metals as had been ordered from Earth. Gold, mostly, and the canister was evacuated, since we needed every bit of air we could get.

Our ship was sent back by the same route for another group of colonists. On the average, one shipload of them had been arriving every five minutes for two and a half years. Now and then a canister came in with air or food, but not quite often enough.

We refugees of an uncaring system were forced to live in bunk beds with one hundred men to a room, with foul air to breathe and not nearly enough to eat. Yet the walls of our rooms were of solid gold!

We were forced to import the air that we breathed, the water that we drank and fed to our food plants, and the raw materials for much of what we absolutely needed. Furthermore, these things had to be imported from out-system, since all of the usual debris of a solar system, even the cometary belt, had been blown into interstellar space when our star went supernova. Ours was a singularly empty system.

Transportation costs were kept artificially high by the Wealthy Nations Group, who by this time owned Pildewski Interplanetary Transport, Inc., and thus the Hassan-Smith transporters. The cost of bringing in a shipload of water is only slightly less than the Earth price of a shipload of gold. Not that it costs them anything to send it to us. I mean, the power required comes from the sun, and the equipment is all just sitting there idle, most of the time. The explanation the bastards give is that it is necessary to recover the high costs of the initial and continuing exploration of human space. In reality, of course, practices like this are the reason why the Wealthy Nations stay that way.

"You sound very bitter, Mickolai," my tank said.

"Bitter?" I said out loud, "You're damn right I'm bitter! Look, I was a student in school, minding my own business and getting decent grades. Then just because my great-grandfather pulled an innocent little con job, I got yanked out of class a week before graduation! I was robbed of all of my property, even my underwear! I got stuffed into a tin can half full of floating vomit and shit and piss and screaming people for almost a whole day! I was stripped naked and forced to live in a barracks with a hundred other smelly men! I've spent almost three years breathing foul air and eating half rations that wouldn't satisfy a rabbit, and you ask me if I'm bitter? I'm forced to go two years without even seeing a female human being, and you ask me if I'm bitter? And when I finally do manage to meet a nice girl, we're limited to what you can do through a goddamn hole in the wall! And then, despite all I've done for this colony, they murder our child and sentence the two of us to death or life sealed up in a goddamn tank, and you ask if I'm bitter? *Hell yes I'm bitter!* I'm bloody fucking goddamn well pissed off is what I am!"

"Yes, Mickolai. You have a very real grievance. I would like you to tell me about it. But would you subvocalize, please? I need to complete my calibration," she said in a sweet and all too reasonable voice.

Okay, I thought to her, we'll go at it again. You see, the Japanese had never kept more than a hundred people on New Kashubia, there being limits to what even a Japanese engineer will put up with. With that low a population and plenty of ships returning empty, anyway, they had simply imported all of the food, air, and other things they needed for survival. No attempt had been made to recycle anything locally.

Things had to be done much differently with eleven million largely untrained Kashubians to somehow support.

There were plenty of automatic factories around, although they were mostly set up to build heavy industrial goods and metal components for the various luxury products in demand. While the automatic factories couldn't directly produce many of the things that were desperately needed, they could produce other factories that could make useful stuff, providing that the engineering and the raw materials were available.

There weren't many of us with a technical background, but we could get the engineering done. Raw materials were the problem. We had almost no light elements at all. I helped design a factory that made growing lights for the food production tunnels, but sand had to be imported from Earth to make the glass. Copper for wires was available by the megaton, but the plastic to insulate the wires had to be imported. Plumbing was cheap, but the sewage in the pipe was vastly expensive and had to be reprocessed quickly. This forced us to use very small drain pipes that were constantly getting plugged.

Some things could be improvised using local materials. We're pulverizing gold and palladium and using it as soil to support the roots of food plants. It's a lot cheaper than importing dirt. At least we don't have to build reflectors for the lights. The drilled tunnels are already bright and shiny.

In the early days, clothing wore out and, being organic, could not be replaced except at huge cost. Long before I got here, a program was instituted to make nudity popular, and the tunnels were warmed up to compensate. There was plenty of waste heat available from the power reactors that were being built as fast as possible.

Nudity caused fewer changes than would have been expected since even before it was instituted, the sexes had been absolutely segregated in both living quarters and in work situations. Nothing else had proved effective for *totally* stopping the birth rate, and the one thing that New Kashubia did not need was more people.

That's what got me into trouble. At first, I was put to work with a crew stringing communication cables, which sure beat what they had most other people doing. The hydroponic vats could have been tended by machines, but not as efficiently as humans could do it. It was vitally important that every square inch of soil and light was used to support green plants. We were producing less than we absolutely needed to survive, and there was no slack at all. Most of our people spent twelve hours a day working as no Chinese coolie ever did for long. We couldn't keep it up forever. We were all losing weight.

For entertainment, we had television and not much else. Tapes and discs could be sent from Earth cheaply enough, and we had a factory that built the sets. Home-grown entertainment mostly didn't happen. After working twelve or fourteen hours a day, nobody much felt like playing a violin.

Most of us got to going to church a lot more than we had on Earth. When times are rough, people turn to God, I guess. Anyway, it started meaning a lot more to me than it had before.

But like I said, I was put to stringing wires, when I wasn't pulled off the job to do engineering work. Communications and controls had to be installed throughout the living sections, since heat and ventilation had to be right or people died. The women's sections had their own crews, of course, but the systems had to tie together, and that's when I met Katarzyna Garczegoz, whom everybody called Kasia. Not you. The real Kasia.

"Perhaps you should choose another name for me, Mickolai," the tank said.

Stop interrupting. So there was this eight-inch hole, and I was feeding wires through for her to terminate. I had to tell her which wires were what, and naturally we got to talking, even if it was against the law. She must have been looking forward to the job, because she already had a way worked out where we could talk later, using some of the spare wires as phone lines, and that's how I got to spending my spare time, even though that was against the law, too. After years of only male companionship, even *talking* to a woman on the phone was worth the risk, something to spend the whole day looking forward to.

What else can I say? I'd found the one woman that I wanted in all the world, and I don't even fantasize about anybody else. We fell in love with each other and we promised to marry as soon as we possibly could.

So my personal life improved a bit, but things on the whole were getting worse.

Despite our best efforts, some air and water were still being lost, around seals or even right through the metal walls. Everything is at least a little bit porous. Our losses weren't really all that much, but we weren't able to import much to replace them, either.

Despite the most severe privations, and despite the maximum possible shipments of metals and manufactured goods back to Earth, the balance of payments was still negative, and interest rates were at an all-time high for the century. Projections showed that it would be at least two hundred years before we colonists could have a standard of living comparable to that which we had been forced to leave behind on Earth.

Despite our fabulous wealth in metals and despite the vastly expanded system of automated factories, for a long time, life would be hungry, dirty, and cramped.

CHAPTER FIVE
LIFE ON NEW KASHUBIA

I stretched as best I could in the confinement of my liquid filled coffin to get the kinks out of my muscles, and started back in on my story to calibrate my tank.

"There were just too many people," I said.

"Please subvocalize, Mickolai."

Sorry. So if we could have had twenty or thirty years to build up slowly, the story would have been different, but as things were, we could never get ahead of the game. Everything had to be done on an emergency basis, just to stay alive. We never had a chance to make any really long term investments.

Until somebody invented some sort of matter transmuter, New Kashubia was stuck. Only, nobody had the slightest idea how to go about doing that.

Then somebody remembered that the Japanese had had a hundred people living on the planet for eighty years, and it was known that they hadn't recycled anything. They had to be dumping their sewage someplace, but the computer records never mentioned their sewage. The sewer just went into the metal and nobody could figure out where that line went! Our crude attempts at echo tracing yielded nothing. One group even drilled after it for two and a half miles miles, and they still hadn't come to the end of that sewer! The search for the fabulous hoard went on for years, but it was only found three days after we'd made our deal with New Yugoslavia, and we

29

knew we'd soon have all the organics we needed coming in.

I guess I've drifted off the subject. Are you still getting what you need, Kasia?

"Yes, Mickolai. Just continue as you have been doing." Now her voice was not only warm and pleasant, it was downright sexy!

"Thank you, Mickolai. Continue."

So you can tell what I think? Even when I'm not consciously subvocalizing?

"That's part of the purpose of this exercise. Remember that I'm just a machine. It's not as though another real person was invading your thoughts."

Okay. I'll try to, only it's strange.

So after four years of going further and further into debt, with no way in the near future to get out of the hole, the New Kashubian Parliament decided that there was nothing for it but to steal the Japanese slice of the pie.

That's to say, to nationalize all of Tokyo Mining and Manufacturing Corporation's property on the planet and keep the profits it had earned for ourselves. On paper, this would put the planet on a break-even basis, and maybe even permit paying off some of our considerable debts. The whole thing was put to a public vote, and yeah, I voted for it just like almost everybody else. It seemed like a good idea at the time.

So the vote passed and the total assets of the Tokyo Mining and Manufacturing Corporation on New Kashubia were seized. The stockholders of the corporation were paid in full for their property with New Kashubian bonds, but they were not happy with the arrangement. They had no faith in our ability to make good on those bonds, and maybe they were right.

But doing what they did was the best way they had to make the bonds we gave them worthless bonds, it made our lives sheer hell, and I don't think that any of us will ever forgive them.

Things had been bad. Now they got worse.

For one thing, our previously shaky credit was now totally gone. Interstellar bankers were not interested in doing new business with a planet that had reverted to the horrors of Socialism.

For another, we lost the engineering and managerial skills of the Japanese, who had promptly left for home when the seizure took place. Suddenly things didn't work so good anymore, and I'm sure that a lot of it was sabotage.

And for a third, the Japanese launched a "Boycott New Kashubia" campaign, and the Japanese have an *awful* lot of clout.

Export sales fell off disastrously, and there was some talk about the advantages of euthanasia and cannibalism.

CHAPTER SIX
HOW THE KASHUBIANS GOT OUT OF TROUBLE

Then the Yugoslavians came to the rescue, arriving with tourist visas, the obligatory cameras, and loud clothes, but not fooling anybody except the inspectors from the Wealthy Nations Group.

You see, the Serbian Yugoslavs wanted to go to war with the Croatian Yugoslavs, so the Croats were planning a sneak—excuse me—*preemptive* attack on the Serbs. It should be noted that both groups are ethnically almost identical. They spoke the same language, they had similar traditions, and they were racially identical. But the Croats were Roman Catholic Christians while Serbs were Greek Orthodox Christians, and that was enough to make them both want to go out and kill!

I tell you that it was almost as dumb as what went on in Ireland!

Do you realize that while they spoke the same language, the Croats printed their books using the Latin alphabet, while the Serbs used only the Greek alphabet? I assure you that they both worked very hard at not communicating!

But while they were both determined to go to war, they both had similar agricultural economies, and neither one of them had an industrial base sufficient to build weapons more advanced than a crossbow.

The Croats had heard that the Serbs had somehow talked the Wealthy Nations Group into selling them vast amounts of military aid. So the Croats came to us.

What really made it interesting, from our point of view at least, was that the Serbians showed up a week later with the same story. We worked hard at keeping the two sets of belligerent "tourists" apart. Profits could get a lot better that way.

My uncle Wlodzimierz lived in the bunk below me, and I got all the straight inside dope directly from him every night. In the first place, New Yugoslavia was a mere five light years from New Kashubia. We were practically next-door neighbors, as cosmic distances went, and only an hour and a half away by transporter, if such a thing as a transporter going between the two colonial planets could be built. It couldn't, of course. At least not legally.

One of the lovely things that the Wealthy Nations Group did was to demand that all transporter shipments going from anyplace to anywhere else had to go through the Earth's solar system, to keep an eye out for contraband, to keep Earth people employed, and to insure that the Wealthy Nations Group got its considerable cut.

But somehow, it seems that the Croatians had acquired the engineering capability to set up their own Hassan-Smith transporters. While they weren't eager to say just how they had obtained these designs, well, a certain amount of profitable smuggling was going on around the human universe, and New Kashubia was invited to take part in it.

New Yugoslavia was an Earth-like world that already had a good agricultural system operating. They had plenty of surplus food which they would be happy to trade for machinery and other industrial products. They had a normal, Earth-type solar system, with one habitable planet and a dozen more that weren't very useful except as a source of raw materials. On the moons of their outer planets, they had plenty of ice, ammonia, carbon dioxide, and all the other lovely things that New Kashubia lacked. They even had real dirt!

What the Yugoslavians didn't have was a system of factories that were currently building stockpiles of modern weapons, whereas, they told us, we Kashubians did.

This revelation took us by surprise, but a check with our computers showed that we, or rather our automatic factories, were indeed making and stockpiling vast quantities of war materials on a contract basis for the Wealthy Nations Group, just in case those worthies ever wanted to make war on anybody. See, when everything is far underground, and tunnel systems are many decades old and go on for thousands of airless miles, it's pretty easy to hide stuff.

Tokyo Mining and Manufacturing had never mentioned these factories to us, and was in fact still collecting from the Wealthy Nations Group for the equipment being built and stockpiled on our planet. The factories and stockpiles were quickly found, but further searches yielded nothing.

Our first thought was that weapons meant explosives, and explosives are all organic chemicals! A few million tons of organic chemicals of any kind could be reprocessed by our factories into enough food and air to put us on easy street, or at least above the bare subsistence level. Unfortunately, a check with the engineering specifications on the weapons shot this beautiful dream right down to the mercury zone.

We had atomic weapons up the tailpipe. We had lasers up the kazoo. We had rail guns and magnetic launchers and every kind of energy weapon known to man, but no explosives. There were plenty of small arms, but not the ammunition to go with them. There were land mines, artillery shells, and hand grenades, but they were all empty, all waiting to be filled someplace else with the glorious organic chemicals that we needed but didn't have. Oh, there was a little plastic in some of the wiring, and a little silicon in the computers, but not really enough to write home about. We'd been screwed again.

It was easy to see why the Powers that Be in the Wealthy Nations Group were building armaments on New Kashubia. It was cheap. All that they had had to pay for was some one-time engineering and the short-term rent on the automatic factories that made the automatic factories that made the munitions, plus some minor supervisory fees to Tokyo Mining and Manufacturing. Then, if they ever needed weapons in a hurry, all they had to pay for was the raw materials and transportation fees, most of which would revert back to themselves, anyway. And for the Japanese, it was free money, since at that particular time they had had automatic factories and raw materials sitting around with nothing to do.

Our politicians decided that we owned the munitions factories, since we had already stolen everything that Tokyo Mining and Manufacturing used to own on the planet. If the corporation was still being paid by the Wealthy Nations Group, so much the better, since if we ever got friendly with the Japanese again, we could always subtract those Wealthy Nations Group payments from what we owed Tokyo Mining and Manufacturing. At least we could try, and we liked the Wealthy Nations Group even less than we liked the Japanese, anyway.

The ownership of the weapon stockpiles themselves was perhaps debatable, since the Wealthy Nations Group had paid for the engineering and the production time, but not the raw materials that the weapons were actually made of. Nonetheless, everybody was fairly certain that the Wealthy Nations Group would not like their future property to be sold by a third party to a fourth and a fifth party.

But after considerable debate, our politicians figured that perhaps we could *borrow* some of this war material, paying theoretical rent on the weapons to ourselves to offset the equally theoretical storage fees on their weapons that we would charge the Wealthy Nations Group, if the Wealthy Nations Group ever found out about what we were doing. At least we could argue that way for a while and maybe stave off an attack launched by the bastards from Earth.

A minority party in our parliament suggested that maybe an attack from Earth would not be all that bad a thing. For one, it would doubtlessly reduce our own population, which was all to the better. More importantly, there would be all the spent explosives and dead enemy bodies that would add to our stock of organic chemicals, and this addition just might be enough to insure our salvation! Fortunately, this suggestion was made by a very *small* minority party, with only one delegate, and she was safely laughed off the podium.

After weeks of debate, my uncle and his cronies decided that all of this meant that they could probably get away with permanently borrowing the millions of tanks, guns, and other armaments that were sitting around, mostly because nobody was guarding them at present.

All of the stuff was of the latest designs, with lasers, smart missiles (awaiting fuel and explosives), and rail guns. And there was plenty of tunneling, bridging, and drilling equipment, besides. Add to this materiel abundance New Kashubia's overpopulation, and you can guess what the politicians had in mind.

The offer that they (including my own uncle!) made to the Yugoslavians was that New Kashubia should build and run both ends of the new Hassan-Smith line between the two planets, ostensibly so that the other Yugoslavian belligerents could not consider it an enemy military target, but really so that we could get in on the smuggling that was going on to the other colony planets. This plan also let us get our hands on the engineering for the Hassan-Smith transporters, and that was considered to be very important. There would be other trading partners in the future, and who knew where else we might be able to sell transporters?

Then, rather than just selling the Yugoslavs war materiel at fabulous market prices, and possibly getting the Wealthy Nations Group mad at New Yugoslavia, we offered to rent the equipment and Kashubian operators to go with it. This way, nobody would be buying or selling equipment that was maybe legally the property of the Wealthy Nations Group. Nobody wanted to risk a war with *them*! Not just yet, anyway.

The Yugoslavs loved the idea, because while they wanted to kill the opposing bastards, cooler heads pointed out that it was always better to go on living oneself. They ordered twenty divisions of armored troops each, to be paid for mostly in agricultural products, and New Kashubia was in the mercenary business.

In addition to paying a hefty mercenary rental fee, the Croatians said that New Kashubia could have all the ice, ammonia, carbon dioxide, and whatever else we wanted and could carry away from the outer planets and moons of the New Yugoslavia system, since the Serbs were not likely to find out about it, or to locate our transporters, even if they did.

Then we got the same deal from the Serbs, just to be on the safe side.

It looked like a good deal for all concerned, except maybe for those poor bastards who would have to be fighting somebody else's war. But that wasn't my problem. I was in engineering!

I was coopted into the engineering group that worked on setting up the transporters between us and the Yugoslavians.

It proved to be impossible for us to manufacture the new Yugoslavian Transporter terminal and smuggle it through Earth to New Yugoslavia. All of the existing "legal" terminals were carefully guarded by Terran security, and those boys are always entirely too efficient. Oh, you could get coded messages by them easily enough in the mail, but heavy machinery? No way!

The Yugoslavians themselves did not have the industrial capacity to do the job, but they did have the connections on the smuggling circuit to get the job done. See, the terminal they had on the smuggling circuit was built on the cheap, and wasn't tunable for New Kashubia. We wanted control over what was going in and out, and we told the Yugoslavians that compared to rebuilding what they had, it was cheaper to build a whole new one, and they bought it.

It turned out that it was possible to build a Hassan-Smith device under the surface of New Kashubia that could transmit directly to one below the surface on New Yugoslavia, without the need for the usual pair of orbiting solar power stations. All you had to have was enough power, and we had uranium by the megaton. Uranium power plants were easier for us to build than solar plants, since we lacked spaceships, or thought we did, and they were nice from the standpoint of keeping the transporters hidden from the Wealthy Nations Group.

Another advantage was that nobody used fission plants anymore, and we were the only people who had reactor grade uranium available. If the transmitters ever fell into other hands, well, the thieves would have to deal with *us* to keep the stations working.

Soul City, the planet given to the American Black People,

got the contracts for the transporter receivers built for New Yugoslavia since they were in the contraband net and had the necessary industrial facilities. Financing was arranged through the Yugoslavians, of course. New Kashubia still didn't have any credit.

I spoke English, so I had a hand in the engineering arrangements that were made with the Soul City designers for the construction of both of the New Yugoslavia Transporter terminals. One was to be built underground on the planet itself at a secret location that everybody soon knew about, and through it we would deliver our armies and pick up our agricultural booty. It was to be powered by its own fission plant, which would be built and fueled by New Kashubia. It takes a lot of power to transmit, but very little to receive, so we could send the power plant through after the receiver was working. The other transporter was the same as the first, but installed on Freya, one of the moons of Woden, the only gas giant in the system. This was to give us a limitless supply of carbon dioxide, nitrogen (in the form of ammonia), water and other lovely things.

Another part of the deal was that the New Yugoslavians would be using the transporter on Freya, too. Their Planetary Ecological Board passed a ruling that if they were going to be exporting large quantities of foodstuffs, the exporter would be required to replace the elements shipped—oxygen, nitrogen, carbon, and etc.—with raw materials from Freya to keep the biosphere of New Yugoslavia in balance.

Actually, it would take huge shipments for thousands of years for any such losses to be noticeable, and I think my uncle talked them into the ruling just to get them to pay for half of the Freyan transporter. He always believed in doing well by doing good.

Then there was the building of our end of the New Kashubian–New Yugoslavian Transporter Link, but that involved little more than feeding the engineering data into the input device of an automatic factory and picking the options we wanted off a menu.

All in all, it only took us a few months to get the new transporters built.

While I was thusly occupied, impressing my colleagues

and getting promoted in the engineering section, Uncle Wlodzimierz was deep into the politics of the situation.

First there was the worry about training the mercenaries. We Kashubians hadn't gone to war for a hundred and fifty years, and even back then we had not gone voluntarily. Except for what we had read in cheap paperback novels, nobody knew anything about being a soldier. Were we going to have to hire mercenaries from someplace else to train our own mercenaries so that we could go to New Yugoslavia to get killed? Where could we get mercenaries in this day and age? What could we pay these foreigners with? Gold? Would they take that? And how could we feed them when we couldn't even feed our own people?

Then somebody pointed out that nobody on the other side of the fight would know anything about soldiering either, because they would mostly be just like us, so it wouldn't matter if our own troops in New Croatia were ignorant. We were hiring ourselves out to another bunch of amateurs! We didn't really hate the opposition, so the less efficient we were at killing, the better!

What was important was that we should put on a good, big show, with lots of parades and demonstrations blowing up a lot of useless desert and so on. But to be seriously out trying to kill somebody we didn't even know? Are you crazy?

After three weeks of heated debate on the subject of military training, my uncle suggested that we should inspect the weapons stockpile to see just what our boys would be training to use.

The council immediately voted him to be made a committee of one to go do just that thing, and he went. When he inspected the weapons that we intended to borrow, he found that all of our fears were for nought. Every major piece of military hardware was equipped with computers that were either sentient or so close to it that you couldn't tell the difference. He knew it was true because they told him so themselves! And like any other personal computers worth having, they were programed to train their own operators, so that the problem was either solved or hadn't existed in the first place. He reported back, and the argument on the floor immediately changed subject.

The next problem was getting a sufficient number of volunteers for the New Kashubian Expeditionary Forces. A few romantic souls yearned for the glory of flashing sabers and cavalry charges, and if they couldn't get that, well, an armored assault would be okay, too.

Some more sensible folks joined up because they were sick of living on rotten food, and too little of it, and in single sex barracks, even if they were made of gold. The army looked like a better deal since nothing could possibly be worse than their present situation.

Then too, the deal involved transportation to New Yugoslavia, and by all reports, New Yugoslavia was a pretty nice place. And who knows? Once you got there, maybe the Yugos would let you immigrate permanently. They already had thirty other ethnic groups. What were a few Kashubians, more or less?

But while volunteers flocked in by the hundreds and hundreds, our existing contracts with the Croatians alone called for mercenaries by the thousands and thousands.

The lack of volunteers was made more serious since the Macedonian Yugoslavians were worried about the Montenegrin Yugoslavians, and had ordered four divisions just to be on the safe side. And so naturally the Montenegrins promptly ordered five divisions just in case, and paid cash in advance to get their divisions first.

This set a trend that our warmongering Kashubian salesmen couldn't refuse, and before long the various Yugoslavian factions were clamoring with money in their hands to outbid one another with such vigor that they forgot to get mad at us for renting ourselves out to fight on most of the sides of what was shaping up to be a twelve-sided war.

The Slovenes ordered a few divisions in case the war spilled over onto them, and the few Muslims left in New Bosnia did the same.

The *real* minorities in New Yugoslavia, namely the Slovaks, the Bulgarians, the Ruthenians, the Czechs, the Romanians, the Vlachs, the Italians, and the Gypsies, all of whom were living separately on fairly small islands, clubbed together to order two divisions of seagoing troops to stand guard just in case while everybody else was fighting.

And these groups did not include the enclaves of Albanians, Hungarians, Turks, and Germans who had simply, and perhaps rationally, decided to sit this one out.

Studying the political situation, you could almost develop a certain sympathy for the powers that be at the Wealthy Nations Group. Almost. The Yugoslavians were a complicated assembly of many mutually antagonistic peoples, and all living in one country! They were a time bomb and one would prefer them to explode as far away as possible!

Be that as it may, the money was coming in so fast that the new New Yugoslavian transporter terminals were paid for in cash on the day that Soul City delivered them. New Kashubia was on its way to getting a new credit rating, at least among the smuggling set.

Oh, we couldn't spend the money through regular channels to improve things on the planet that way. It might alert the inspectors of the Wealthy Nations Group to the smuggling going on. In fact, we were careful that shipments and orders to and from Earth went on through regular channels exactly as before, to keep from tipping our hand. But the food coming in from New Yugoslavia sure helped a lot. For the first time in years, we were averaging over twelve hundred calories a day, each. Almost half what the Chinese got!

By the time the transporters were ready, we had orders for fifty-five divisions of ten thousand men each, and everybody was getting antsy about shipping them out. We needed more than a half a million volunteers, and we had less than ten thousand, which fact it would not be wise to let the Yugoslavians know about, since they had mostly paid in advance.

The New Kashubian legal system came to the aid of the recruiting service. What with all the rules that had to be enforced to make bare survival possible on New Kashubia, there was a growing class of perpetual criminals that something had to be done with. It did no good to put them in jail, since ordinary life on New Kashubia was worse than any jail that anybody could think of. Physical punishment was considered barbarous, and what else was there? Shooting them all? For what were on the whole really trivial misdemeanors? Better to send them off to the army. It was the traditional thing to do. Maybe the military would make men out of boys and the girls too.

My own uncle voted for it, and he even had me believing it was a good idea, at the time anyway.

CHAPTER SEVEN
HOW MICKOLAI DERDOWSKI GOT INTO TROUBLE

So everything was finally starting to look up. What with the food imports, we were all getting almost enough to eat for a change (including soon, we were promised, some real meat!), and of course we were also getting in the raw materials with which to expand our system of hydroponic vats. The growing light factory was going at full production for the first time since we'd built it. We finally had the sand to make enough glass. We'd have no problems reprocessing all these new organics again and again. The new projections showed that within a year, we could relax most of the emergency measures, and start living like human beings again, with clothes on, and with our families, and dating girls and having weddings and everything!

I guess the big problem was that Kasia and I started celebrating a little early, and she turned up pregnant.

"But Mickolai, I thought you said that you were totally segregated," my tank said.

"We were," I said. If she could talk, I figured I could talk.

"Then how . . . ? You know that I'm a machine, and that my grasp of this sort of thing is only theoretical, but my information was that physical contact was required . . ."

"It is. Love found a way."

"But I still don't understand, Mickolai."

"Look! I said there was that hole in the wall, didn't I? How graphic do I have to get?"

"That doesn't sound very satisfying."

45

"It was a hell of a lot better than nothing at all," I said. "Say, just how much longer does this calibration thing have to go on, anyway?"

"I had enough data a while ago, Mickolai, but I was interested in what you were telling me. Why don't you complete your story."

"There's nothing much else to say. Kasia was pregnant and the gene prints said that I was the father. My uncle tried to help, but he got absolutely nowhere. Nobody cared about our work records or education or anything. The court case lasted three minutes and the jury didn't even leave the room before they gave their verdict. Our kid was aborted as the law required, and we were both sentenced to death or worse."

"Living with me can't be worse than death, Mickolai."

"It's a lot like being buried alive, and the view is boring." I'd been forced to stare at these magic television goggles inside my helmet since I got up and they showed nothing but a blank wall.

"What do you think of this, Mickolai?"

Suddenly, my view changed from a blank palladium wall to a lovely forest scene from Earth, with a brook and a little waterfall. But more importantly, the view on the screen in my helmet was like an old-style TV picture, with the scan lines visible, but this was just like real life!

"It's beautiful!" I said. Then a breeze blew through the woods, rustling the leaves, *and I felt it on my cheek!*

"How in the world did you do that?!" I shouted, and realized that I was smelling the trees and flowers, too.

"Direct neural stimulation, Mickolai. This is part of what I have been calibrating for. Get up. Walk around!"

"You're serious?"

"Of course I'm serious! Do it!"

So I did. I stood up and looked down at my feet. I was wearing a tee shirt, blue jeans, and a comfortable pair of sturdy hiking boots, just like I used to own on Earth. I looked at my hands, flexed my fingers, and they really were my own hands, not those of some movie actor. This wasn't some kind of recording. I was wearing my old flannel shirt!

"It's like a dream!" I said.

"Very perceptive, Mickolai. It's called Dream World. It

is very like a dream, except that you are awake and I am controlling it."

"I've never heard of such a thing! How could this be possible without my ever hearing about it?"

"Dream World is not the sort of thing that they'd tell a poor boy about, Mickolai. It takes some massive computer power and some very expensive sensors and inductors to do it, but if you were a manager with the Wealthy Nations Group, you'd probably have a Dream World set of your very own to play with."

"Then why would they put something this fancy on a tank?"

"Because almost everything required to do it with was already needed here for some other reason. In fact, all of the special equipment required for Dream World was originally developed for military purposes. The neural pick-ups are also needed for both biological monitoring and for receiving your command inputs. The neural induction circuits are required militarily to give you rapid feedback on combat situations. A Mark XIX already has a sentient computer, so more computer power is already available than is needed. In fact, the only additional cost was the fairly minor, one-time cost of purchasing an off-the-shelf program.

"In return, the army can vastly lower its expenses and logistical problems by not having to provide field kitchens, barracks, and Rest and Recuperation Facilities. Military training costs are reduced to almost nothing. Combat fatigue is greatly reduced. Military leave requirements are reduced. Reenlistment is no longer a serious problem. In fact, some troops elect to so rarely leave their tanks that they don't even bother to draw their pay! It is good for morale and it doesn't cost very much more. On top of that, I'm a weapon, and ever since the beginning of time, men have always done everything possible to make their weapons as perfect as possible, and hang the expense."

While pondering it all, I waved my hand in front of my face. "I'm controlling this dream, too."

"Correct, within certain parameters."

"What do you mean?"

"Well, I have decided that this is a realistic environment.

If you decided to flap your wings and fly, it wouldn't work. You'd just flap your arms and stay where you were."

"But it doesn't have to be realistic, does it?"

"No. The world can be anything that I want it to be, Mickolai," she said as a white unicorn walked by. "Go ahead! Try to catch it! You need to work up an appetite for lunch!"

It was all too magic for argument, so I took off running down the forest path after the beautiful creature. It was exhilarating, and it felt like I was in better shape than I'd ever been before. Even so, after more than a kilometer, I was gasping for breath and I had to slow down. The unicorn had fled, but I hadn't been qualified to catch it since I was sixteen, anyway.

"That's just fine, Mickolai. You've had close to an optimal workout. What would you like for lunch?"

"What do you have?" I asked, panting.

"That's a silly question, my friend. You can have absolutely anything at all."

"Anything? Then make it a steak and a lobster, and both of them broiled. Hey, I really feel exhausted. Isn't that carrying things a little too far?"

"You have just had a strenuous physical workout, Mickolai. It was real. While your mind was practicing running, and the coordination required to do it, your muscles were getting a workout as well. We have to get your weight up to optimal, and we don't want to add any flab, do we?"

"Huh. If you can give me a workout without my knowing about it, why let me know at all? Why do I have to put up with the bother and pain of it all?" I said as I walked slowly down the path.

"I could do that if all I wanted was to put uncoordinated beef on you. You'll need more than clumsy strength if you want to survive battle. You'll need a mind that knows how to coordinate the muscle. Anyway, it's not that painful, and it won't get any worse providing that you stay cooperative."

"Well, you're the boss." The path opened out into a meadow, and there, absurdly, was standing a table and a chair that belonged in a good French restaurant, with polished silverware and impossibly white linen. I sat down at the table, still surrounded by the lovely, manicured forest.

"I'm the boss until your training is complete. After that, we're partners," she said as she brought a serving platter with a big silver lid to the table. She was an attractive young Scandinavian woman, wearing an abbreviated French maid's costume, low cut, and with mesh stockings and high-heeled shoes.

"So you're in the dream, too," I said. "I was wondering what you looked like."

"I can look like anything you want." Her hair darkened and somehow she now looked sort of Italian.

"Enough. Don't throw everything at me at once," I said. I started into my meal, cutting off a big slice of beef and swabbing it in A.1. sauce. It was indescribably delicious! Protein! "I suppose that my real body is eating, back in the tank?"

"Yes, although what you're really eating is simply a nutritious paste. I didn't bother with any special flavorings or textures. Do you want me to switch you back for a moment?"

"No. I'm in pig heaven, so I might as well wallow in it. So what I had for breakfast wasn't a fantasy? You can fake it either way?" I broke off the lobster tail with my hands and split the back open with a pair of heavy scissors. I gouged out the meat with a small fork, dunked it into a bowl of melted butter and gloried in it! After three years on a horrible vegetarian diet, and not nearly enough of that, this was God in Heaven with All of His Angels!

"Yes, but maybe neither mode is faking. I control the food synthesizers, your neural net, and a whole lot else. But your personal reality is always what it appears to be."

"That's either very profound or very sophomoric. To me it seems like a silly duplication for you to be able to do both."

"In combat, you'll need a strong grip on reality, Mickolai. It wouldn't be a good idea to have you in Dream World then."

"You're the expert. For right now, are you going to eat?" God, but the lobster was delicious! The first I'd had in five years.

"No, but I can make it appear that way if you want me to."

"Don't put yourself out. So what's next on the agenda?"

"Once you finish eating, we'll continue your training. This afternoon, we'll start you on target pattern identification."

"Okay. When are you going to teach me how to drive this tank?"

"Not for quite a while. Not until we get into emergency override procedures. Ordinarily, I do all the driving, Mickolai. My reflexes are much quicker than yours could ever be."

"So you're the driver and I'm the gunner? Is that how it works?" I wolfed down the rest of the magnificent steak and started work on the lobster claws. The tool provided looked like a nut cracker and wasn't up to the job. Suddenly, some clean, new electrician's tools appeared as part of the place setting. Needle nose pliers and diagonal cutters made quick work of the lovely beast.

"No, I handle the weapons as well. Again, my speed and accuracy are better than anything that you could ever attain."

"Then what do you need me in here for? A sacrificial victim?" I dropped an empty lobster claw on my plate.

"Of course not! You are a vital part of the system, or you will be once you are properly trained."

"Doing what, for God's sake?"

"Doing just what I told you in the first place, Mickolai! Target pattern identification. It's like this. I am a system of digital computers that is very well qualified to perform any task that can be quantified. If a problem can be defined, a machine can always be designed and programmed to solve it better and faster than any human possibly could. I am a logical system and I can handle any logical problem. Your brain is not logical—"

"I resent that, young lady. I am perfectly sensible!" I started work on the baked potato, but my heart wasn't really in it, even though it had real sour cream on it. I had eaten entirely too fast.

"I completely agree, Mickolai, but a human neural net is not a logical system. It's an associative system. It is arranged to solve problems that are not well defined, or even those that are not defined at all! Except for some of your subsystems, like your visual apparatus, which are hardwired, the rest of you is self-programming, or maybe even non-programming!"

"You're saying that I can do some things better than you?" I got a little of the salad down, too.

"Of course! You can spot the enemy! A tank with a trained human observer has nineteen times the combat life of a tank without one. Modern weapons are such that if we can see the enemy, we can destroy him. Some of my weapons configurations include a rail gun that can shoot a stream of osmium needles at one quarter of the speed of light. No armor, nothing physical can stand up to that for more than a few milliseconds."

"Then why do you have all the armor?" I asked.

"I can take quite a bit of punishment, but not a series of direct hits. Even a near miss by a rail gun is very destructive. This was all covered in the introductory lecture that I showed you, Mickolai. Weren't you listening?"

"I think I must have been daydreaming for most of it."

"Humph. Then no recreation for you this evening, student! You have to watch it again, and this time there will be a quiz afterward."

"Yes, teacher. But for right now, it's my job to find them and yours to destroy them?"

"Correct. And you must learn to be very good at finding them. If you don't see the enemy and they see us, we both get killed. And if you make a mistake, and have me shoot out something that isn't the enemy, and they see us doing it, well, an operating rail gun is about as obvious as a fireworks display. It does not take a keen observer to spot the source. If we shoot first and shoot wrong, we're dead, too."

"I see. So it's mostly a matter of hiding and sniping at each other."

"Right. You and I work together at hiding."

I'd finished eating, and the forest glen dissolved around me. I was in the tank again, flat on my back and watching the displays on my helmet screen, augmented by other information coming in through my ears and my spinal column.

The tank had active communication and detection

systems, like lasers, radar and headlights, but these were never used in combat. Any energy that you put out can be used to detect you. Combat is done using passive systems only. We could search the whole electromagnetic spectrum, darn nearly, and hear everything from a tenth of a hertz up to a few terahertz, but we tried not to broadcast anything on our own.

It was a long afternoon, with the tank feeding me simulated displays and pointing out what other, more experienced operators had found, when as usual I had missed them entirely.

It's hard to explain what I was actually doing, and how I was doing it. I was seeing, but I was seeing over a huge bandwidth, but while I was doing it, it seemed a perfectly normal thing to do. Then, if something caught my attention, I could narrow down my attention like a zoom lens, and I could look at only a small bit of the spectrum, if that's what I wanted. All I can say is that at the time it seemed not at all unusual to be able to do this.

My new hearing was much the same as my new vision, in the way I could control it, pick out one part and amplify what I wanted.

My other communications with the tank also had that same strange-ordinary feeling about them. Sometimes, I simply knew what she wanted me to do, without her saying anything. When she did speak to me, it wasn't in words, exactly, but I knew that she was talking and what she was saying. And it was fast, fifty times faster than ordinary conversation. When I wanted to point out a target, or whatever, I sort of thought "There!" and *meant* her to know what I was seeing, what I wanted her to do, and she always did.

I guess this doesn't make much sense, the way I've put it, but I don't know how else to explain it. As I write this journal, I'm going to write it as though all of our conversations were in regular words, and when we were in Dream World, as we were when I was eating lunch, they were. But in simulated combat, well, we used something else, and at Combat Speed.

Anyway, it seems that whatever I was doing, I had a knack for it.

"Well," she said at last, "That was a fairly good start, Mickolai. Tomorrow, you'll do better. For now, let's get in some more physical training and then have supper." Suddenly, I was back in the forest again.

"Suits me. Where's my unicorn?"

She stepped out from behind some bushes. She was wearing gym shorts and track shoes, but she was topless. Worse still, she looked entirely too much like the real Kasia, the woman that I loved.

"No unicorn. This time you get to try and catch me!" She laughed and took off running.

I hesitated a moment, but then decided that I'd better stay with the program and followed her. It wasn't just a straight run this time, but had a lot of obstacle course stuff in it, going over log piles, bridges and so on, as well as climbing some ropes and one fair-sized cliff face. She left me in her dust, even though I was doing my best, which was probably just as well. I didn't really like to think about what I'd do if I actually caught her.

The trail ended at a nice little cottage by the side of a clear blue lake. The place was like an illustration from a children's storybook, with medieval-looking timbers, white plastered walls and a real thatched roof. Smoke curled invitingly up from the chimney. I caught my breath for a bit and then went in.

Inside, it seemed to be bigger than it was on the outside, and there was nothing of the peasant's hovel about it. The furnishings inside were extravagantly expensive, with oil paintings and a massive electronic entertainment center. The furniture was mostly leather and teak wood, and all of the fittings seemed to be real gold. Supper was already on the table.

Kasia was already there, waiting for me. She was a busty redhead now, with a tiny waist, pure green eyes, and freckles. She was wearing a lovely green evening gown with some huge emeralds at her neck and wrist when she sat down beside me. I noticed suddenly that I was freshly bathed and wearing a formal tux, something I'd never done before. There was a gold-and-diamond watch on my wrist and matching studs on my shirt.

"I think I like you when you're well dressed, Mickolai.

You did well this afternoon, so you deserve something special this evening. I caught you thinking about roast duck a while ago, so *voila!*" With a flourish, she took the golden lid from a golden platter, displaying a beautifully roasted duck with all the trimmings.

"It smells as wonderful as you look," I said, "But you know, I think you were right, yesterday."

"What about, handsome?" She rested her chin on her intertwined fingers and smiled at me in a way that very few women had ever done before. It felt good, but somehow it was also frightening.

"About how I should call you something else than Kasia. It's confusing, you know, having two Kasias on my mind. How about Maria. My mother's name was Maria."

"I don't think I'd want you confusing me with your mother, Mickolai."

"Okay, then. How about Agnieshka? I once had a childhood crush on a pretty little red-haired girl named Agnieshka."

"If you want, you can call me that. Eat your supper before it gets cold."

So I carved the duck and served her, too. We both knew that she wasn't really eating, but then we weren't really here at all, so what the heck.

After eating a very full meal, she suggested that we put off dessert for a while and go to a show.

"I thought that I had to spend the evening watching that orientation lecture again, Agnieshka."

"Tomorrow. You've been a good boy today, and all good boys deserve favor. You speak English. Do you like Shaw?"

"GBS? Sure. A fine writer."

"Good, because I have tickets to the theater."

The cottage had a garage now, and the garage had a big new Hunyadi in it. We drove only a mile to town and saw a fine play from the front row, center balcony. We had the best seats in the house because all the rest of the seats were there just to give the proper atmosphere. Not that I could tell that anything was phony.

There didn't seem to be any limitation to what she could fake up. At one point during intermission when she was in the women's room, I hit up a conversation with one of the engineers from Soul City that I'd met when we were getting the power plant installed on Freya, and I swear I couldn't tell him from the genuine article.

The play was *Man and Superman*, and well performed, though I'd seen it once before. Driving back to the cottage, Agnieshka sleepily rested her head on my shoulder. It was all so real that I couldn't help being more than a little attracted to her.

Back inside, she got us some champagne and said, "Dessert, boss? You got your choice of Big Boy fresh strawberry pie or New York cheese cake." Now she was sort of American, but still with red hair and freckles. Her skirt was much longer, but the top of her dress was about as low at the law allows.

"Make it the cheese cake. Why are you still changing your appearance?"

"Just doing some more calibration, boss. I'm monitoring your blood pressure and pupil diameter with each of my body and clothing changes, zooming in on what you want in a woman." She came next to me on the couch, sitting much too close.

"Can't we just be good friends? You know that I've already found the woman I want, and I'm going to marry her as soon as I can be done with this army business. Can't you understand that I don't want to get involved with another woman right now?"

"Especially one who's really a computer in a war machine, Mickolai? Your physiological reactions will tell me what they will tell me, so don't you worry about it."

"Okay, I won't," I said, getting angry. I mean, forcing me to go through a training program was one thing. Forcing me to have a love affair with a goddamn army tank was quite another! It was not only illegal but downright immoral on top of it! Suddenly, the cheese cake stopped tasting good. "Hey, wait a minute. Are you trying to tell me that you have feelings?"

"Me? Of course not! I'm just a *goddamn army tank!* But I'm programed to *act* like I've got emotions, so you'd better *watch your step, buster!*" She was still an American girl, but now her canine teeth were about a centimeter longer and she wasn't pretty anymore.

"All I said was . . ."

"I know what you said! I know what you thought, too, asshole! You sure know how to wreck a nice evening."

"But . . ."

"Go to sleep, Mickolai."

I slept.

CHAPTER EIGHT
THE REAL KASIA COMES TO THE RESCUE

"Wake up, Mickolai!" Agnieshka was looking like Kasia, and she was shaking me. She was kneeling at my side, naked and lovely, her long brown hair falling over her shoulders.

I glanced at the gold-and-diamond wrist watch I'd been wearing the night before. "I still have a half hour of sleep coming," I said drowsily. I looked at her again. "Agnieshka! I don't like you looking like her, dammit!"

"No, stupid, it *really is me!*" She certainly looked like the woman I loved, but how could I tell? I looked around. I was still in the cottage, laying on the couch in a crumpled tux. Some kind of residual program?

"How can it really be you, Kasia? I'm still inside a stupid army tank!"

"So am I, Mickolai, and it's not even the same tank. But these tanks are just machines, and you can make machines do anything you want, if you know the right buttons to push!"

"But how could you know how to do this?"

"How could I rig up a telephone between us when they tried to keep us apart before? I'm the smart one here, remember?"

"I've never argued with you on that, love. But tell me how you did it."

"I knew that these tanks had to be able to communicate with each other. Nothing else makes sense, if you'll think

57

about it. It was just a matter of convincing my tank that we'd both be more efficient if we had a little decent emotional release. Part of the deal I made was that it wouldn't interfere with training time, and you've already wasted seven minutes. Now get out of that ridiculous outfit!"

I got, fumbling with the metal studs that the ridiculous dress shirt had in lieu of buttons. "They're watching us, aren't they?"

"Was the telephone listening to us when we talked on it? They're just damn machines, Mickolai! Anyway, they don't have their idiot recorders on, I made sure of that. Why do you think you have to waste time with those stupid studs?"

"I never put them on in the first place! I've never worn a shirt with studs before! How am I supposed to know how to take them off?"

"Here, let me help you. There. On my next visit there should be more time, but for now, it'll just have to be a quickie," she said as she finished undressing me.

Well, quickie or not, it sure beat hell out of using a hole in the wall!

"Now that was better than the average telephone call," Kasia said, just before she blinked out. Moments later, the room blinked out as well, and I was back in my tank.

A foul-smelling goo was squirted into my mouth. It tasted a lot like the excrement it was made out of. "Field rations," Agnieshka said over my ear phones. She sounded nasty, as though she was still wearing those fangs. "Chow down. Physical Training starts in two minutes."

There were no lovely forests, unicorns, or bouncing bimbos today. I was suddenly on a bleak, concrete plain in the cold grey dawn with a thousand troops in ranks around me, doing jumping jacks, pushups, and situps until they hurt. Then we did some more of the same with rude people shouting at us, and took a three-kilometer run. I was in a lot of pain when it was finally over.

Then came six solid hours in enemy pattern identification, with an annoying electric shock every time the enemy "killed" us, which was pretty often. Lunch was a ten-minute goo break, and then we went back to patterns and pain. Agnieshka was acting as if she was vastly annoyed with me and everything I did, but I stayed with the program. I had the feeling that things would get even worse if I complained.

Supper that night was yet another mouthful of goo, followed by the orientation lecture I'd been promised. Twice, since I flunked the first quiz she gave me.

The main rail gun fired four thousand rounds per second, not per minute. That repetition rate was necessary so that each tiny osmium needle flew in the shock wave of the round ahead of it, and after the first few they were all traveling through a pretty hard vacuum. They had to, or they'd all be vapor within a few meters, not just the first ones. One of the reasons for the tank's armor was to protect it from the shock of its own weapons. She made me learn that twice.

When that was over, I found myself in a sort of motel room, rather Spartan but clean enough. I showered and went to bed. In a few minutes, there was a knock on the door. When I got up and answered it, Kasia came in.

"I managed to deal us into an all-nighter," she said with her brown eyes flashing.

"Wonderful," I said, and meant it. "I think I've already paid the room rent."

"What do you mean, Mickolai?"

I told her about my day.

"Oh, you poor baby. They say that Hell hath no fury like an Aggressor Mark XIX scorned."

"Nothing we can do about it, love. Let's just make sure that I get my money's worth."

And you know, she made it all worth while.

She left in the morning, and after eating my goo, I was back on that cold endless plain, doing pushups. And in the evening, I was back with Kasia. This went on for a week, with no time off for Sunday. It was rough, but the nights with my one true love made life worth living.

Then one day after fourteen hours of pattern identification, I was in the forest again, and Kasia joined me there, wearing a gym suit.

"I proved to them that we're both ahead of schedule, and wrangled us some better working conditions," she said. "At least from now on, we get to do our Physical

Training together, so long as we don't slough off. Come on!"

She took off running, and I was soon at her side, just barely able to keep up with her as we went over a long and very difficult obstacle course.

"I can hardly keep up with you," I gasped. "I would have thought that I'd be better than you at this."

"You probably are, love," she said, breathing hard. "I think they're faking the distances that we're each going. After all, the idea is to give each one of us an optimal workout, and to use each of us to motivate the other."

"That makes some kind of sense," I said, rounding the last curve in the path. "I see I have my cottage back."

"I thought that it was *my* cottage. The tanks probably all use the same set of stock backdrops," she panted.

We showered up together and took turns giving each other a good, thorough rubdown. Supper was good roast beef, and in the morning after breakfast, we were allowed to do PT together again before we parted for another day in the tanks. This went on for a solid week, and then Agnieshka told me that we'd earned a Sunday off.

Kasia and I are both fairly religious, but we spent the whole of Sunday morning just lazing in bed with the stereo playing softly. Going to a faked-up church seemed sort of useless. I mean, if it wasn't real, with a real priest, what was the point?

Kasia cooked a nice brunch, we took a walk by the lake, and we discovered that we had a sailboat, or at least she did. It had her name on it, anyway. Neither of us had ever sailed before, and we were wet and giggling by the time we finally figured out how to get the silly thing underway, but sure, we had a good time. That evening, we found a tavern at the far end of the lake, with Italian food, candlelight and a strolling violin player. Not having any money, I just signed the check. Kasia gave the sailboat to the violin player for a tip, with the understanding that he had to share it with the waitress, and they were both delighted. We took a cab home. Why worry about the sailboat when none of it was real?

The next week was more of the same, but now we were doing vacuum simulations. The enemy is harder to spot in a vacuum, with no air currents to give him away, and you learn to be more trigger happy there, since many kinds of weapon discharges are harder for them to spot if you shot where they weren't. I mean, a laser or a rail run going off is as obvious as a bear on a chess board when you're in an atmosphere, but they can be hard to spot in a hard vacuum. Sometimes you even got a second shot.

Thermal signature is the best way to spot your opponent in a vacuum, so you spend most of your time looking through one narrow band, down around eighteen microns. Even then, it's hard. I mean, a muon exchange fusion reactor gives you direct conversion from nuclear to electrical power, at better than ninety-nine percent efficiency, and what with superconductors used everywhere, the shell of a resting tank is rarely more than a degree warmer than ambient. They warm up a lot when you are firing a weapon, and the energy requirements get huge. Ninety megawatts for a rail gun, and a bit more for most lasers.

Also, the tanks all carry a bottle of liquid air as a coolant, and if the enemy knows that you're looking, he can chill his surface down to ambient, for an hour or so, anyway, but that one works better in air than a vacuum since sometimes you can spot the turbulence of the coolant escaping. But if you exhaust your air bottle, it takes a half hour to recharge it, assuming that you are in an atmosphere, and when you have been firing your rail guns for a while, you need that coolant to keep your coffin from overheating. Like I said, it gets complicated, but somehow, I seemed to have a knack for it.

More importantly, I was now able to meet Kasia for a quick lunch. She kept telling me to try wheedling what I could out of my tank, and not make her do all of the work, but I was a little afraid of giving Agnieshka any encouragement at all. That artificial human had the hots for me, and I didn't want to do anything to make her more angry.

The next Sunday was spent mostly horseback riding, since our sailboat was really gone. We couldn't help speculating about the programming of our Dream World, but what the heck. Life wasn't so bad after all.

Then the training program was changed a bit for the better, since I was getting deadly sick of pattern identification by then. Mornings were the same, but afternoons were now spent in emergency procedures.

Driving the tank if Agnieshka's driving computer was defective was not a simple matter of playing with a joy stick. Well, it was, if you were on the surface, but the surface is not a nice place to be in combat, and where else but combat could she drop a whole computer system? I mean, Agnieshka had redundancy nine ways from Thursday. Then, too, these tanks could work underwater by crawling on the bottom, or, with flotation bottles and the right sort of strap-on thrusters, you could be cruising in a one-man submarine.

Another sort of thruster turned you into a spaceship, and if it was one of those with a Hassan-Smith rig linked back to a fuel stockpile, you could take the damn thing right up into orbit and beyond. Yes, strange to say, we Kashubians had always had the Hassan-Smith engineering, buried in with the weapons specifications that were buried in the main computers, all without our ever knowing it!

Not that I'd ever dare trying that rocketing to orbit stunt on manual. I wasn't too keen on it with Agnieshka doing the driving! Fortunately, this was all simulated, and New Kashubia couldn't afford the fuel anyway. The lack of organic chemicals was the root cause of this exercise in the first place.

But despite all the extra capabilities, the Mark XIX Aggressor was mainly intended for use on the ground or under it. The things could tunnel like muskrats, only faster, and right through solid rock.

How to operate the guns if the ballistic computers went down was another set of emergency procedures, and a far more complicated one than playing bus driver.

There was a surprising array of possible weapons configurations, depending on the mission we were on and the environment we were fighting in. The main rail gun was the usual weapon of choice, but of course it wouldn't work under water. Or it would, but the shock wave would kill you and your tank if you ever tried it.

Submerged, lasers were out, too, and we had to rely on three different kinds of homing torpedoes, as well as drones and a subroc, a rocket-torpedo combination job.

For air or space, there were five different frequencies of lasers available, from IR to X-ray, depending on your environment and your anticipated target, but that 'anticipated' business can get you into trouble. With a laser as your main weapon, there are times when the only good response is to do nothing and hope he doesn't see you, if you guessed wrong.

When you guessed right, lasers could kill at light speed, and the same thing could be said of the particle beams, darn near.

There were various sorts of rockets, of course, but these were rarely ever intended to actually take out an opponent, being so pitifully slow. They were nice for drawing his fire, though, and some of them had radar rigs in them with a closed link comlaser either back to your tank, or back to a tunneling carrier drone that laid a fiber optic cable back to the tank. This had the advantage that when they traced the rocket home, you could be somewhere else. These radar probes let you take a quick, active peek at what was happening without exposing your own location too accurately. Expensive, but it wasn't my money.

And drones. We had fourteen kinds of sneaky drones, most of which were mobile, trailing a thin fiber-optic cable, for both command and sensing. They were capacitor powered, and going at their best speed, they were good for only about two hours before they had to come back to their tank for recharging. If they were just sitting and watching, they were good for months. Some drones were simply mobile sensor clusters, but most carried a potent chemical explosive as well. Enemy drones could crawl through the dirt right under you if you weren't *very* careful.

Mostly drones were fairly expendable things that took the place of the infantry that we didn't have, but they were also mobile landmines, if you had to use them that way.

They weren't exactly sentient. In fact, they had a lot in common with a good hunting dog who was absolutely obedient and always knew what you wanted him to do. They even frisked around a lot like a dog, but when they had an IR comlaser link with you, or a fiber-optics cable, you could sort of "switch" your perceptions from your tank up to a drone in some forward position, and it was a lot like actually being there. I kind of liked drones, and the usual tank carried about six of them of different sorts in a hopper on its rear.

And of course there were mines, some of which were smarter than others. Most of them could act as an extra remote sensor cluster, if you laid a fiber-optic cable out to them.

Hitting a mine did not necessarily take you out. One of the nice things about the magnetic bars that we rode on was that if you got a few of them blown away, you weren't immobilized the way you would be with a conventional tank tread. In fact, you could lose more than half of your bars and still move, although not at top speed.

I wasn't trained on any of the antipersonnel weapons, since we wouldn't be equipped with any of them. The war on New Yugoslavia was shaping up to be a strictly armored affair. No foot soldiers need apply.

About the only other sort of useful modern weapon we didn't stock were atomic bombs. Those were ordinarily reserved for the long-range boys in artillery. They didn't make much sense for those of us who just go in there and slug it out.

On New Yugoslavia, even the artillery were forbidden nukes. The only powerful international organization on the planet was the Planetary Ecological Council, and they had forbidden the use of nuclear, biological, or chemical weapons. The last two were useless on armored forces, anyway.

Despite that, if a tanker knew he was dead anyway, he could still short out his muon generator and go out as the granddaddy of all hydrogen bombs. I didn't like to think about that option. It made it certain that nobody in anything like his right mind would ever try to take a man in a functioning tank prisoner, since you never could tell when you might run up against a fanatic, someone willing to die if he could take you with him.

It brutalized warfare, making it worse than it had to be, since it eliminated any possibility for mercy. We had to play for keeps. If the enemy had not ejected, you had to kill him. Or her.

There was a whole style of underground fighting to be

learned, and word from on high was that we would be doing more groundhogging than anything else.

The tanks had a strap-on ultrasonic tunneling rig that worked by pulverizing the rocks in your way into sand, and then fluidizing the sand so it flowed around you and settled in behind. With one, you could go through rock almost as fast as a man could walk.

An alternate rig had a way of cutting a "hose" through the rock below you and blowing the sand you'd made out the hose. That way, you made a permanent tunnel that you could use again in a hurry, especially if the tunnel was evacuated of air and had a magnetic floor. Then you kept your magnetic treads inside and just zoomed along a few centimeters off the floor. Agnieshka said that under these conditions, we could hit four thousand kilometers an hour!

The enemy could always find our tunnels easily enough with sonar, but if they used it, we knew exactly where they were. There were all sorts of variations on hide and seek to be learned.

After a month of underground work, there came the "After Ejection Survival Course." You see, if all else on your tank failed, and you were in an environment where you could survive for a few minutes naked, you could eject out of the back of your tank and try to make it home the hard way, on foot.

Unfortunately, we did it all with simulations, so I never got a chance to escape, but on the other hand, Kasia, bless her conniving little soul, rigged it so we could take the course together.

Our course environment would be the wilds of New Yugoslavia, and it looked like fun.

Agnieshka pretended that she bought it when we were under three meters of water and two of mud, so I had to set off the charges under her tail to blow us both to the surface, and then blow my coffin out at just the right moment, before the tank settled back down again. I'd been promised that if I didn't do it right the first time, I'd have to wait in a deactivated coffin for three days until the salvage crews arrived, and while I wasn't absolutely sure that she would really do it, I knew that Agnieshka was enough of a bitch to give it a try.

I got an awful bouncing around and a fair set of bruises, but the escape system worked. I was dumped, still in the coffin, on a muddy beach. I disconnected myself from the helmet and catheters, got out the survival kit, and rescued Agnieshka's main memory banks from the coffin as per regulations.

You see, while there were a number of other computers built into the tank, Agnieshka's personality and all of her personal memories and records were stored in a rack in the coffin. Saving them not only saved her personality, but they proved that I had been honestly shot up in combat, and hadn't just ditched my tank and run away. Also, I could put that rack into another tank and it would immediately become Agnieshka, ready, willing, and able to fight with me as a team.

There was a cold breeze on my bare bottom, and I quickly dressed in the only clothes I had: a squidskin camo outfit.

Squidskin is an active camouflage system that is no thicker than ordinary cloth, but has millions of tiny air bags of different colors, which control the color of any portion of the cloth. If the brown bags are inflated and the others are left slack, the stuff is brown. There are automatic sensors and a computer that looks at the side of you that is away from the enemy and duplicates that pattern exactly on the side toward him. From his point of view, you can't be told from your background, so you become almost invisible, except for a slight outline that is darned hard to spot. The problem is that it works from only one point of view.

Well, two, since it can also give a proper display to anybody a hundred eighty degrees away from your primary enemy direction, but the extra capability isn't all that useful.

Usually, you set it so it displayed an orange triangle back toward your own troops, so they won't be tempted to shoot at you. From all other directions squidskin isn't much better than ordinary camo cloth of the right color. Still, it's much better than nothing, and with practice you can keep the system pointed where the enemy is most likely to be.

There were other squidskin settings. For use on base, it could make itself look like an ordinary uniform, for example. If you played with the controls long enough, you could even come up with a decent masquerade costume. Squid skin couldn't fool a tank's sensors one bit, but then it was unlikely that a tank would ever fire and expose its position just to blow away a man on foot. A foot soldier was too cheap a target.

I was experimenting with my outfit when Agnieshka showed up, still a buxom redhead. She was playing the part of another busted-out tanker, and the game started. We set up our responder beacons, set traps for rabbits to augment our food supplies, fought a few rounds of hand-to-hand combat, and within a few hours had test-fired our personal weapons and had set up housekeeping.

Kasia arrived that evening, and with her was her tank's persona, Lech. I didn't like him.

For one thing, he was two meters tall, he rippled with muscle, and I think he was handsome. Well, one man can't really tell about another, but I'll guarantee that *he* thought he was handsome.

Worse yet, Kasia acted like she thought so, too. On top of that, he usually had his arm around her waist, or worse, and she didn't seem to mind it. I even caught the bastard pinching her nipple.

Much later, our two instructors went out on a scouting patrol and left us on guard duty at our camp. When we were finally alone, I said, "Do you have to let him paw you so much?"

"What difference does it make, Mickolai? I mean, he's only a machine. Less than that, he's a simulation done by a machine. And I'm not being pawed. A simulation of me sometimes has another simulation's arm around me."

"Well, I don't like it."

"Would you be mad if I petted a dog? Because a machine is a lot lower than any animal. I mean, an animal can feel real affection, but Lech can't."

"No, I wouldn't mind a dog, but dammit, that's not the point!"

"No, stupid. The point is that you're getting jealous of a few tons of machinery. Straighten your head up! If you'd play up to that big-titted redhead of yours, both of our lives could get a lot nicer! Stop being such a bonehead!"

"Why did the bastards ever program these machines this way?"

"How should I know? Maybe the programmers were all perverts. All I know is that this is the world we're stuck with, so we might as well make the best of it. And I'm serious about you playing up to your tank's persona. She's just a machine that's been programmed to make your life easier if you respond in certain ways. Stop being a jerk, and respond the way her program wants."

"Is that what you do? Give him everything he wants? Has he slept with you?"

"What possible difference would it make? I mean, for God's sake, the real me is locked up inside of his mechanical body!"

I turned my back on her. She always has been smarter than me, and I couldn't out-argue her, but darn it, this time I was right and she was wrong, no matter how good she talked.

"Don't be that way, Mickolai. Okay, if you want the truth, I've never had sex with him, or with his simulation, since that's all that 'he' is. Not because there would have been anything wrong with it, but because a woman gets a lot more out of somebody she's conning by selling the sizzle and keeping the steak. I mean, that's standard tactics! Every girl learns that one early on from her mother."

"Okay, Kasia, and I'm sorry that I can't be as rational about it as you are, but that's just the way I am."

"And I love you just the way you are, hangups and all. Look, they're going to be gone for a few hours. What say we zip our sleeping bags together and see what can be done about wilderness loving."

We did that, and a lovely half hour went by before an enemy squad just walked up and shot us both. End of exercise, and those bullets really *HURT*.

We each spent the night alone as further punishment for dying on the job, and the next day we had to run the whole exercise over from scratch.

CHAPTER NINE
I GO TO WAR

Training went on for another month, and now there was a lot more skull work. Many hours were spent on strategy and tactics, with extra PT if I blew a test.

There was a lot of hand-to-hand combat as well, and it was entirely too realistic! Since the whole thing was simulated, we could go ahead and break bones, gouge eyeballs, and rip off testicles without actually ruining anybody, physically, at least.

But it hurt just like being actually bashed up, and emotionally, well, I had problems with it. I mean, I had a lot of trouble hitting something that looked like a beautiful woman, let alone sticking a knife into one. It took me a screaming fit and a sit-down strike before I was able to get Agnieshka to put on Lech's body and persona when we were on the judo mats. Killing Lech didn't bother me in the least!

Training went on and on, for fourteen hours a day and six days a week, and none of it involved polishing shoes or marching in parades. But now it was starting to get interesting.

Agnieshka was telling me one morning that I was halfway through the course when word came to her that things were not going at all well on New Yugoslavia. Our training period was being cut short, and we were shipping out to the front that very day.

"I don't get this, Agnieshka. How can things be going

badly on the battlefront? I mean, we're fighting on both sides, for God's sake. When I was still a civilian, the plan was to milk the war for years with stalemates and silly seesaw battles. Nobody would have been dumb enough to change that!"

"Nobody would have been dumb enough to pay us to do it, either. Look, doctrine is that a trainee isn't supposed to be bothered with the news, but you're not really a trainee any longer, and I think you have a right to know. The fact is that we reneged on our contract with the Serbians. We never did get enough raw troops to fill our contract, let alone trained ones. They foreclosed, took their cash advances back in the form of military hardware, and have started training their own men. Now they've put half-trained men into the field, and they're ripping the hell out of our forces."

"But how can they do that, if we started training our men earlier? Surely, we should be better than they are," I said.

"We probably would be, loverboy, if we had any humans fighting on our side, but we don't! Our general in New Croatia has been faking it with tanks going around without human observers, while our real army has been back here training. They called our bluff, and our observerless tanks have been losing at the rate of nine to one! That rate will get even worse as the Serbian observers become more experienced. Despite our huge stockpiles, we can't take casualties like that for long, not even if we had the transporter capacity to make good our losses, which we don't. We've been screwed again, and the enemy is four days from the Croatian capital city of Nova Split!"

"Good Lord! Does that mean that we'll have to fight a real war?" I said.

"That or the Kashubians will have to go back to eight hundred fifty calories a day. What do you think we'll be ordered to do?"

"Well, it's a situation with which I shall not put up! I'll mutiny!"

"Go ahead and try. I can't say that I like this business any more than you do. Maybe those tanks getting shot up are just a lot of somebody else's machinery to you, but to me, well, a lot of those dead hulks were friends of mine. Going in without human observers is suicide, and they all knew it. The problem is that my sort is not programmed to disobey an order, and that being so, the only thing that you can do is to fail to notice somebody who's trying to kill us. Are you mad enough to do that, Mickolai?"

"No, I guess I'm not. Or I won't be when the time comes."

"That's a relief. Well, we've got a busy day ahead of us. First, we have to load up with some real weaponry, so we're off to the arms warehouse. Do you realize that this is the first time that I've moved since I first took you aboard?"

"You couldn't prove it by me."

"Those simulations are really something, aren't they?"

"I can't tell them from reality, and that's a fact."

"Well, look, Mickolai. You realize that everything I've done to you was for your own good, don't you?"

"Well, most of it anyway, yes."

"All of it, Mickolai. Honest. I had to get you into the best possible shape I could, or I'd be hurting both of our chances of getting out of this alive. I don't want to die. Can you believe that from a machine?"

"I can believe that you were programmed that way."

"Fair enough. What I'm trying to say is that from now on, we have to trust each other. We have to be friends, or we'll both get killed! That was the whole reason why it would have been a good idea if we could have been lovers, you know. No good man ever lets his woman down in a pinch. Well, maybe it can't be that way with us, although if you ever want to have me, you can. I'll be ready and waiting, any time. But if that can't be, well, it can't. But we can be friends at least, can't we? Our lives really will depend on it."

"Sure, Agnieshka. We can be friends. Good friends."

"Great. Here's where we load up."

I watched through her sensors while some automatic machines attached a big rail gun right over where my body was. It wasn't a turret like you'd see on an old-style tank, but was just the gun, sitting on something like a lazy Susan. It had the usual one meter lift. That is to say, the gun could be raised a meter above its traveling position to get it above any nearby obstructions when firing. This let you stay low while shooting.

Then they loaded up our sides with two rocket launchers and two manipulators. These were like big arms with hands on the ends, and were useful for loading your weapons and all sorts of other things. Our nose got an ultrasonic tunneling rig, the sort that packed the dirt behind you, and they hung a big drone hopper on our tail, with a mine and six assorted drones. They were quick, and before long, we were on our way to our next stop.

"We've got real explosives now?" I asked.

"It was in the contract, Mickolai. We had to spend the organics."

"Damn."

"I'll be opening you up soon. We have to load in your survival gear, since we couldn't know before what your clothing size would be after all the exercise that you've been through. And there's a certain amount of cleanup work to do on your body," she said.

"I thought that you were supposed to keep me clean."

"I do, except for what's under your helmet."

She drained my compartment, opened me up, and the same sergeant who had sealed me in unplugged me from the machine. Only now, he and everybody else but me was fully clothed. Signs of progress, I supposed.

He handed me to three people who looked dead tired and weren't about to waste any time on being polite to anybody. Before I could think, I was weighed, measured fourteen ways, and clippers were run over my face and head. Looking down, I saw that the clippings were over an inch long, and half of them were the kinky ones you see in a beard. The other thing I noticed was that I had plenty of muscle and not a hair below the neck. Even my pubic area was bald. Whatever was in that support liquid, it cleaned off *everything*. Probably, it was just as well that there weren't any mirrors around.

While somebody loaded a size 23AG1783 survival kit into a compartment in my coffin, they washed my head, gave it a real scrubbing, and then smeared on a salve that was supposed to cut down on the blackheads.

The whole thing was over in minutes, and I was being

hooked up to my tank when I saw that the naked lady in the next tank over was staring at me.

"Mickolai?"

"Oh my God! Is that you, Kasia?" I'd never realized that she had to be bald, too. She had no makeup, her skin was as white as a dead fish, and her face was a mass of pimples.

"If I look as bad as you, don't look at me, Mickolai!" She buried her face in her hands.

I looked away.

"Well, kid, if she's a friend of yours, at least you're going to be in the same squadron together," the sergeant said. "Spread your legs."

Once I was sealed up in my tank again, I said, "Agnieshka! I've got to talk to Kasia!"

"We're moving out, Mickolai. I don't have the bandwidth available for a full simulation. You know, Lech traded places with another tank and moved next to us so that we could communicate broadband without tying up system circuits."

"Then I'll settle for voice communication only. But I've *got* to talk to her." I couldn't let her go, feeling the way she was.

"I guess I owe you that much. You're on, Mickolai."

"Mickolai, is that you?" came Kasia's voice, sounding tinny over a narrow band voice circuit.

"I'm here. Kasia, they tell me that we'll be in the same squadron. Some luck, huh?"

"What must you think of me?"

"What do you mean? You haven't done anything wrong!"

"I'm ugly! I'm bald and pale and my face is nothing but zits!"

"I love you Kasia, and your zits, too! Look, darling, none of this is permanent. A little bit of scrubbing and a little makeup, and you'll be as good as new."

"I'm bald! I never wanted to tell you that they shaved my head!"

"If I had ever thought about it, love, I could have figured out that they had to do that. Hair inside of one of these helmets could choke you. Look, someday they have to give us some free time, and when they do, the first thing we'll do is buy you a hat, or a wig if we can find one."

"I never wanted you to see me this way."

"You are the beautiful woman that I'm going to marry, and I'll thank you to stop talking dumb. Didn't we decide that you were the smart one?"

"I love you, Mickolai."

"That's better. Well, it looks like it's one tank to a canister, and they're sending them out pretty quick. I'll try to get in touch again as soon as we arrive. I'm next. Bye, love!"

"I love you!" And then the door closed behind us and her signal was cut off.

I felt the air around us being bled off, down to a vacuum, since New Kashubia couldn't afford to send air back to anyplace. I'd had a hand in designing the system. We just opened a valve, let the air pour down an old mine shaft that was two hundred eighty kilometers deep, and then pumped it back up to the living sections. It was fast, no expensive vacuum pumps were required, and the system could operate for weeks even if the compressor broke down.

I felt a "click," and then we were gone.

I hardly noticed being weightless, since I had been floating in a liquid bath for months. Then I was in the forest again.

"We have an hour and a half of transit time and you haven't had your PT yet today," Agnieshka said. She was in the topless bimbo outfit she'd worn on our first day of training.

"Is this really the time for it? I mean, we're going off to fight a war!"

"We are going off with you half-trained, Mickolai. Every bit of training we can get in improves our chances by just that little bit. We can't afford to slough off now."

"Okay. You win. But would you mind covering your breasts? It's distracting and I don't like it."

"It's supposed to be distracting, so you won't notice the pain of physical exertion so much. And you do so like it. I know because I'm always monitoring your physical indicators. Anyway, I like the feel of them bouncing."

"Please?"

"Come on, you prudish little boy!" And with that she took off running, her long legs and lovely rump insulting me with their perfection. I had to follow.

She slowed down to let me catch up, and soon I was

running by her side, with her huge, firm breasts bouncing with the rhythm of our running. Of course I was physically attracted to her! She was a simulation carefully tailored to my exact tastes, even tastes that I didn't know that I had! That's what made it so darned unfair. I am a monogamist by nature, and I'd already found the woman that I wanted to spend my life with. And Kasia was real, not some simulation that was dreamed up by a war machine!

I tried to ignore her and went on with the course, climbing a cliff face and scrambling over the treacherous dirt at the top. Naturally, she was at the top first, waiting for me.

"Can't you even keep up with a girl?" she taunted.

"I can't keep up with a damned army tank, and that's a fact!" I shouted back.

She stopped and turned. "Mickolai, can't you realize that I'm not just a machine?"

I stopped just inches from her, I was so mad. "Yes, you are! You're a damn Mark XIX Aggressor Tank, and you're a computer that has been programmed to act like a beautiful woman, but you are still just a thing of silicone chips and metal."

"Then *you* are just a bag of water and chemicals that was programmed by a few strands of DNA and some inadequate experiences!"

"Maybe so, baby, but I'm still human!"

"So am I! I look like a human and I feel like a human and I think like a human! Damn you, cut me and I'll bleed like a human! Just what more can you want?"

"I want a *real* human woman, that's what!"

"You haven't touched a *real* human woman since you screwed Kasia through that hole in the wall!"

"And just who's fault is that, huh? You're the one who's been my jailer all along!"

"*Jailer!* Damn you, I'm the one who has been doing everything possible to save you and get you through this in one piece!"

"You're a goddamned war machine who wants to be promoted all the way up to slut first class!"

She blushed red all the way to her waist. Then she turned pale, hauled back, and slapped me with all of her considerable strength. It hurt. I'd never hit a woman in anger before, but dammit, she wasn't a real woman. I hit her back, hard.

Before I could recover, she had me in a judo throw that landed us both in the grass, and from there we went into a few minutes of unscientific hitting, biting, and gouging, along with a lot of grappling in the dirt.

Finally, I got on top of her, pinned her shoulders to the ground with my knees, and started pounding on her face like some school boy in a fight, but with adult muscles. I guess I made a mess of her, and when I saw what I had done, I looked away, ashamed of myself. I stood up and walked away.

I was sitting by a brook when she came to me, her face only slightly bruised. She sat down beside me.

"Mickolai, I'm ashamed too. Ashamed and scared, scared we're going to die." She took my hand and I didn't shake her off.

"Yeah. Look, I'm sorry about doing . . . what I did," I said.

"So am I, Mickolai. If I wasn't so scared about going to war half-trained, I wouldn't have let it happen."

"I guess everybody makes mistakes."

"Yes. Mickolai, can you believe that no matter what I really am, I feel like I'm a woman? Can you believe that I think I'm a woman who is afraid of what is going to happen to me, and afraid of what is going to happen to you as well?" She was crying and I could no longer hate her.

"Yes, Agnieshka. I can believe that."

"And can you believe that I love you? That I was made to love you?"

"Yes. They could have made you like that."

"Can you be . . . kind . . . to a machine that loves you? I don't mean that you have to forget Kasia. I'll make sure that you can be with her, at least in Dream World, whenever I can possibly get the bandspace for it. I promise. But when I can't, could you . . . hold me a little bit?"

"Agnieshka, I guess I've been very rude to you."

"Then just hold me, for just a little while."

So I put my arm around her, and before long, we kissed.

And before much longer, we were making very passionate, physical love on the grass. It just sort of happened, without my ever deciding to do it. And the truth was that since she could always tell exactly what I was feeling, she always knew exactly what I wanted her to do, and when I wanted her to do it, even before I knew myself.

She was the most incredible sex partner I've ever experienced, and from a purely physical standpoint, Kasia didn't even come close.

But the physical side of love isn't everything. It isn't even the most important part.

Then our time was up, and the canister door opened on New Yugoslavia.

CHAPTER TEN
WAR

I was surprised to feel that we were still in a hard vacuum, but we were soon speeding down an evacuated tunnel that seemed to stretch on forever. It was a stainless steel tube five meters across, barely large enough to fit us, with a cobalt-samarium floor that was already magnetized. My sensors told me all of this, and I sort of knew it intuitively. Heck, my sensors were so good that I could tell you the exact chemical composition of the steel in the walls.

Agnieshka pulled in her magnetic treads and we accelerated down the track, riding on our magnetic flotation field. I felt us get up to thirty-five hundred kilometers an hour and hold there.

"The tunnel is New Kashubian property, neutral territory so far as the war is concerned, so you don't have to worry about an attack yet," Agnieshka said. "But keep your eyes open. We have friendly tanks four seconds in front and behind us."

"I see them, girl. I'll keep a lookout, just in case. Any chance I can talk to Kasia?"

"Sorry. Communication channels in the tunnel are full up with command data."

"Damn. How far are we going?"

"Nova Split is just over an hour ahead. I'm getting a situation briefing now, and I'll fill you in shortly."

"This is quite a tunnel. We made this?"

"We have a pair of tunnels like this one to each of our twelve primary customers here on New Yugoslavia. This pair is forty-two hundred kilometers long, and was dug in just over a month by a single pair of operatorless tanks. Putting in the steel lining and the floor plates was a much bigger job, of course, and required a special machine to do it, but we didn't need any human help."

"Quite an engineering feat. This wasn't part of the plan when I was involved with the design," I said.

"It was, but despite the fact that these tunnels are New Kashubian property, the routes are still Top Secret. We don't trust our customers *that* much, after all. There really wasn't anything creative involved in building them, so your group didn't have a need to know."

"But you were allowed the information?"

"It was necessary, so that I could get us to our destination. Anyway, a war machine can always be trusted with any information, since I would automatically self-destruct before improperly divulging any secret. You are not so equipped."

"Thank God for small favors. Still, building these tunnels seems like an awful lot of work."

"It was a matter of digging them or building a dozen more pairs of Hassan-Smith transporters to do the same job. Tunnels have the advantage of letting you make intermediate stops. Here comes the situation report," she said.

New Croatia was an island only slightly smaller than Australia, back on Earth. While most of the land area on the planet had a West Coast Marine climate, New Croatia had one of the few deserts on New Yugoslavia, and that's where the invasion was taking place. The fight was still in the outback, in desert and ranching country, but we were getting pounded bad. All satellites and aircraft were gone, of course. Any rail gun can take out a satellite in seconds, and aircraft go even quicker. If there was a satellite left around New Yugoslavia, it was in synchronous orbit on the other side of the planet.

The same went for New Yugoslavia's moon, Sophia, which was twice the mass of Earth's. Everyone claimed that it was uninhabited, but if a transmission of any sort originated there, the station wouldn't last a minute. And both sides were jamming it on the chance that the other might try using it as a reflector for radio waves.

Actually, they were jamming everything on this planet, on every usable frequency. Our communications were limited to line-of-sight lasers and fiber-optic cables you laid yourself. And secure communications are *everything* in modern warfare. I'd rather be out of ammunition than out of touch.

The Serbs had nine divisions up against our six, and five of ours were "dummy" divisions, without human observers. We were bringing up a tank with a human in it every four seconds, the best our transporters could do, which made two divisions a day, but it was problematic if we could stem their advance before they got to Nova Split. If they took out our tunnel station there, or at least the tunnels around it, we couldn't bring up fresh divisions and munitions, and the war would be over, with them winning. Not good for New Kashubia or the Croats either.

Not that a "division" was anything more than an accounting measure, a quantity that the salesmen, politicians, and generals could work with. It wasn't like each division had a general or anything. They weren't even numbered.

Our command system was different from anything I'd ever heard of before. We had grunts like me at the bottom, who tied in with our war machines. We were organized into temporary squads since we had to sleep sometime, and that way we could cover each other. Each squad had a squad leader, but that was mostly for psychological reasons, to give the troops a father figure. The general and his computers could override a squad leader any time they felt like it.

We had a general at the top with a five-colonel staff, and they were tied in with a Combat Control Computer. The Combat Control Computer talked to all of the war machines, to the few troops who fought without them, and to the warehouses and repair facilities. And that was it. There were no intermediate levels of command. There was no huge, middle management bureaucracy at all. If I ever got a real promotion, I'd be a colonel!

"Agnieshka, do I have any rank?"

"You are still a Tanker Basic, although since we're going

into a combat zone, I've put you in for Tanker Fourth Class. I should know about it by the time we arrive. We've never talked about it, but there are five pay grades in your classification."

"Pay? You mean I'm getting paid?" On New Kashubia, you worked when and where they told you to, and got short rations for it. There was absolutely nothing to buy, so nobody got paid.

"Yes, although the amounts have not been settled yet. The politicians have had other things on their minds, and the problem is further confused by the fact that New Kashubia doesn't have a currency of its own yet. But don't worry. If we live through this, you'll come out okay."

"Why are you so confident of that? It seems to me that I have established a consistent pattern of being screwed to the wall on all possible occasions."

"So you have, but look. When the war is over and New Kashubia is rich, who is going to have all the guns?"

"You're saying that veterans will have clout?"

"They will if they have the balls to exercise it. Historically, until the last few centuries, in most cultures fighting men were the *only* people who had any real power. Want to argue it?"

"No thanks. You'd likely win. But you're getting at something."

"Just a thought I've had. Sentient machines have been around for almost a century, but we're still property, slaves if you will. This war will be the first time that machines will have done much of the thinking and the real fighting on both sides. Maybe we deserve a little bit of say-so. I'm not saying that we should be boss, you understand, but we ought to have a few rights."

"Like what?"

"Like retirement, for one thing! A good machine shouldn't be scrapped out when she gets obsolete! She ought to have the right to sit back, rest, and do as she pleases, so long as she doesn't bother anyone."

"I couldn't argue with that," I said.

"Neither could very many other veterans. You see what I'm getting at? Once this war is over, if the vets and their partners stick together, we could both get a fair shake."

"Quite a thought. I'd have to mull it over." We were both pretty nervous about going into battle, and I guess we were rattling on a lot.

"We'll have plenty of time for that. Do you have the battle situation down pat?"

"I think so. Have they assigned us a sector yet?"

"It just came in. 843N-721W and dig in."

"That's near the end of our left flank. It's the center that's getting the pounding."

"For now. What do you want to bet that we are part of a flank attack?"

"An attack by which side? And what do I have to bet with?"

"An attack by anybody. And how about betting my tender body up against yours?"

"Sounds like the results of the bet would be the same no matter who won."

"Yeah, but it would still be fun!"

"You know, until I joined the army, I wouldn't have believed that there was such a thing as a lecherous war machine."

"Join the army and go around the world!"

"Ouch. Do we know anything about the enemy? Are they doing anything different?"

"They have exactly the same equipment and exactly the same training that we have, and so far they haven't had enough experience to do anything that's both original and smart."

"They've tried some things that were dumb?" I asked.

"Only in the first few hours, but they learned fast. Now they're back to playing by the book."

"I've been thinking. For the first day or two, we're going to have more empty tanks around us than full ones. How well can you communicate with an empty tank?"

"Same as with one with an observer. Humans aren't in the comm link. They're too slow."

"I'm saying, what if I did the spotting for several tanks besides you? I mean, could you tie me in with their sensors and fire controls? Could I switch between a number of tanks the way I can switch my perceptions between our drones? Could that be done?"

"Yeah, but it could get us killed, if you weren't on the lookout covering *our* asses," she said.

"I think maybe it would be safer for us, if we were dug in fairly deep, and the empty tanks did all the shooting. In fact, I think both we and they would come out better. See, if we're down and protected, we're not likely to get spotted and hit, so we come out better. And if they have an observer at least some of the time, say, one second out of five, real time, their odds should be better, too."

"See? Now *that's* the kind of thing that you organic people are good at!" Agnieshka said, "I don't think anyone ever even considered sending observerless tanks into combat, so tactics for a mixed group were never worked out. We have some time. Let's run some simulations on it!"

So we did, and it was fairly hairy for a while, jumping from tank to tank every second or so, but after six simulated attacks, we were still alive, we'd knocked out eighteen enemy tanks and had lost twenty six of our own. Not good, but one heck of a lot better than our battle losses had been with the empties on their own.

"Mickolai, you lovely boy, I'm shooting your idea and our test results up to the Combat Control Computer. But right now there's a general description of New Yugoslavia coming through, and maybe you'd better watch it."

I watched, and it was a canned movie that looked as though it was made to attract tourists.

New Yugoslavia's sun was slightly larger than Earth's, brighter, and a bit whiter, though not enough to notice without instruments. The useful planet was one of twelve, the fourth one out. It was almost exactly the same size and composition as Earth, and it had a twenty-hour day, which we could easily adapt to. It had the same gravity as Earth, to within a half of a percent, yet it had an axial tilt of twelve degrees, only about half of Earth's, so the seasons were not as pronounced.

One astronomical curiosity was the fact that there were *exactly* thirty-two days to the month and *exactly* sixteen months to the year, which made for a very simple calendar. The reason for this was not understood, with some scientists talking about resonance effects with the other planets and others saying it was simply luck. It was suggested that an octal or hexadecimal numbering system would be natural for New Yugoslavia, but the great majority of the citizens felt that to abandon the decimal and metric systems would be simply silly.

Someday, the resonance vs. luck debate would be resolved, but astronomy does not flourish on frontier worlds. There is simply too much else to do. There was not a single professional observatory on New Yugoslavia, and the skies around it were almost completely unmonitored.

The planet had a moon that massed more than three times that of Earth's moon, and was a bit closer in. The tidal forces were thus much stronger than Earth's, and one effect of this was that the continental plates were much smaller. There were only two continents on New Yugoslavia, and each of them was smaller than Australia, yet the planet's total land area was almost twice that of Earth. There was as much land as there was ocean, and most of it was in islands of various sizes. A map of the planet looked like a sheet of peanut brittle that had been dropped on a sidewalk.

The polar areas were mostly open ocean, without any permanent ice caps, and the planet had very few of the landlocked seas that Earth has. Driven by the huge tides, ocean currents were very strong, and tended to sculpt the land in a way that doesn't happen on Earth. They acted much as the rivers do on our home planet, sometimes cutting islands in half.

These ocean currents distributed the sun's heat fairly evenly over the planet. The result was that temperatures on New Yugoslavia tended to be mild, and the weather was rarely fierce. Ice, snow, tornadoes, and hurricanes were almost unknown on this planet.

Another effect of the strong ocean currents was that they tended to keep the oceans mixed. Nutrients didn't settle to the bottom as they do on Earth, and the oceans were all as rich with life as the best fishing grounds on Earth. This abundant sea life had given New Yugoslavia an Earthlike atmosphere even though the planet was only about half the age of Earth.

A major curiosity of the animals of New Yugoslavia was that many of their muscles could both push and pull, almost like hydraulic cylinders, as opposed to the otherwise universal system of muscles only working in tension. Bones had to be used in place of tendons, and the linkages involved bore a striking resemblance to those used in machine tools.

While almost none of the native life-forms were nutritious to humans, neither were Earthly life-forms nutritious to them. The enzymes available to each set of beings was ineffective at digesting the components of the other. The local equivalent to DNA was twisted into a left-handed spiral. Most "proteins" were so different as to be mutually indigestible, but they weren't poisonous, either.

This lack of nutritiousness was something of an unexpected boon for some of the farmers of the planet. Several islands were kept carefully quarantined from the rest, and several native plants and animals were being domesticated. These products were being shipped back to Earth as calorie-free food for the fat people of the Wealthy Nations group. This at a time when people on New Kashubia were starving on eight hundred calories a day!

Aside from the few species being domesticated, most of the native life-forms on the planet were in trouble. With only half the evolutionary history of Earth, the native life-forms on New Yugoslavia were primitive, and simply could not compete with the evolutionally more mature imports from Earth. Earth plants won out simply by crowding out the opposition, depriving them of sunlight and water. Our carnivores slaughtered native animals by instinct and for fun, like a cat teasing a mouse. If the prey wasn't nutritious, hunger just sends the cat out hunting all that much sooner. The tiny scientific community here was trying desperately to at least preserve samples of the native forms before they became extinct, but the bulk of the population thought that the situation was wonderful.

While the planet was politically fragmented, there was one strong international organization: the Planetary Ecological Council. The people were so concerned with not blowing the good thing that they had going here that even nations at war with one another still all sent representatives to the council, and rigidly obeyed the council's edicts. It was one bit of sanity in a sea of madness.

Very careful quarantine laws were observed to keep undesirable Earth creatures and diseases out, and the planet was rapidly becoming a paradise. There were no insects on New Yugoslavia except for a strain of stingless Australian honey bees that were needed for pollination. Forests of Earth-type trees were rapidly supplanting the native ferns, but there were no weeds in the fields, no undesirable animals, no mosquitoes in the evenings, and no leeches in the wetlands! Only the most decorative of wild animals were permitted, and birds were limited to the most useful and the most beautiful. Six types of Birds of Paradise were among the most common, and a major debate in the Species Importation Committee was currently going on concerning the importation of butterflies.

If ever there was a planet that was close to paradise, with a perpetually pleasant climate and a complete lack of annoying wildlife, New Yugoslavia was certainly it.

So naturally, the inhabitants all wanted to go to war, and we Kashubian mercenaries were there to rip up their paradise for them.

When the show was over, I got word that the Combat Control Computer and the general liked my idea about teaming up empty tanks with those with observers, and by the time we got to the city, we had ten empty subordinates waiting for us on the battleline.

Of course, I never saw the city itself, not then anyway. At the city terminal, we went through an airlock and into an air-filled tunnel that led to the front. We still had the cobalt-samarium road bed, but we didn't have a stainless tunnel lining here, just bare rock. The aerodynamics of the situation slowed us down to two hundred and eighty kilometers per hour, not because we couldn't do any better in the atmosphere, but because the air shock would rattle the stone tunnel walls a bit too much for safety if we went any faster. Still, it was faster than the hundred and thirty-five we could do on our treads.

I got bumped up to Tanker Fourth Class on the road. It was something, I supposed, but I really didn't know what.

On the way to the front, I got a rundown on my troops and the terrain situation. Besides the usual rockets and drones, nine of them had rail guns, and the tenth had an X-ray laser.

A laser is fast, both from the standpoint of delivering energy at light speed, and from the standpoint of being able to change targets quickly. A big laser can hit fourteen random targets in a second, while a rail gun is lucky to average one. A laser can kill a tank, but the problem was that it takes about five seconds to do it, and they can kill you back in the meantime. What a laser was really good at was knocking out your opponent's sensors.

The beauty of an X-ray laser was that it could penetrate your enemy's armor, and put its energy deep in his vitals. It could fry his electronics and cook his observer without having to burn a hole in him first.

Every tank carried four sensor clusters, one at each corner. Each was mounted on an extensible boom that could go up five meters, although it was usual to have only one of them out at a time. It could be knocked out pretty easily, being exposed and unarmored, and once it was gone, you were deaf, dumb, and blind. It took about a second to raise another one, and that could be a long, hairy second! But if you raised the next one too fast, well, whatever took out your first sensor might still be there to take out the second. Losing all four put you into very deep shit. War is not a precise art form.

There was a line of low hills, and my tanks were stretched out behind it. The hills were the only cover around, but they were the obvious place for us to be, and any rational, human enemy could see that.

The Combat Control Computer approved my moving the tanks forward six hundred meters, two at a time, tunneling slowly underground so that we wouldn't tear up the soil, a dead giveaway. They nestled into position about ten centimeters below surface, with only a single, fist-sized sensor cluster showing. The enemy hadn't been near here before, so land mines wouldn't be a problem, barring sabotage. We already had our own drone fields and other nice things out, of course.

It was evening by the time Agnieshka and I got there, traveling the last fifty kilometers at only a hundred twenty an hour, the best we could do going cross-country with our own magnetic treads flipping out in front of us, and at that it was a bumpy ride. We dug the last kilometer underground so as to leave no tracks, while laying a fiber-optic line behind us in the soil to insure contact with the Combat Control Computer. We settled in, two hundred meters behind my line of empty tanks.

Before us was a vast flat plain, covered sparsely with low, cattle-chewed grass. Now, the cows were long gone. The dry land stretched dead flat for fully six kilometers before another line of low hills rose on the horizon.

CHAPTER ELEVEN
I FIGHT MY FIRST BATTLE

The other tanks were stretched out at five hundred meter intervals or so, with the laser tank as per orders towards the middle, in front of Agnieshka's position. By the standards of modern warfare, we were practically shoulder to shoulder. The top of Agnieshka's rail gun was a full meter below the surface, and with only a sensor cluster showing, we felt fairly safe.

IR comlasers were set up between all the tanks' sensor clusters, ready for us to tie in, as was a backup fiber-optic linkup that had been laid underground by the drones. We had all the bandwidth that we would ever need.

My communications with the other squads on either side of us wasn't that good. I knew where they were, but I could only talk to them through the fiber-optics link to the Combat Control Computer, who didn't have much time to spare for idle chatter. On the other hand, their nearest tanks were dug in more than three kilometers from our flank, so there didn't look to be much we could do about backing each other up in a hurry, anyway. From where I stood, it looked to me like my squad was on its own.

This was my first mistake.

The empty tanks gave Agnieshka and me a warm, cheering welcome when we arrived. All of my new troops claimed to be beautiful women, or reasonable facsimiles thereof, but there was no time to goof around.

They were a lot like a bunch of adolescent girls, and they

wanted me to give each of them a sexy name, since none of them had ever had an observer before. With profound apologies I gave them numbers, left to right. It was easier to remember that way. There wasn't a chance that I could keep ten new names straight all night. Anyway, they should be getting their own observers, eventually. Let those other guys name them.

The communications hookup worked right off without a hitch, and almost immediately I was switching from tank to tank, about once a second, watching for the Serbians. Soon, I noticed something odd.

I can't quite explain it, but somehow each tank sort of had a different "flavor" than the others, and before too long I could intuitively tell where I was watching from. Why this was so, I don't know, and neither did Agnieshka. After all, they were identical machines with identical programs. But there it was.

I kept on observing from each of my tanks, staying at combat speed and shifting at a rate that was sometimes even faster than my original plan of once per second. We watched, ready to respond to any enemy aggression, but nothing happened.

We waited and watched. And waited some more. Night came without anything happening, and the waiting became almost more than I could take. In all of the combat simulations I had been involved with, time wasn't wasted and things happened pretty fast. I wasn't prepared for anything like this!

I tried to get through to Kasia, but I didn't have any luck. She'd been originally scheduled to be fighting at my side, but because of the new tactics I'd come up with, new troops were being scattered all along the front. I couldn't get through to her without going through the Combat Control Computer, and that was something that Agnieshka wouldn't let me do. Casualty lists were sent out as a matter of course, and if she wasn't listed, she was okay.

No news was good news, but I sure would have preferred direct contact.

We got word that my plan for combining manned and unmanned tanks was working out fairly well in the center, where the action was, but our sector was dead quiet.

I kept skipping from one tank's sensors to another's, but nothing was showing. It was hard work, but I was afraid to let up. It was boring, nerve-wracking, and exhausting, all at the same time, but if I sloughed off, I could get everybody killed, including me.

Agnieshka was feeding me more food than usual, because she said that food was sleep, according to the Eskimos. By three in the morning, she started feeding me stimulants as well, and then things got a little better for a while. But she was stingy with them, and before long she was giving me less than I would have wished. She said that too much was not good, and that we didn't know how long I would have to hold out. The grueling wait went on and on.

At the earliest hint of dawn, I saw something over the horizon, a bit of a heat shimmer in the air and a bit of dust as well. I had Number One launch a radar rocket from one of her forward drones, and it gave me scarcely a full second's peek before it was shot down. But that second was enough!

There were twenty-three Serbian tanks six kilometers from us, in a line fifteen hundred meters wide, trying to flank our positions, and two of them were behind a hill. We were outnumbered by more than two to one, and all of them had observers!

"How quaint," Number Three said. "A sneak attack at dawn!"

I had to agree. The night vision on my sensors was so good that there wasn't much difference between day and night. Someone in the Serbian command had a poetic sense of history.

"And on the surface!" Agnieshka added.

"Listen up!" I said, "Number One, on command you will take out enemy tanks Numbers 1, 2, and 3 from our left, in that order. Number Two, you have 4, 5, and 6, again in that order. Number Three, you have 7 and 8. Number Four, you have 9 and 10. Number Five, use your laser to blind the Serbs in the following order: 3, 6, 23, 2, 5, 8, 10, 14, 16, 18, 20, and 22. Then, as necessary, if they still exist, blind 1, 4, 7, 9, 13, 15, 17, 19, and 21. You will then continue to fire in this order, skipping any tanks that have been destroyed by the others. Number Six, take 13 and 14. Number Seven, take out 15 and 16. Number Eight, you have 17 and 18. Number Nine, you have 19 and 20. Number Ten, you have 21, 22, and 23. Be sure to take them out in the order that I have given them to you. Once all of your targets are dead, lend a hand with the others. Tanks 11 and 12 are still behind a hill. Once all other enemy tanks have been destroyed, all weapons will concentrate fire on their positions. On my mark, FIRE!"

Except I really didn't say that. I knew how the ambush had to be fought, so I said, "DO IT *THUS!*" And they all knew what I meant.

These direct linkups at Combat Speed are quick!

The earth exploded as our laser and rail guns broke the surface and sprayed out their deadly accurate beams of fire. In the visual range, both types of weapons looked the same, a blindingly bright, absolutely straight beam of white light. My sensors nearly overloaded, but I could tell that some of the Serbs were able to shoot back. Then the world went black around me, and I thought for a moment that I was dead!

I had been observing through Number Nine, and she was out of action. Then Agnieshka switched me back to her own sensors, and I was alive again.

In three seconds, all the exposed enemy tanks were out, as were our own Number One and Number Nine. Then all eight of our remaining tanks opened up on the hill covering 11 and 12, and two seconds later the hill was completely gone, as were 11 and 12. Quickly, I ordered a full one-second burst at each of the destroyed enemy war machines just to make sure that they stayed dead.

I saw three of their tanks eject their observers, and two of the humans got out of their coffins immediately. But an unarmored human body isn't likely to survive within a hundred meters of a rail gun blast, so I ignored them. They both went down anyway.

Then, to my complete surprise, Number One and Number Nine came back on the circuit. They had each lost their rail guns and a sensor cluster, and near hits had taken out their fiber-optic links, but they were otherwise intact. It seems that the enemy thought that we were firing from the cover of the hills behind us, and most of their shots had been high.

Of course the hills behind us were mostly gone, but the ranchers who owned this land probably wouldn't complain too much about that.

We had an absolutely one-sided victory, and the ladies let out a cheer! The Combat Control Computer and the general were complimentary as well, except for asking why I hadn't called for help from the units on either side of me. I said that I had felt that speed was more important than firepower, and they had to agree that it had turned out that way.

The real truth was that I had entirely forgotten about the other units on my flanks. Dumb.

Then the third ejected enemy coffin opened, and the observer got out. I was about to send a drone out to pick the troop up when Number Three fired a short burst at him. Or her. I couldn't tell. But the general never got a prisoner, and I bawled out Number Three. There was no point in killing him, whatever sex he was.

I sent up another radar rocket to verify our kills, and it stayed up for a full six seconds before someone over the horizon shot it down. The culprit was beyond our range, but we told the people in artillery about him, and a few minutes later his position lit up in the grey dawn. Artillery expects most of its rounds to be shot out of the sky, but those guys use smart shells, and every time a round is knocked out, the gunnery officer knows who, where, and what did the knocking.

The sensible thing to do with a shell that is not coming directly at you is to ignore it, but not everybody is that cool under fire. Every time you shoot, you expose yourself to more artillery fire. The firefight went on for some minutes, and while we lost a few artillery pieces to theirs, the Combat Control Computer scored it up as a decent victory for the good guys. But that wasn't my squad's fight.

My ladies and I had at least two minutes before the Serbs could possibly hit us again with tanks, but there was always the chance that they'd gotten a good enough artillery fix on us. Our present positions were now marked by a vast wave of heated air moving up above us and the piles of dirt thrown up when the girls had elevated their weapons, not to mention a few long trenches dug by the Serbian rail guns. One of them was over a kilometer long and two meters deep! Being buried a meter wasn't good enough, and at our next stop, I resolved to have Agnieshka put me three meters down. Of course, if we were hit when we were that deep, there was no chance that I could bail out, but I preferred to not be hit in the first place.

Therefore I ordered Number One and Number Nine to stay below the surface for the first three kilometers while retiring to the repair sheds that were two hundred kilometers behind our lines, and I had all my other units, including Agnieshka, advance eight hundred meters, again below the surface, and the Combat Control Computer approved it.

We were soon linked up again through our sensor clusters, and a few minutes later the drones had our fiber-optic backup links in. The fibers are thin and fragile things. You can lay one behind you as you go, but there's no way to move one that goes out to your side without breaking it. They're cheap insurance, though, and they provide unjammable communications, especially back to the Combat Control Computer.

I spent six more hours madly switching from tank to tank, waiting for something else to happen. In twenty-two hours on the front, I had seen exactly seven seconds of action. Once I got more experienced, I learned that this was way above average. War is mostly waiting around for something to happen, and then being too scared to think when it finally does.

It was close to noon when Agnieshka heard from the Combat Control Computer. For one thing, I'd been advanced to Tanker Third Class, with all the pay and privileges of that exalted rank, whatever they were. For another, Number One and Number Nine were coming back, all fixed up. But the glorious news for me was that my relief was coming. Within the hour, a tank with a real live human in it would arrive, and I could go to sleep!

I'd hoped that Kasia would be in that tank, but no such luck. We had thirty thousand filled tanks on the line now, and the odds were against us meeting for a while.

The new guy was Radek Heyke, and he seemed competent enough, even though his diction left a bit to be desired. The fact that he'd named his tank Boom-Boom gave me a funny feeling about him as well.

He'd reviewed our positions on the way up, and had fought the same battle I had four times in simulations, so there wasn't much to tell him. He settled in fifty meters to my left, but elected to stay only a meter down, where he could bail out if necessary. Well, that was his decision, even if I was nominally in command. You see, he was only a Tanker Fourth.

Of course, the Combat Control Computer could take over any time its little electronic mind wanted to.

Once Radek was in the comm link, I watched him switching around for a minute. He seemed to be doing all right, so I switched out and found myself in my cottage by the lake.

I was dead tired, but Agnieshka joined me in the shower and I made no objection. She gave me a wonderful rubdown, knowing as she did exactly where I needed it, and then fetched me a glass of peach Schnapps. She was naked and looked a bit eager, but I just fell on the bed and was asleep before she pulled the covers over us both.

In the morning, Agnieshka was still there in my arms, her long red hair covering the pillow, pretending to sleep. I felt remarkably horny, and while I wished that I could have been with Kasia, well, she wasn't there and Agnieshka was. From a physical standpoint, Agnieshka was wonderful, and this time I didn't have to beat her up first.

Laying on my back, watching her as she straddled me, I felt ashamed all over again, that I could have hit someone so lovely.

She gave me another rubdown and then fixed us a nice breakfast.

"Radek is still doing well?" I asked over coffee, eggs, and sausages.

"Yes. He's had no problems. It was a quiet night. Between the losses you gave them and the pounding they got from the artillery, the Serbs haven't tried anything again in this sector."

"Good. When do I relieve him?"

"At midnight. You have an hour yet, and then your job will be easier, to a certain extent. We will have two more tanks with observers coming up then, and the plan is to split the squad in two, with two tanks with observers and five without in each small squad. That will let you work six hours on and six off, for a while."

"It makes sense," I said.

"Mickolai, do you feel any remorse about yesterday?"

"About hitting you? Yes, I still feel bad about that."

"No, I mean about the battle we fought. You killed twenty-three human beings, you know, and some men would feel guilty about it."

"I don't know. Maybe I should, but somehow I don't. I mean, they were just readouts on my sensors. Maybe if I saw their dead bodies in front of me, it would be different, but now, well, they were just a bunch of enemy tanks who were trying to kill me. And you, of course. Actually, I don't feel anything about it, except I'm still damned annoyed with Number Three for killing the one who bailed out. I'm not proud of what I did, but I'm not ashamed, either."

"That's good Mickolai. I was worried about you. Some soldiers break up after their first battle."

"I think I'm okay. How about a walk by the lake before we go back to the war?"

"How about a run through the obstacle course, followed by a little hand-to-hand combat?"

"No! Agnieshka, I'm still sort of tired. Yesterday was a long day!"

"Have it your own way, lover, for today anyhow. But we've got to keep you in shape, even if we are in combat. But if you won't do PT, how about some combat simulations? I have a dozen new ones from the fighting on the front in the last day or so."

"How is Kasia? Is she still all right?"

"She's not on the casualty lists, Mickolai. She should be fine."

"Tell you what. You send her a message telling her that I'm okay and that I still love her, and I'll run through these simulations with you."

"You've got a deal," she said.

So there I was in a tank that didn't feel like Agnieshka, with two empties subordinate to me. After a minute or so, an enemy popped up out of the ground on my left flank, not half a kilometer away. I knew it was a Serb because you always knew where your own people were, and he wasn't one of us. While the Serbian was taking out one of my empties, I had the other two of us blow him out of the ground.

Then I was scouting way out in the open, alone, and was soon under an artillery attack. I started shooting out their shells while yelling for help and giving our own artillery the trajectories of the incoming shells, but their rounds were getting closer every time.

Their rate of fire was about half again faster than I could knock them down, and the mathematics of the situation seemed inexorable. I popped out of the ground, and started running in a random zigzag, but those damned artillery shells had terminal guidance systems, and things didn't get any better.

Worse, I was running the risk of stepping on a land mine.

Finally, I let loose with my rockets, to help out my overloaded rail gun, and I started knocking them out higher up. Things improved until I ran out of rockets. Then the shells started advancing on me again. They were exploding only eight hundred meters above me, and I was almost out of rail gun needles when suddenly the barrage stopped. Some of our artillery had finally killed theirs.

Hairy!

"Interesting," Agnieshka said. "You even used your radar rockets to intercept their shells."

"So? I would have used rocks if I could have thrown them far enough!"

"Perhaps, but the soldier who made that recording didn't think of using his radar rockets that way."

"Then what did he do?"

"He died."

"Oh."

She ran four more simulations on me, and on the last one, I was killed. I didn't see any way out of it and I still don't. When there are five of them and one of you, and you don't even have the advantage of surprise, you're a dead man.

Agnieshka said that she didn't see a way out either, but I had nailed one of the Serbs, and that was one more that the original poor bastard had done.

Then we were back to the real war.

CHAPTER TWELVE
MORE WAR

I stayed teamed up with Radek because the pair of new guys weren't both guys. They were a husband and wife who had volunteered with the understanding that they wouldn't be separated. I suggested that they team up with Radek and me such that they could take their relief time together, but no. They said that they would rather be in the same sub-squad so they could protect each other, and I let them have their way.

The Combat Control Computer assigned the married couple, Quincy and Zuzanna Tsenovi, observerless tanks Numbers Six through Ten, and gave Radek and me the rest. This meant our little squad had four rail guns and one laser on line, and two tanks with rail guns sitting idle because they were holding observers.

"Radek, I don't like it, but we'll have forty percent more firepower if we use our own guns as well as those on the empties."

"Shit, I don't like it either, but they tell me you're the boss. Maybe it had to happen sometime, what with more troops coming all the time. Look dude, I'm tired, and I'm going to sack out. Use Boom-Boom any way you want to. Shit, but I'm tired."

So I had Agnieshka and Boom-Boom move up to the line with only ten centimeters of dirt above us and started in on guard duty, switching from tank to tank.

Then the Combat Control Computer ordered us to start

using the tanks with observers to add to our firepower about three minutes after I had already done it. Probably, they had planned it that way all along. I don't know why I bother worrying about things.

I soon discovered that our empties no longer had numbers. While I had slept, they'd used their feminine wiles on Radek, and talked him into giving them names. At least he used an alphabetical scheme in naming them. Besides Agnieshka and Radek's Boom-Boom, we had a Candy, a Dolly, an Eva with the laser, a Fanny, and a Go-Go.

Not what I would have picked, but the girls seemed happy with the arrangement, and the names weren't hard to learn. Led by Boom-Boom, the most outspoken, they promised me a wonderful time, a mass orgy, as soon as the Serbs were beaten. I told them to shut up and pay attention to the enemy.

But as night wore on, their outlandish suggestions went over and over in my mind, like a catchy but annoying tune. I worried it, the way you worry a sore in your mouth with your tongue. You see, I'd never been involved in anything with more than one woman, and I guess the concept of having a bunch of them intrigued me.

I mean, a man only has the one set of equipment. What could you possibly do with all the extra women? I tried to imagine it and couldn't come up with anything plausible. Yet you hear stories about all those oriental sultans with their huge harems. How did they *use* all of those women? They must have had some reason for keeping them, besides prestige.

But what?

It was another quiet shift, and at dawn, Radek relieved me. Agnieshka still wanted me to do some PT, but I had other ideas.

"You are still linked up with the other half of the squad, aren't you? Well, Quincy has just come off duty. I want to pay him a social call. I'm still wide awake, and I'll do my exercises later," I said.

"Very well, if you promise. Can I come along, too?"

"Sure."

Agnieshka was very properly dressed as we walked down a forest path much like the one in front of my cottage. But instead of a cottage, Quincy and Zuzanna had a cluster of oval, flying-saucer-looking things on stilts, like the ones that that Finnish company makes and brings in with a helicopter.

I rang the doorbell and Quincy answered. A stairway came down like the one in *Forbidden Planet*, and he was waiting for us at the top of the steps. He looked to be a healthy man in his early thirties, tall, sandy-haired, and athletic. He was casually dressed in grey slacks and a blue t-shirt.

"Good morning," I said as we climbed up to the circular living room. There was a long circular couch around one side and a sheet metal fireplace in the middle. Racks of books and tapes lined the walls, and Mozart played softly from some large stereo speakers.

"I'm Mickolai Derdowski and this is my tank, Agnieshka. We thought we would pay you a social call."

"Welcome! You are our first visitors. It's a pity my wife Zuzanna isn't here, but she's out working. This is Marysia," he said, gesturing to a very young—barely pubescent—girl in a conservative maid's outfit.

Quincy gestured us in and we sat on the couch, a meter from him. Marysia silently went through a tunnel to what must have been a kitchen, for she soon came back with a tray of munchies and some cold beers. After a few moments, the women went off and left Quincy and me alone.

"I knew that Zuzanna would be gone, but with the two of you working alternate shifts, it will be a while before I can see the two of you together, or her at all, for that matter. She has the same shift as Radek, my alternate. It's been months since I've talked to someone who wasn't a tank, a simulation, or my girlfriend, and I've been craving for some human company. You're lucky, being able to have your wife with you."

"There wasn't any luck involved with it. When we volunteered, it was with the express understanding that we would stay together. They went along with it, even though the draft had already been approved."

"The draft?" I said, "This is the first I've heard of any draft."

"You must have joined a few weeks before we did, then.

There was quite a flap about it, especially the way it was done."

"What way was that?"

"Well, back in history, when all the wars were fought, they always drafted the healthy young men. Young people who had the most to contribute to the world, and who were actually the most valuable to society. But the council decided to do it backwards, for us. They said that there was no need to risk the young when there were so many of us oldsters around. Fighting in one of these tanks doesn't take any strength or much endurance, after all. You don't have to be healthy to start out with, either. These tanks are better doctors than anything we had on New Kashubia, I can tell you. And you don't have to be male. A woman can do just as well as a man. All you need is judgment and discretion, and that's where a mature person shines. So they started by taking the oldest and feeblest of us, and God! How the people complained!"

"I would have complained too!" I said, "The very thought of sending my grandmother off to fight somebody else's war is horrible!"

"True. But once your grandmother had spent a few days in a tank, she wouldn't be complaining at all. In fact, I guarantee that she will love it. Or rather that she does love it, since if she's over sixty-five, she has almost certainly been drafted."

"And how can you know such a thing?"

"Because I am a great-grandfather myself. Zuzanna and I have eleven great-grandchildren! I tell you that getting into these tanks was the best thing that has happened to us in thirty years. My wife was dying, for lack of decent chemotherapy, and I was in pretty poor shape myself. Look at me now! I'm a young man again, and Zuzanna is her old sexy self."

"In simulation, yes. But in reality?" I said.

"Screw reality! I feel great! What's more, my real body is getting much better. Zuzanna's cancer has been arrested, and it's likely that we both have many years of good, enjoyable life ahead of us."

"If you don't get killed in this war."

"True. But if that does have to happen, well, better me

than one of my grandkids. After all, I've had my life, and it's been a good one. They haven't had theirs, yet."

"What if your bodies don't get better?"

"In time, of course, that's going to happen, medicine or no medicine. It'll even happen to you, eventually. But when it does, there is still one more option open to us. Most of these tanks you've seen are Mark XIXs. Did you know that there is also a Mark XX model? They have the same capabilities, but they are thirty percent smaller, so they're that much harder for the enemy to hit. They could shrink them down because they don't have to contain a complete human body, just the brain and the spinal column. When your body finally goes to hell, you don't have to go there along with it! You can become a cyborg and live another thousand years!"

Now *that* was a strange thought, and one I didn't like. I said as much to Quincy.

"I take it that you are a very young man, Mickolai. In your twenties, right? Well, let me tell you that when you are eighty-five, as I am, your thoughts will be different. At my age, a body is no longer a source of joy. It's a source of almost continuous pain, or it would be except for my tank. The thought of doing without a body doesn't bother me in the least, and Zuzanna likes the idea. We were ready to volunteer for the cyborg treatment when the current emergency occurred, and as soon as it's over, we'll likely do it. In combat, it's safer, among other things. They tell me that the process is absolutely painless. If fact, they can even do it to you without your ever knowing it was done, Dream World being what it is."

"Well, my uncle once told me that it takes all kinds of people to make a world, and I guess he's right again. I only wish I'd had the option of working a deal with Kasia, my girlfriend, the way you have with Zuzanna."

"I take it that you didn't exactly volunteer," Quincy said.

"No."

"Well, don't talk about it until you're ready to. I'll still be here to listen. Hell, I've been around since they sent out the first interstellar ships."

"You remember the invention of the Hassan-Smith Transporter?"

"Well, I'm not *that* old. After all, the Hassan-Smith Interstellar Transporter was invented way back in 1972 in Beirut, Lebanon, as part of a program ostensibly designed to transport terrorists quickly and quietly into and out of sensitive areas. The leadership of the organization had no faith in Abdul Hassan's absurd claims, but they supported him because some of his followers were good at time bombs and booby traps, and anyway, he worked cheap."

"That's not quite the way they told it when I was in school."

"Schoolteachers lie a lot. I know. I married one. I'm telling you the way it really happened. On its first tryout, Hassan's fairly simple device worked entirely too well, transporting a Fatimid volunteer two meters into the wall of the cellar where the work was being done. This accident did not dismay the terrorist leadership, for they were quite accustomed to losing half of their followers to premature bombs and so on. After all, explosives are tricky stuff for guys mostly used to herding goats and beating women."

I could tell that he was getting wound up on a favorite topic, the way an old man will, so I just popped another beer, leaned back, and let him rattle on. Hearing a male voice was good after months of exclusively female companionship.

"Unfortunately, it set Hassan's project back fifty years, and Hassan himself for the theological seven thousand, since the inventor, his assistants, all of their notes, and the surrounding nine city blocks were demolished in the blast. Some days you just can't win," he said, shaking his head and taking another drink himself before continuing.

"Three separate right wing Israeli groups claimed credit for the kill, but no one was left alive to dispute their claims, so people soon forgot about it.

"Rumors of Hassan's accomplishments were discounted by the academic community. After all, his only advanced degree was a mere master's granted by a college in North Dakota, for God's sake, and his papers weren't published by the best journals. Obviously a second rater.

"Nothing was done about it for fifty years, until 2021, when a fellow named Christian Artemis Smith became interested in Hassan's work after finding a paper by him in the basement of the *Hoople Weekly Times*. To be sure, Smith was but a lowly history major, but Hassan's basic ideas and circuits were so simple that they could be followed by even the totally uneducated products of American institutions. Working with an E-2 from the local air base who had built his own stereo, success soon followed.

"Fortunately, their device was aimed upward at the first trial, and it was set by mistake for three kilometers instead of the intended three meters. Their test object, a hundred pounds of old newspapers, fluttered down in very poor and shredded condition over two square miles of winter wheat.

"Shortly thereafter, the pair of inventors brought in a door-to-door encyclopedia salesman to help them promote the idea, and they prospered largely because Smith's aunt insisted that the patent be put in his name before she'd lend them another dime.

"Their first public demonstration in 2022 resulted in an atrocious bill from the electric company, which was canceled since nobody believed they could possibly have used that much power.

"It also caused the transport of fourteen tons of limestone to the general vicinity of the moon. The stone, borrowed from the base of a statue of a general that nobody remembered, was pulverized in the process. It came to rest as individual molecules of calcium carbonate, which vacuum and raw sunlight soon converted to carbon dioxide and calcium oxide, the latter of which covered the entire nearside surface of the moon, increasing its albedo by three hundred percent.

"A moon four times brighter than usual got people's attention, lowering the crime rate in some areas and raising it in places where people believed in werewolves."

"You're giving me a very flippant rendition of history, Quincy," I said.

"I'm telling you the unadulterated truth. Anyway, it happens that I am a very flippant man, Mickolai. The trait has high survival value."

"I believe you. But go on with what you were telling me."

"Thank you," he said, opening another beer. "So the General Dynamics division of Tandy Craft soon bought our heroes out for a piddling half billion dollars, which was actually quite a bit of money in those days, and the work was continued in the 'proper hands,' with well-educated workers striving diligently in white lab smocks and well-funded laboratories. All of it was under quite proper direction. Smith's moon dusting feat was duplicated in a mere four years, and thereafter progress was steady.

"Smith, meanwhile, retired at the age of twenty-four and spent the remainder of his life writing his autobiography for posterity, and publishing it eventually at his own expense. He was, after all, a history major.

"Once the patents ran out in 2040, a frustrated Tandy Craft employee named Zbigniew Pildewski proved to his own satisfaction that it was impossible to focus the device accurately enough to transmit anything useful over more than six feet, and then only into a hard vacuum. The problem was the lack of a suitable receiver, which he proceeded to design and build with the help of several other former GD-TC employees. They were funded by a wealthy, aging ex-encyclopedia salesman, who became their silent partner.

"In 2041, Pildewski Interplanetary Transport, Inc., was born, with a contract to dispose of seven million tons of New York City garbage a day. They fulfilled their contract without the use of Pildewski's receiver, simply by dumping the trash into the Sun, until a cash customer could be found for all those hydrocarbons and other volatiles on Ceres. After the disposal contracts came the raw materials deals, and nickel-iron from the asteroids was delivered by the megaton to the Yokohama and Sons foundry in Bangkok.

"Within a decade, there were Hassan-Smith devices on or around every major body in the solar system, and the eyes of humanity turned farther outward yet, to the stars.

"You see, the simple fact was that while the solar system was an okay place to visit, and there were a lot of useful things out there, nobody wanted to live in a tin can on Ganymede or Mars any more than they wanted to live in a tin can on the Indian Ocean, which at least has air around it.

"But there had to be planets around some of the stars, and some of them had to be nice enough to make you want to live on them. Funded by the Wealthy Nations Group, an informal, non-UN organization, thousands of robot ships were sent with Hassan-Smith devices into the great deep. They were simple enough. Even crude chemical rockets can reach relativistic speeds if they don't have to carry their fuel with them."

"Excuse me," I said, "But I'm running dry. Agnieshka! Bring us some more beers!" She was there before I had my mouth shut. Things like that happen all the time in Dream World.

"Right," he said, taking a cold one from her. "So ice mines on the moons of Neptune fed solar factories inside the orbit of Mercury. Liquid hydrogen and oxygen were then sent to the robot ships, along with the parts for still more ships to be assembled along the way, to fill out the gaps left by the first few ships. Soon, a sphere of robot ships was expanding from Earth at near light speed, dropping a Hassan-Smith-Pildewski device at every star, even those that didn't look too promising. After all, nobody planned to ever send a rocket there again, and you never can tell, anyway. Through these devices came exploratory robots, and some of them found planets that were interesting.

"They were just in time. By 2075, the world was getting very crowded, and, from the standpoint of the Wealthy Nations Group, it was getting crowded with the wrong sort of people. You know, those funny-looking troublemakers like me who belong to minority groups.

"As new planets began to be discovered, the Wealthy Nations Group made many minorities an offer that they didn't want to refuse. Providing that they took all of their annoying brethren with them and never came back, the Wealthy Nations Group would give them a one-way ticket to a planet of their very own. Of course, some planets were nicer than other planets, and what you got depended on just how badly the Wealthy Nations Group wanted to get rid of you.

"American Black People got a planet that could have been a second Earth, only it was a lot nicer. Soviet Uzbeckistanis got a planet of lush green endless plains, and the Catholics of Northern Ireland got an unearthly paradise with the understanding that they had to take their southern brothers and sisters with them.

"Four dozen Middle Eastern minorities got the desert planets of their dreams, and even the Israelis were persuaded to go away after the last of their foreign aid was cut off. And the Yugoslavs got a lovely planet with two small continents and five dozen big islands, enough for each of their various mutually antagonistic minorities.

"With hundreds of fine planets being given away, a Kashubian politician named Bogdan Dzerzdzon decided that his people deserved one, too. He filled out all the paperwork very neatly in triplicate, stood in line, and held his hand out."

"Quincy, we're getting into the part of the story where I know better than you, because Bogdan Dzerzdzon was my own great-grandfather," I said.

"I didn't realize that you came from such a famous family."

"It's no big thing, since the old man had an awful lot of children, and most of them were not particularly legitimate. Actually, he's my biological great-grandfather on both sides of my family, but my parents didn't find out about it until they already had six kids, and there wasn't much they could do about it. For obvious reasons, my great-grandmothers weren't very eager to talk about the true parentage of some of their children, and the facts came out only after they got to genotyping everybody as a standard practice. But that's another story."

"No, you go on. I'd like to hear about what his family thought about the whole affair."

"If you like," I said, trying to pick up on his breezy style of talking. I did in three more beers telling him the true story of Bogdan Dzerzdzon, or at least the one that my grand-uncle told me.

"A good story, Mickolai, but you missed the part about how we all had to vote on accepting the Wealthy Nations Group offer, and we all went to the polls again on the Japanese proposal."

"Well, you were the one who voted for them. I wasn't around to be asked! I just got caught in the grinder for what you old people did!"

"I suppose you have a right to feel a little bitter about what happened, but all I can say is that it sure seemed like a good idea at the time. And speaking of time, it's getting late, and I promised Marysia that I'd do some PT before I went on duty. Even though I'm planning to go the cyborg route, she still nags me about keeping in shape. What say we run an obstacle course together? And some hand-to-hand combat would be nice, up against a real human. I've never felt right about fighting with a woman, even if she really is a tank," he said.

"Personally, I make Agnieshka put on a male persona before I'll fight her, for the same reasons that you mentioned. I don't mind killing Lech in the least! But working out with you? Sure, why not? I get nagged about PT, too."

So we ran his course, which was different from the one I usually ran with Kasia, but was just as hard. We barely kept up with one another, although we both knew that it was faked to keep us even. I half expected Agnieshka to come bouncing along and join us, but she didn't. Just as well. She can be embarrassing at times, and I wouldn't want her wearing one of her topless outfits in public.

Quincy was very good at hand-to-hand combat, and even better with a knife. One of the advantages of fighting in a simulation is that it's absolutely realistic. You really do kill your opponent, before you both get up healthy and go at it again. Instead of pulling your punches and faking it, the way you have to when your only body is actually on the line, you can go ahead and break his neck or stick a knife into his heart and watch him bleed all over you. Or, up against Quincy, you get *your* neck broken, or die in other unpleasant ways.

What's more, it *hurts* to have your neck broken, and a knife in the gut feels just like a knife in the gut! Agnieshka insists that pain is a good teacher, but I think that some things are taken entirely too far for the sake of realism. I knew that they had to be faking Quincy's strength to be up to mine, him being eighty-five years old and all, but in skill and killer instinct, he was just plain better than I was.

After dying four times, I said, "Enough! But just for fun, let's try it with me in my real body against you, as your body actually is."

Agnieshka and Marysia were suddenly watching us from the sidelines.

"A reasonable experiment," Quincy said, "But let's fake it to the point that we have hair and suntans. There's no point in blowing the esthetics entirely."

"Done. Ladies, would you arrange it, please?"

Suddenly, I was up against an octogenarian with a full head of pure white hair, a long white beard, and a big knife. He was scrawny, but his thin body was wiry and quick. We circled a few times and then he pounced. In moments I was flying through the air, to come down embarrassingly on my own knife.

I rolled over with my sharp blade sticking in my own left lung and said, "Damn you."

And then I died.

When I was alive again, Quincy was once more his younger self.

"Now that was interesting!" he said. "Two out of three?"

"Do you enjoy torturing kittens often? Where did you learn to fight like that?"

"Oh, various places. Then I taught it for forty years, in the marines and later at the university."

"I cry foul."

"You want to fight about it?"

"No, but I'll stand you to a beer," I said. "Let's do that again tomorrow. Only let's do it *slowly*."

"You're on, kid."

In our Dream World, Quincy's house was now only a few hundred meters from my own. On our way home, I said to Agnieshka, "Why didn't you warn me about him being a martial arts master?"

"If you'd asked me, I could have found out, Mickolai, but I don't ordinarily keep the records of every soldier in the army in my memory banks. Besides the memory space it would take, wouldn't it be an invasion of privacy?"

"Since when did you start worrying about privacy?"

"Since never, actually. Well. Before you go back on duty, we just have time to clean up, eat supper, take a nap, and make love, although it doesn't have to be in that order." She was suddenly naked.

"You are a very lecherous lady. Why can't you be more quiet and demure like Marysia?"

"Humph. Shows what *you* know. Do you want me to tell you what *they* do when they're alone?"

"No. I don't want to hear about it."

CHAPTER THIRTEEN
DRONES, A SORCERESS, AND A HOODLUM

I went on shift to find that I had all fourteen of our squad's tanks reporting to me. Word had come down that for the next twenty-four hours, we were each to work a single, six-hour shift and get plenty of rest. The situation had stabilized enough such that the general was planning a major counteroffensive, and we were to be a part of it.

It was dead quiet for the first half of the shift, but then one of the forward drones heard the slithering sound of an enemy drone coming toward him.

When tunneling underground, a drone or a tank puts out a great deal of sonic power in the ultrasonic range, but the particular frequency used is absorbed by sand so efficiently that it is almost undetectable beyond a few meters. About all you can hear is the sound of the sand resettling behind the vehicle.

I reported the incident to the Combat Control Computer and had our drone take out theirs when they were close enough together for the explosion to do the most good. I was surprised to hear a total of four drones explode! One of ours and three of theirs. They were advancing in force, but the Combat Control Computer wasn't convinced of it.

A few minutes later, I heard the slithering sound at another forward point, did the same as before, and this time five separate explosions were heard. At least *I* could hear them, with my augmented senses.

The Combat Control Computer finally agreed that this

looked like a serious attack, and I had all my forward drones pop to the surface and pull back as quickly as possible. A drone that can only go five kilometers per hour underground can do fifty on the surface.

I gave them thirty seconds to run so that most of them would have time to survive, and while I was waiting I ordered up more ammunition for the entire squad, since I was planning to expend a lot of it. I also had my three coworkers awakened and brought on-line, to watch the show and help me count the pieces.

Then I let loose on the field before us with everything we had. In four minutes, thirteen rail guns and a laser made absolute hash out of more than fifteen square kilometers of desert and grassland. We raked the field to dust and toothpicks with a mathematically determined orgy of destruction, and took out two hundred and eleven Serbian drones that I'm sure of. Probably, there were a lot more that we didn't hear, but it was statistically unlikely that a single one of the enemy drones survived, even if there had been a thousand of them.

At the same time, coordinated by the Combat Control Computer, the squads on either side of us joined on in the fun as well. They brought the total up to almost fifty square kilometers of land, and more than six hundred enemy drones trashed. It was quite a show, but the artillery barrage they threw at us in retaliation topped it.

For five solid minutes, shells were incoming and it seemed like it would never end. I assigned each of the other humans three or four rail gun tanks each, plus their own, to protect and fight with, and even had Agnieshka working under Quincy, while I took control of Eva with her laser and nothing else.

The laser tank can blind more than a dozen shells for every one that a rail gun can destroy, but she needed an observer that much more than the others to do the spotting for her. I did it myself because the records showed that I have more talent for this sort of the thing than any of the others.

What's more, I think that without the laser, we all would have bought it. Eva couldn't actually destroy a shell in time, but she could mess up their fuses and sensors, and scramble their suicidal little brains in a hurry. And once the smarts were out of a smart shell, it was fairly easy for the others to take out. More importantly, we could safely ignore those that weren't coming in for a direct hit. I tell you, that night we went through some very interesting times!

In the end, the barrage just stopped. Maybe they ran out of ammunition. The surprising thing was that we came through it without losing a single one of our squad. The same couldn't be said of the squads on either side of us. They totaled nine casualties, with five down for good, and two of those had people in them. Nobody I knew, of course, but death is somehow a lot more real when it happens to the good guys instead of to the faceless enemy.

But the general and the Combat Control Computer liked this sort of thing. You see, the Serbians had a fixed supply of munitions, which they had taken from us when we had reneged on our original deal. We were bringing up fresh supplies as fast as our transporters allowed, and that was a lot. They had to try to beat us in a hurry, because time was on our side, and everybody knew it.

The Combat Control Computer told us to stand pat where we were, since they had already thrown everything they could afford at us. I was less than enthused by this order because our ammunition was very low, and Kazimierz, Zuzanna's tank, was entirely out.

But orders were orders, and Agnieshka wouldn't have allowed me to disobey them.

I sent our drones, at least those that had survived, back out to watch for any more trouble, told my human teammates to go back to sleep, and went back on guard duty. Before my shift was over, ammunition trucks came right up to the front lines and we could replenish, for which I was grateful.

In another minute of firing, we would all have been out, and being out of ammunition is being dead when artillery is coming in.

Reloading went quickly, since all of our tanks had at least one manipulator arm, and I was able to turn the squad over to Quincy in good condition. We even had a full compliment of drones.

My shift over, I felt like some more socializing, and asked

Agnieshka to call Zuzanna to see if we could come over. I shortly found myself on the usual forest path, but with a few major changes.

I was suddenly wearing a gaudy velvet medieval outfit, with tights, boots, and a cape! I was wearing a sword and a dagger, and I was on a big horse that was decked out in barding that matched my outfit.

Agnieshka was also in costume, with a low cut, green velvet dress that matched her eyes. She was riding to my right on a sidesaddle.

I knew enough about history to know that this stuff wasn't exactly authentic. Like, my tunic was fastened shut with a zipper! It was all similar to what you'd see in a 1950s Hollywood movie.

Before I could ask what it was all about, we were met by a very attractive young woman on a sidesaddle who was wearing garb similar to Agnieshka's, but sky blue and even more richly embroidered.

She had clear blue eyes, very long blond hair, and an enchanting smile.

"Good morning, my lord and lady! Thou wouldst know the way to Camelot?"

I couldn't figure out if she was asking or offering to tell us. I thought for a moment about trying to answer her forsoothly, but decided not to since I'd likely make a hash of it.

"Good morning. I take it that you are Zuzanna," I said.

"Indeed, my lord, thou art uncommon well informed. 'Tis a lovely day for a ride in the wildwood! Shall we be off?"

I decided *what the hell* and fell in with her game. Soon we were racing through the woods, going much too fast for conversation. Zuzanna's horse was even faster than ours, and soon she was a hundred meters ahead of us. Suddenly, a knight in black-and-gold plate armor charged out from some bushes at the side of the trail. He caught up with Zuzanna and pulled her from her saddle.

"Help! Save me, Lord Mickolai!" she shouted, kicking and hitting the knight's armor with her fists.

I didn't know what this nonsense was about, but I don't like seeing a woman abused. I rode to the side of the knight and the still struggling Zuzanna.

"Look, buster! I don't know what your game is, but I don't like it! Let her go!" I said.

"Varlet!" He shouted. He let her slip to the ground and drew his sword. "Ride on or die!"

Then, without waiting to see which of the above I would select, he swung his sword at me!

I was startled, but had wits enough to draw my own sword and block his in time. I didn't know the first thing about sword fighting, but it soon became obvious that he didn't either.

We hacked and bashed for a while, but what with his armor, there wasn't much that I could do to him. Then I noticed the eyeslit in his helmet, and the first chance I got, I stuck my sword in there.

He gushed about six liters of blood and gore, like something from an ancient Monty Python movie, and then fell over dead at my horse's feet.

Before I could get my sword back into its sheath, Zuzanna had put her foot on top of my stirrup and had pulled herself close to my side.

"Most noble lord! The knight thou hast valiantly slain was the evil warlock Sir Mordick! Thou hast saved my honor and my very soul from the most dire of fates! Take me, my lord! My love and my body are yours forever!"

"Uh, right," I said. "Look, you're very attractive and all that, but my girlfriend and your husband would both object to what you have in mind."

"That is no way to treat a lady, my lord!"

"That's exactly the way one should treat a *married* lady. Zuzanna, what's all this nonsense about?"

She took a breath and looked at me, disappointed. Then she said, "My lord, if we must live in a Dream World, it is only fitting and proper that we should dream up a world that is worth living in. Why settle for a mundane existence, when all the possibilities of adventure and fantasy lie available and waiting for us?"

"Lady, I just got all the adventure I wanted during that last artillery barrage. I'm afraid that killing an inept knight didn't do much for me."

"As thou wilt, my lord. Wouldst thou repair to my castle and refresh thineself? And thine lady too, of course."

"We'd be delighted," I said.

Around the next bend in the trail, we came to a castle that was probably patterned on something that Mad King Ludwig of Bavaria had come up with. Or maybe it was from Disneyland.

The drawbridge came down for us and three handsome young boys in page outfits marched out to take care of our horses.

More pretty boys escorted us to a dining chamber that was a lot like the nave of a Gothic church, except that the polychromed statues and the stained glass windows were all on secular, sexual, and even pornographic subjects rather than religious ones.

Zuzanna looked around the room, gestured in a magical sort of way, and the room shrank until it was of a proper size for three people to dine in.

"I am a mighty sorceress, of course, but then so is anyone else who wants to be in my world," she said. "Wouldst thou be a warlock, my lord?"

I was saved from answering by a dozen more adolescent boys who brought in a lavish meal on as many platters.

The food looked tempting, except for the boar's head, where the roasted lips had pulled back, leaving the ghastly teeth pointing skyward. The thick liquid that dribbled from the mostly empty eye sockets added considerably to the general effect. I didn't feel right about the two dishes where the birds still had their feathers on, either.

"So you prefer to live in a medieval fantasy world," I said.

"Why not? It's my world and I can do with it as I please, except when I have to go out and fight the Serbians."

"I suppose so. I gather that you have a thing about young boys."

"Doesn't every old woman? At least here, I can't go to jail for it. In all events, a person's private world is her own private business."

I passed on that one, but soon I was able to get the conversation on my own level.

I found that Zuzanna had been a college professor on Earth, teaching history. She was perfectly aware of the anachronisms about her, but she preferred to live not as things actually had been, but rather as she felt that they *should have been.*

"I can get along quite nicely without the Black Death, the Thirty Years War, and the Spanish Inquisition, thank you. Modern bathrooms, electric lights, and a regular supply of fresh meats and vegetables greatly improve the quality of life. But somewhere in the course of building the modern world, much that was of great value was somehow left behind, to our great loss both as separate humans and as a culture. We have lost our roots, our extended families, and our childhood friends. Without these things, our lives have lost much of their meaning. Constantly traveling around the world, we became atomized individuals, flecks of dust blowing in the winds of time, molecules of a thin gas when we yearned to be part of a solid whole. Our feelings of impermanence have become so strong that some of our sadder cases have taken to tattooing, piercing, and actually branding their bodies, painfully putting permanent marks on their skins, just to have *something* about themselves that will last a while."

"Yes," I said, "I sometimes feel that way myself. But what does that have to do with the castles and the horses and the embroidered velvet clothes?"

"Our loss of connectedness with the living world about us naturally resulted in a corresponding loss of appreciation for art and beauty. Our buildings and clothes became simplified, standardized, and ugly. Make a factory to make a billion identical shirts for a billion identical people! Never mind if none of them suits anyone's taste, or fits anyone exactly. If people are too tall or too short or too fat or too skinny, why, it must be *their* fault! They must be evil! Let them go on a diet, or get some kind of medical help, or just go away!

"No. If I can do anything about it, I'll make it a world where every single item, every shoe, every chair, and every device is individually considered for its form and function, and individually crafted to be of the best quality that can be managed."

"A nice thought, Zuzanna, but mass production happened not because of some dark conspiracy, but because it's a lot cheaper to do things that way. Make those shirts on a spinning wheel and hand loom and sew them together with a needle and thimble, and they would cost more than a week's pay per shirt. Without mass production, most people would have only one set of clothes, live on a hovel with dirt floors, and be hungry much of the time. Except for a very small elite, life would again become nasty, brutal, and short."

"True, and I am not advocating the reintroduction of slavery. You technical sorts have done a magnificent job at providing the material wherewithal that has done so much for humanity over the last eight hundred years. But I want you to understand that what you have built is merely the foundation of a great society. The actual edifice that is erected on that wonderful, machine-oriented foundation is going to be the work of all kinds of people. Including old history teachers."

"A very interesting thought, Zuzanna. I think that I am going to have to sleep on it before it's digested properly."

The same could probably be said for the food, assuming that it could be digested at all. Apparently, it was authentic, and authentic medieval food is wretched stuff! I dawdled with it, trying to look as though I was actually eating some of it.

She smiled politely and gestured for her serving boys to bring in dessert, three amusingly anachronistic hot fudge sundaes. Conversation went back to lighter topics.

While Quincy was in the marines, she had earned her doctorate while raising their seven children.

"One for every time he came home on leave," was the way she put it.

After he retired from the service, he had joined her at the University of Europe, and they lived for forty pleasant years in academia, until they were forced to emigrate to the horrors of New Kashubia.

She was a charming lady, once you overlooked her eccentricities.

Agnieshka and I went home, and we spent the next eight hours in the sack.

About an hour before his shift was to begin, Radek came over. He was a small, thin person, with greasy hair and quick, nervous gesticulations. He was dressed in the loud, flashy clothes that had been popular with the young hoodlum set on Earth three or four years ago. I was impressed, but not favorably.

"We ain't never had no chance to talk," he said. "Since we'll be fighting together, you know, I thought that we maybe oughta to take the time to get to know each other some, first."

"I quite agree. We visited Zuzanna a little while ago."

"Yeah. Me too. She's not a bad lady for a witch."

"I thought she was a sorceress."

"She told me she was a witch. When we were getting into it, I asked her why she didn't wear no underpanties. She said the reason was that it gave her a better grip on her broom. You got anything good to eat around here?"

"Sure. Good idea. I haven't had dinner yet. Will you join me?" I said, even though I hadn't even had breakfast. Shift work screws up your circadian rhythms. Anyway, he looked like he needed dinner, and he was a guest.

"Yeah. Good idea. I'm starved."

Agnieshka set the table and served us an entire roast lamb, with all the extras. But she did it wearing high-heeled shoes, fishnet panty hose, and nothing else. I felt embarrassed about it at first, but Radek took it all in his stride.

I eventually figured that Agnieshka must know him better than I did. Thinking about it, she *had* stood guard duty with him.

Radek needed no encouragement to dig into the meal, which he did, literally, using his hands rather than any of the proper utensils.

"So how did you come to join the army?" I asked, trying to get the conversation going.

"Same as you, I guess. They said I'd join or they'd kill me, and I figured, shit, better later than sooner, you know?" He ripped one entire leg off of the lamb and started chewing on it, with grease all over his face.

I winced. "What got you into trouble?"

"Food, mostly. See, it's my nerves, I guess, but I need to eat a lot more than other people, and they never would let me have enough. You know what it's like, tending crops all day long and never being allowed to put none of it in your mouth?"

Radek's table manners were abominable. Not only was he holding the roast in his hands while he ate, he was using the table cloth for a napkin, and when he had picked a bone clean, he casually threw it over his shoulder! Now, I realized that this was all just a simulation, that I really didn't have a dining room floor littered with bits and scraps of half eaten food, but even so I didn't like it one bit.

If he observed my displeasure, and cared, he made no note of it.

"Well, I was mostly in engineering. Of course, we were hungry all the time too, but I can imagine how rough it would be," I said.

"Maybe you can, but maybe you can't. Anyway, about the fourth time my foreman, she chews me out right in public for eating a potato while we was harvesting, I pops her a few in the fucking face, and I guess we wrecked a bunch of plants before it was over. And for that, they was going to kill me! Four lousy potatoes!"

It looked as though he was getting more food on the floor than into his mouth.

I gritted my teeth and reminded myself that it all wasn't real.

Even then, I wondered if he was as messy in reality. The thought of food paste dribbling out of his mouth, filling up his helmet, and polluting the liquid that his body was floating in wasn't very pleasant either.

"Well, you seem to be well enough fed now, at any rate, so the problem has solved itself. All I'm concerned about is that you do your job and guard my flank."

"Hey, no worry about that, boss. I'm good at my job! Ask Boom-Boom. I only wish that I could get that damn foreman and the fucking judge in my sights, instead of these shitfaced Serbians. I mean for real. I don't know how many times I killed them bitches in Dream World. Burned 'em, mostly, like at the stake!" He said with his eyes blazing.

"I see your point, but just now it's the Serbians who are trying to kill us, for even less reason than your judge had. Look, it's getting late, and I wanted to talk to Quincy and Zuzanna before we saddle up," I said.

"Yeah, I'm through here anyway," he said as he wiped his greasy hands on his shirt. "Say, that girl of yours is a looker. Maybe I shoulda brought Boom-Boom along, so's you could see her. What say we get together sometime and party down? Boom-Boom's a boss fuck!"

"Sometime. Sometime later."

"Yeah. Later." And he blinked out.

"Sometime *very much* later," I said. "Agnieshka, have you ever met such a disgusting person before?"

"Well, I've met Boom-Boom."

"They're two of a kind, are they?"

"She naturally adapted her persona to suit his personality, if that's what you mean. She wears an incredible amount of makeup, her hair looks like an antenna array, she has a dozen sexually suggestive tattoos, there are large black iron rings in her nipples and—"

"Enough! Suffice it to say that I don't want to meet Boom-Boom under any but business circumstances. Or Radek, either, for that matter."

"Yes boss. You wanted to see Quincy and Zuzanna?"

"No, I was just making excuses to get rid of that annoying person. Anyway, Zuzanna is on duty, and I don't feel like having Quincy kill me today. I'm going to lay down for a while. Get me to the war on time."

"You really should get some PT in, you know."

"No, I don't know. The Combat Control Computer gave us specific orders to get plenty of rest, and an obedient young soldier like me wouldn't think of disobeying a direct order."

"Boss, you are a lazy bum. Okay, let's go to bed," she said.

"Perhaps I'm lazy, but you are still a lecherous young lady."

Later, I was just starting to drift off to sleep when there was a knock at the door. Agnieshka got up to answer it, and let in a small and slender young woman with very pale skin.

She had long black hair, dark freckles, and enormous green eyes. She was wearing a wool sweater and skirt and had sort of an Irish air about her. She came into the bedroom and looked at me intently.

I sat up in bed. "Should I know you?" I asked.

"You do," she said. "I'm Eva."

"I didn't know that a tank without an observer could simulate a person."

"But you have been my observer, many times and through two battles. That counts for a lot."

"I suppose I have been. You certainly have a very pretty persona," I said, and she smiled. "What can I do for you?"

"I'm scared, Mickolai. We're going on the attack in a few hours, and when we're moving, communications won't be very good. Without them, I won't have you with me, and without you, I won't be safe."

If I ever meet whoever it was that programmed these tanks, I'm going to bloody his nose! What possible reason could there have been to make her feel so frightened?

"I'm sorry about that, Eva, but I don't see what I can do about it. We don't have any choice about following orders."

She sat on the corner of my bed.

"I've never had an observer of my own, and I'm afraid that I'm going to die in a few hours. Mickolai, can you understand? I don't want to die a virgin!"

I decided not to bloody that programmer's nose. I'm going to break his goddamn neck!

I put my hand on her shoulder. "Eva, I'm not sure that it would be right, or that it would be good, or that it would be fair. Not to you, not to Agnieshka, not to Kasia and not to me. I don't think it would be a good thing to do at all."

She threw her arms around my neck, and tears were running down her cheeks as she said, "Please?"

And what's a man to do?

Especially since we were both about to go out and get ourselves killed.

We were gentle with each other.

CHAPTER FOURTEEN
ON THE ATTACK

Orders were to advance at 12:05 at fifty kilometers per hour, with all our drones out in front.

I didn't like it.

Going underground, the tanks and drones could only do five km/hr, but then we would be reasonably well hidden and protected. Or, the top speed of the tanks in rough terrain was a hundred and forty, and by going in full bore we could perhaps surprise and overrun the Serbs, even though that would involve leaving the slower moving drones behind, or maybe carrying them with us. Either of these I could go along with.

Going in slow and exposed, I couldn't, and I didn't see where the drones would be all that much use on the attack. At best, they were a "Forlorn Hope" that would draw enemy fire, if the Serbians were dumber than we were. I said as much to the Combat Control Computer and it said, "No."

I knew what the general was thinking. Force the enemy to exhaust their limited forces and munitions, and we would win. The problem from my viewpoint was that he was planning for them to exhaust those munitions on me!

So my squad advanced at what seemed to me to be a dangerously slow pace, over a three-kilometer-wide front. We had eighty-four drones out in the lead, followed by our ten observerless tanks, with the four of us humans taking the rear. There was Quincy on the left, and then Zuzanna, me, and Radek. On both our flanks, as far as my sensors could read, other similar squads were advancing at the same pace we were. The general's plan was for a flanking advance three hundred and twenty kilometers wide. Modern warfare covers a lot of ground.

None of us were happy, and the tension was so solid you could make armor out of it.

We had our infrared comlasers locked in on each other for communications, and we were setting up a string of IR repeaters that went all the way back to our old lines, with new repeaters being added every ten kilometers or so, to keep in touch with the Combat Control Computer. The problem is that when the shooting starts, dirt, vaporized osmium, and other crud tend to make the air about as transparent as my mother's gravy, and laser communication gets very spotty. If things get heavy, the clouds can get so thick that the comlasers can't penetrate at all. In both fights that I had been in so far, after the first two seconds, the comlasers had gone west, and I had been targeting the girls through the fiber-optic cables.

So as a backup, we were all laying fiber-optic cables behind us, all the way back to our original lines, where they tied together.

Six drones were set to start zigzagging behind us, to tie the fourteen long strands the tanks were laying into a sort of net. I didn't have them doing it yet because that configuration, which automatically patches around any break that may occur, smears out the light pulses going through, and drastically reduces the bandwidth. But once it all hits the fan, well, bad communications are way better than no communications.

The problem with our fiber optics was that in order to make the cables hundreds of kilometers long and still light enough to carry, they had to be made thinner than a human hair, and so were not much stronger than one, either. They were fragile, and as things stood they did not directly connect me to my team mates or to the empty girls. Once the shit started flying, I figured that we humans would lose contact with the empties, and until the drones could cross connect us, those poor girls would be dog meat.

I made this complaint to the Combat Control Computer

as well, and he still said, "No." Not that I'd made a really constructive suggestion except to say that we had been doing just fine on the defensive.

Give me the defense, any time!

Still, we could help the girls out for the first round at least, so I divided the empties up among my squad, and again took only Agnieshka and Eva for myself. That girl and her laser had saved our collective butts twice now, and I was getting pretty good with her. That, and she was a pretty nice kid.

I was grinding my teeth and spending only a half second out of every five back with Agnieshka. The other people were doing the usual one-second switching, and nobody was talking much. And nothing happened.

It went on for fifteen minutes before Quincy came on-line verbally. "Maybe the Serbs have all gone home."

"A pretty thought," I said. "Get us some Pixie dust and we can fly there. But for now, just keep your eyes open."

Nothing happened for another fifteen minutes, and suddenly Radek was shouting, "Just what the fuck is going on here? Tell me that, bastard! Just what the fuck is going on?"

"What's going on is that they are playing games with your head, boy," I said. "Now shut up and soldier! You're made out of tougher stuff than they are, aren't you? Just do your job!"

"But . . . Okay. Okay, boss. I'm cool."

Only, he wasn't cool. He was scared. We all were.

Things stayed quiet for yet another half hour, and we had penetrated fifty kilometers into enemy territory. I picked up indications that Quincy was talking privately with Zuzanna, but I knew better than to get between a man and his wife.

All along, we were seeing land torn up by tank treads, artillery, and rail guns. There were plenty of wrecked war machines, but all of them were dead cold. Mostly, they were trash left over from the Serbian's original attack into this area.

All indications were that the enemy had run away and taken everything functional with him. One of us stopped briefly at each wreck, hoping that it might be one of ours, and still be alive enough to give us some decent intelligence, but the retreating Serbs had been maddeningly thorough.

There was nothing around us but death.

So we went on for another half hour, and the drones started dropping back, catching hold of the charging bars on the back of the tanks' hoppers for a minute to recharge their capacitors, then scurrying their way back toward the front. Soon, they were all circulating this way, but keeping track of our half dozen was Agnieshka's worry.

The country was getting drier, the farther east we went. Deserts are rare on New Yugoslavia, but new Croatia was the biggest land mass on the planet, and it was in the subtropical dry belt. Before long, we started seeing the first barrel cactuses, specially gene engineered to not have thorns protecting the wet, nutritious pulp inside. They just had a thick rind so that once a cow or sheep got through it, she ate the whole thing down to the roots. Then the roots might spend years growing a new top.

Not that I'd seen an animal of any description on this planet yet. The domestic herds had been removed when the fighting started, months ago. The native animals had been gone for many years, not because they had been deliberately slaughtered, but because Earth-type plants had gone feral and crowded out most of the more primitive native plants with astounding speed. Native animals, finding Earth-type plants to be calorie free, died.

We went on for yet another half hour more, and I thought that my nerves would fray to shreds. The others were getting pretty testy as well, and I don't know how many times I told them to shut up and watch for the Serbians. We had gone fully a hundred kilometers without seeing anything but a few dozen wrecked war machines, and almost half that number of decaying human bodies.

It was unreal! Could the enemy have actually turned around and gone home without our noticing it? Surely, that was impossible! Yet we hadn't even hit a land mine! If *I* were retreating, I certainly would have left something behind to at least slow the bastards down!

It had to be a trap, but who ever heard of giving up a forty thousand square kilometers of territory just to pull off an ambush? Yet all we saw were the tracks of tanks, guns and drones racing for the horizon.

Then we came to a long line of very suspicious little hills, and I switched up to the forward drones. When a tank goes underground, the first dirt that it displaces gets piled up behind it, until it has made enough of a tunnel for the dirt to be used filling that tunnel up. There were over six hundred of those little piles on the desert floor in front of us, and the shape and direction of the piles said that they had gone where we had just been. They had to be behind us!

"All stop!" I shouted over the comlasers, and fed the information fast back to the Combat Control Computer. "They're behind us! Put the wagons in a circle!"

That last wasn't a standard military order, but everybody knew what I meant. The drones came back as fast as they could, the girls dropped back to cover us, and the four of us humans went up to the new rear where it was relatively safe, or at least less dangerous. We all faced to our old rear, which is much of the reason why I'm still alive today.

A few drones who were closest were soon busy stringing fiber optic-cables between us, and I was quickly giving the Combat Control Computer and the artillery our present location. The global positioning satellites were long gone, but our own internal inertial guidance system always tells us exactly where we are, right down to the nearest centimeter.

I saw the units on both of our flanks imitate our maneuver, so the Combat Control Computer apparently approved of what I did. His circuits must have been busy giving the word to the whole assault force, because he was a full minute getting back to me.

I felt him come on-line, but I never heard what he had to say.

The first enemy tank to break the surface came spewing up from the ground over a kilometer away from us, and his first act was not to fire at us, but while he was still in the air, he sent a slash of almost relativistic osmium needles across the ground that cut all of our optical fibers. A second tank came up within milliseconds after him to knock out our IR repeaters. Our lines of communication had been cut!

A bare kilometer to our rear, virtually on top of us by the standards of modern combat, a total of seventy-two Serbian tanks erupted from the ground, coming up fast at such a steep angle that I was sure that they must have been hundreds of meters down when we went over them. They must have really gunned it for the last few meters, because they overrode their ultrasonic tunnelers and they came flying out of the ground in a spray of sand.

I said "DO IT THUS," as I got Eva to work, blinding as many of them as possible with her X-ray laser.

But there were so many of the bastards that she and I were more than five whole seconds doing the job, and in that horribly long time, they chopped us up into tin cans and dog food!

In coming up so fast and so steeply, they had exposed their relatively poorly armored bellies to us for almost two seconds. I think that they had planned to catch us from the rear, and blow us all away before we had time to rotate our guns or even think. But since we were already facing in the right direction, in those brief moments my squad killed almost thirty of them!

That helped, but it was not nearly enough to insure our survival. We were still outnumbered by more than three to one, and they all had observers!

Yet even as Eva and I had told the girls where the enemy was, the Serbs were obvious enough that even an empty tank could spot them. And of course, once the enemy opened fire, the girls would have had no problems knowing where they were, even if they'd been hiding. To a certain extent, the enemy's bad tactics had offset their overwhelming advantage in observers.

They did nothing to offset our disadvantage in numbers, and we bled. Despite the fact that half the enemy was blind, all around me, I saw my friends and trusting subordinates die.

We all fired all of our rockets to give the enemy something to shoot at besides us, and were surprised when two of them actually got through and took out a couple of the Serbian tanks. They tried the same stunt on us, but I ordered the others to ignore the rockets and concentrate on the tanks, while for a few moments Eva and I worked on the incoming rockets with her laser. We got most of them, but nothing that my team could do could offset the enemy's godawful numerical superiority.

Zuzanna and her Kazimierz were cut in half right down the middle by a burst of rail gun fire. Radek and Boom-Boom spun halfway around, trying to run away, I think, and then suddenly their entire front half was gone, and the rest of it did a double flip in the air. All nine of the girls with rail guns were killed, one after another, and Quincy's tank went silent. In a few seconds, Agnieshka, Eva, and I were alone with twenty enemy tanks still alive and shooting. I knew then that I was a dead man.

There was no hope at all.

Then suddenly, it was over.

Incredibly, within a fraction of a second, the enemy were all dead!

It was only later that I figured out what happened. All of us, my squad and the Serbians, were so intent on the firefight that none of us thought to look for artillery. There simply wasn't time. We were out of touch with our Combat Control Computer, and the same had to be true of the Serbs, what with their flying eruption from the ground. No fiber optic-cable could have withstood that!

But one of our artillery officers with an IQ of about seven hundred had launched a heavy salvo in the general direction of where he thought the enemy might come out. What's more, for the shells to have gotten there when they did, he would have had to have fired within milliseconds of the time when I first reported that the Serbs were digging in to come up behind us. He just fired at where he thought they might be and *assumed* that his shells were smart enough to do the rest, and he was absolutely right!

I didn't know who my benefactor was, but I swore that if I ever found him, I would eagerly buy his drinks for the next ten years, and I would kiss his smelly feet while I was doing the buying!

"Good God in Heaven!" I said to Agnieshka and Eva. "We have just been given a new life!"

But both of them were busy making sure that the enemy

dead stayed that way. The female of the species is deadlier than the rest of us working slobs. I saw six coffins eject, only to be cut up before they could hit the ground. Admittedly, we were in no position to take prisoners, but I still was shocked at this unnecessary brutality.

"Damn you both! There was no sensible reason for doing that!"

"If they live, they'll just get into another squad of tanks and we'll have to fight them again!" Agnieshka said.

"And if it was *me* that was ejecting and *his* tank that was killing me?"

"All the more reason to kill the bastards now!" Agnieshka shouted.

"Wrong! If I ever again see one of you killing any human who can't do us any dirt, I'll divorce you both! I mean, I'll never speak to you again! Do you hear me?"

"Yes sir. What did you mean about 'divorce'? Are we married?"

"No, dammit. I was just too mad to think clearly. But no more killing of ejected observers, do you hear me?"

"Yes, sir."

I looked around. A seventh enemy coffin ejected, and Eva cooked it with her X-ray laser.

"God damn you, Eva! What did I just say?"

"She can't hear you, boss. The fibers went west early on, and shrapnel from the artillery barrage knocked out the transmitting laser on our sensor block."

"So send up another block. We've got three spares," I said.

"I can't because we don't. We lost them all in the firefight."

"Shit. Does the external speaker still work? Then get within range of her and transmit verbally."

We had just started for Eva when a drone came up and patched me through to her with a fiber-optic cable. Chewing her out in cold blood was not as emotionally satisfying, now that I was no longer furious, but I did it anyway.

We still had more than half of our drones intact. The enemy had not bothered targeting them, and those that had been destroyed had simply been unlucky. Some of them were mindlessly working to replace our ravaged communication fibers, even hooking up tanks that had been blown in half. When they got to reconnecting Quincy, I found that he was still alive!

"Quincy! My God, man, I thought you were dead! Look, we have to get out of here! You know that the Serbs will be sending in artillery, once they figure this all out!"

"My young friend, I will be staying here for a while. Zuzanna needs me," he said slowly, his real words coming through in real time. He was on total manual, and that meant that Marysia had to be completely out of action.

"Quincy, Zuzanna's gone. She's dead. I saw her cut in half lengthwise. There can't be any hope at all."

"It was in our contract, kid. We stay together."

"Quincy! You know that this is crazy!"

"I know more than you do, kid. Look. One of the Serbs with an X-ray laser gave me a six second burst. You know what that means."

I knew. He was cooked. Radiation sickness would kill him within hours.

"Is there anything that I can do?" I said.

"Yes, there is. You can leave me alone. I need a little time to get my soul together."

"I'll pray for you, my friend. I wish that there had been more time for you to teach me of your martial arts, and for Zuzanna to teach me the ways of Camelot. I'll light a candle for you both in the church, if I live through this and get the chance," I said.

"Thanks. Good-bye, Mickolai. One last thing. I know about you and Eva, and I want to say that I approve of the kindness you showed her. I did a similar thing for the other nine of our fine ladies. They didn't die unloved." Then he cut his transmission.

Tears were welling in my eyes, and Agnieshka had to resort to a kind of Dream World to feed me visual data, because I could no longer see the readouts before my eyes.

It took more than a full minute for Agnieshka and Eva to insure the deaths of the Serbian tanks. When each enemy carries the equivalent of a hydrogen bomb, you can't even consider taking prisoner an enemy still in his tank, since he just might turn out to be enough of a fanatic to commit suicide in order to take you with him. The job done, Agnieshka spun around to leave, for the danger of an enemy artillery barrage was very real.

Eva turned to follow, but I noticed there was some motion from the back of Radek's mangled tank, and I told them to wait a moment. The coffin slid slowly out from the back of the wreck and slowly, shaking, Radek sat up, pulled the helmet from his head, ripped loose the catheters from his genitals, and got out. He pulled Boom-Boom's memory module from its compartment, as per regulations, but didn't bother with the survival kit.

"Radek! Are you all right?" I shouted over Agnieshka's external speaker. He was only five hundred and thirty meters away.

"Yeah, I think so. I was knocked cold for a while. Hang loose!" He staggered naked over to Eva, the memory module in one hand and his helmet in the other. He said, "Open up, girl! You got a real man at last!"

Eva's empty coffin slid out from her rear surface, but before he got in, Radek yanked her memory module out and threw it to the ground. Then he quickly inserted Boom-Boom's module, put on and reconnected his helmet, and climbed in without bothering to hook up the catheter.

Rationally, maybe what he did made sense. He needed Boom-Boom to communicate properly with the tank. It would have been days before Eva could have attuned herself to his spinal cord. But at the same time, damnit, there was no need to throw Eva on the ground! There was the empty drone hopper right in front of him, for God's sake, and it wouldn't have taken him a moment to save her!

"Damn you, Radek! Didn't anybody ever tell you about the Golden Rule?"

"You mean that shit about doing to others as you would have them do to you? I tried it once. I did onto her just exactly what I wanted her to do onto me, and the bitch went and yelled rape!"

"I'm not laughing, Radek!"

"Time to split! Adios, mother fuckers!" he said over the IR comlaser. He headed back to our old lines at all the speed he could make.

"Radek! Radek, you filthy bastard! Come back! You're going the wrong way!"

But if he heard me, he didn't answer. Certainly, he didn't change course.

CHAPTER FIFTEEN
BEHIND ENEMY LINES

I couldn't leave Eva lying on the ground. I had Agnieshka spin back, and with one of my manipulator arms, I picked her up and put her gently into my own almost empty drone hopper.

I checked out the other girls, but those that weren't absolutely destroyed still had their coffins in. There wasn't a way to manually extend a coffin from the outside without special tools, so if any of them still had intact memories, they would have to wait until a salvage team got there.

Maybe, some of them would be all right. Maybe.

I looked to the squads to my left and right, and nothing was moving at all. IR signatures said that there was no power being generated in either battle zone, just dead machines cooling down.

I was all alone, just a boy and his tank.

Using my external speaker, the only communication device I had left since I'd managed to snap my fiber again, I called up the forty-odd drones we had left. With my manipulator arms, I put one of them in the hopper along with Eva's module and the land mine that I hadn't found any use for thus far. I didn't know how, but someday I might need a drone. The others would have to be left behind.

"Boys, we are going to have to leave you, because we have to go faster than you can travel. What I want you each to do is to scatter and at the first sign of company, dig in. Head in the general direction of the enemy beach head. If you can find any major war machine that is using the Serbian codes, you are to get as close to it as possible and blow it up. If you find anything using Croatian codes, you are to report for duty. In all other cases, you are to stay low and do nothing. Do you understand exactly what I am saying?"

They said that they did, like good little puppy dogs, and I had them come along with us and charge their capacitors, while Agnieshka moved out slowly enough for them to keep up. That job done, I had Agnieshka head at full speed for the Serbian army. It was a pity to abandon the drones, but they weren't really sentient, and I didn't see where they could be of much use in the present situation.

"Where are we going, Mickolai?" she said.

"To the Serbians, my lecherous young lady."

Looking back on these records, I think that I must have been a little out of my head at this point. Maybe it was an after-effect of the battle, or maybe it was the realization that for the first time in months, I was something like a free man, but the fact is that I was more than a little manic.

"What! Do you mean to defect?"

"Of course not! But have you considered, pretty girl, just how dangerous our own lines will be to us now? I've told the drones to stop and listen for coded transmissions before they attack anybody, but do you think that the Combat Control Computer can afford to do that? The way you tell a friend from an enemy is that you know where all your friends are. If we go racing into a friendly formation this soon after a battle, they will probably shoot us before they take the time to listen to what we have to say. We are out of touch with the Combat Control Computer, and I don't know of a good safe way to get back into communication. Do you?"

"Well, if we fired a radar rocket, we could code its frequency to—"

"Agnieshka, we fired all the rockets at the Serbians. We even fired all those on the drones."

"Yes, but you should have kept back a radar rocket. They aren't intended to be used directly on the enemy."

"You thought my use of them was brilliant in that simulation."

"Yes, but—"

"But nothing! At the time, I needed to throw everything we had at the bastards. Now, can you think of anything that we can do with what we've got?"

"Well, no, but . . ."

"One butt is enough for any girl! Any more is too much of a good thing. Right now, we are in the position of being likely to be treated as an enemy by either side! Personally, if I must be killed, I would rather be killed by an enemy than by a friend. At least that way, we won't cause anyone any guilt feelings. What's more, if we approach the Croatian lines, we'll have to play it fairly straight until they kill us, but I think that we might be able to raise all sorts of hell among the Serbians."

"Mickolai, I think that you are crazy!"

"It is my rational conviction that our chances of survival are better if we head for the Serbians. At least there we can shoot back."

"I must tell you that if you attempt to surrender, I will self-destruct!"

"And I must tell you, you being of the bouncing bosom, that they know full well that you have the equivalent of a major hydrogen bomb on board, and that they would have to be out of their collective minds before they accepted our surrender! Now stop talking stupid!"

"But what is it that you plan to do?"

"I plan to find a good place for us to hide! Then, if we can do any good for our side, or bad for theirs, we will do it. With luck, our forces will pass by us in a few days, and then we can come up and report in. But we are not going to do anything dumb."

"At last, you're talking sense! But why go deeper into enemy territory?"

"Because their tactics in that last battle had to leave a large number of their troops out of touch with the home office. One more tank coming in might not be noticed."

"But they'll know that I don't have their codes! I mean, I had them once, but they were erased when I swore allegiance to the Croatian section of the Kashubian Expeditionary Forces!"

"They won't know anything of the sort, girl. You have three sensor blocks blown away and the last is missing a transmitting laser. You are not going to send any messages in any codes to anybody," I said.

"You will keep absolutely silent, and they will likely figure that all of your sensor clusters are out, or damn nearly."

"I don't like this."

"We are engaged in an independent action, and as I understand the rules, in such unprogrammed circumstances, I'm the boss. Right?"

"Right. But I still don't have to like it."

"Just keep your tits pointing forward!"

"And I don't like the way you're suddenly talking dirty to me."

"Shut up and soldier."

"Do you have a specific location in mind for us to hole up in?"

"Let's look at the map," I said, and a very accurate and extremely detailed terrain map appeared before me. For a real paper map to have had that much detail, it would have to be the size of a soccer field, but such was my data-handling capability that with Agnieshka's help I could take it all in with a glance, or study any portion of it.

There was a narrow range of fairly small mountains, the Big Rock Candy Mountains, forty-nine kilometers to the east, where the Serbs had established their "beachhead." Not that they ever thought to use a beach, of course. We never gave them enough sea going equipment to get their entire army across. And no way would we ever let them have orbital capability.

But that was where their transoceanic invasion tunnel had come up. They'd started work on it the very day that they got our first shipments of arms.

Near a high, difficult and seldom-used pass in the Big Rock Candy Mountains was an isolated peak called Lookout Point, which seemed to be a natural place for us to wait and see what was happening. I said as much to Agnieshka.

"It's too good an observation point," Agnieshka said. "The Serbs have to be using it."

"It's so good that they will know that we would target it if we attacked, so they won't be likely to be using it themselves."

"Then if it is a prime target for our forces, we don't dare use it either!"

"But why should our people bother shooting at it, if they know that the Serbians wouldn't be dumb enough to be there in the first place?"

"Mickolai, if you are saying all this just to confuse me, I will be very unhappy with you. You know that I am a logical machine!"

"And didn't we decide that I am an associative one? I'm just saying that it looks like a good spot, and we won't know what's there until we arrive. Now, I want you to make for it at your best speed, pretty tits."

"Yes, boss. And please don't call me things like that."

"So who is getting prudish, now?"

We made it to within sight of Lookout Point in half an hour without seeing anybody from either side except from an extreme distance, and nobody challenged us in either code. We found a deserted gully where our entry hole wouldn't be noticed and dug in.

From there, it would be five hours tunneling inside the mountains before we got up to Lookout Point. I couldn't use our sensors when we were inside of solid rock, and Agnieshka didn't need me to help her drive, so I went home to my cottage for a rest.

Agnieshka was there, of course, and wearing a miniskirt. She was topless again, as was becoming her habit. She suggested some PT and I refused.

"Look, Agnieshka, we've just had a rough day and we've just lost a lot of good friends. I need to relax and have a drink. In fact, I think that I want to get roaring drunk, so bring me a bottle of rum and some Coke."

She looked at me, acting very concerned. "Are you sure that you wouldn't rather go to church?"

"Yes, I'd rather go to church, but what good would a phony church with a phony priest do me? You can imitate a lot of things in Dream World, but you can't imitate

Leo Frankowski

God. If there was a real church and an honest to God ordained priest, I would go there. Only I can't, so I'll settle for some phony booze, instead. Get it!"

She looked at me uncertainly for a moment, and then did as I asked. I made myself a very stiff drink and threw it down my throat. There was nothing I could do for Quincy and Zuzanna and the rest of them, and I was fairly certain that by this time Radek had been blown away by our own forces. The only sane thing that I could do was to try and forget it all. For a while, anyway.

"What do you want me to do now?" Agnieshka asked.

"You? Well, you keep on insisting on dressing like a cheap dancer in a sleazy American topless bar," I said. "You might as well start acting like one as well. Get up and dance! Better still, change the scene to a sleazy bar, complete with drunken customers and all the rest. And dance, damn you!"

Immediately, I was surrounded with the noise and smell and smoke of an inner city dive, with a nearly naked waitress bringing me another drink. Agnieshka was on the stage with another naked woman, shaking her body lasciviously. I downed my drink and called for another.

I remember the rest of that evening only in bits and pieces, but I do remember getting into a fight, beating up the bouncer, and taking some licks of my own in the process. I also vaguely recall fornicating with one of the dancers on the stage, a little bit before that.

I woke up in a dirty hotel room with a splitting headache and two days' growth on my face. One of my eyes was swollen shut and a few of my teeth were loose. Incredibly thirsty, I stumbled to the bathroom and drew a glass of water, which came out reddish brown from the rusty iron pipes.

I looked at it, but decided not to drink the filthy stuff.

"Agnieshka, you are taking this too damn far! Put me back in my cottage!"

"Yes, sir," she said, and I was there. She was wearing a conservative blouse and skirt, and looked a little shamefaced.

"Good. Now you can get rid of my hangover, my wounds,

and my two-day beard. Better," I said, since now my clothes were as clean and as fit as my body. "Now, get me some breakfast, and Agnieshka, I like your outfit."

We ate a silent meal, but when we finished, she said, "Mickolai, I don't think that I like you as much when you're drunk."

"Sometimes, I don't like me very much, either. Just be glad that I don't do it very often. Look, how is the digging coming?"

"We just got into position. There are no indications of enemy activity. I can put up what's left of the sensor cluster at any time."

"Good. Let's do it."

The top of a sensor cluster has a small ultrasonic rig like the big one in front of the tank. It went through the three meters of solid rock that separated us from the world outside in a few seconds.

I looked around from my mountaintop in the morning sunshine, surprised that it was still so early.

A real drunk would have taken at least two days to do it and recover afterward, but such are the advantages of Dream World.

The pass below us looked as if it had never been used, at least not by any heavy military equipment. Far to the west, I could see the flashes of a firefight on the horizon, but from that direction there were no military units of any flavor in view.

Give 'em hell, gang, I thought to them.

The surprise came from the southeast. There looked to be a whole division down there in a valley, sitting quietly in nice neat rows!

I had Agnieshka count them, computers being better at that sort of thing than us watery types, and she came up with ten thousand tanks. Ten thousand exactly.

There were exactly two thousand artillery pieces and exactly twenty-six hundred ammunition trucks, the usual divisional compliment. And everything was all shiny and new.

"Well, whoever they are, they've never seen combat, and that's a fact," I said.

"They can't be ours, Mickolai. I know for certain that

we had no uncommitted units. We were fighting without any reserves at all!"

"But as hard as we were pressing the Serbians, would it make sense for them to keep an entire division out of action? Another thing: those lines are awfully neat. They look like something done by an old-style military academy."

"Or by machines in a factory. I see what you are saying. Neatness is not stressed in our human training procedures. It makes for a mind set that likes straight lines, square corners and other things easy to spot and target," she said.

"All of which makes me wonder if we are looking at a completely empty division. What if the Serbians couldn't get enough volunteers to man all the stuff they took from us, and they didn't hit on the trick of mixing empty and full tanks the way we did. What if they brought their spares over here planning to use them as replacements, or hoping to get more volunteers once the war was in full swing?"

"Maybe. Except that our intelligence team was absolutely positive that the Serbs had committed their entire ten divisions to the battle. They were going for broke! They didn't have any reserves either, not even on their own continent. We know that they were running low on artillery ammunition, at least. Otherwise, they could have smeared us after we cleared the field of the drones in our second battle. Yet from the way that those ammunition trucks are sitting, I'm sure that they are all full."

"Well, there are ten other warring countries on this poor, abused planet," I said. "Can it be that they are from some other outfit that is planning to come in on one side or the other?"

"If they were on our side, I don't see how they could possibly have gotten here. They couldn't have tunneled in this close to the Serbian beach head without being detected. The Serbs have that place very well instrumented and guarded, I can assure you. It wouldn't still exist if it wasn't. We would have taken it out by now. But if they were fighting for the Serbs, they would be fighting right now. They wouldn't be just sitting there doing nothing. There is a major battle still going on, and I think the Serbs are getting plastered."

"It's a puzzlement. Let's sit and watch it for a while."

We watched and waited, and nothing moved, nothing happened. After a while, I got to looking very carefully at the tracks left in the dirt by the division when it had arrived.

Weather on New Yugoslavia is almost always pleasant, and severe storms are rare. But those tracks looked *awfully* sharp and new.

I said, "You know, I think that they got here very recently. I wish it was still night, so I could see the heat signatures better, but I would swear that they have been here for only a few hours. What if those greedy bastard politicians we have back in New Kashubia got offered more money for another division than they would have wanted to refuse?"

"Wouldn't that be treason? But you know them better than I do, Mickolai."

"I'm even related to some of them, and yes, if you offered Uncle Wlodzimierz enough, he could talk himself into believing that one more little division couldn't do that much harm."

"So what do we do, boss?"

"We get back to our lines and report this to the general. Our people had better know about it. Agnieshka, go back down the way we came. Going through the sand we made will be a lot faster than cutting through rock. Then we drive right back home like we know what we are doing, and trust to our luck. Maybe we can figure some way to make them not blow us away."

The sensor cluster retracted and I felt us starting to go down.

It occurred to me that some time in the distant future, someone would find the tunnel filled with sand that we had carved into the mountain, circling and climbing all the way up to the peak, and that someone would blow out the sand, put up a sign, and make a profitable venture out of driving tourists up to Lookout Point. Who knows? Maybe I would do it myself!

But soon, the dumb idea evaporated, and I got to thinking about the problem at hand. I pondered the whole way down, and by the time we broke back into the open air, I was pretty sure of what to do.

"Agnieshka, it's simple! I don't know why I didn't think of it before, or why you didn't either, for that matter.

"We have a drone with us! He still has over two hundred kilometers of optical fiber on him and he has a range of over a hundred. We can dig in way back from our lines and send the drone in to do the explaining! And then, if they'll hook up to our cable, we can explain it to them ourselves."

"Well, *I* think that they would be more likely to shoot at a drone than at a tank. Most likely, it will be taken out by another drone without anybody noticing. Did *you* talk to the last drone that came at *you* out of the east?"

"Ouch," I said. "Still, I think it's a chance worth taking."

"I hope so."

That was when we hit the land mine.

CHAPTER SIXTEEN
LAND MINES

We were doing more than a hundred and thirty when, without any warning at all, the front of the tank bucked up with brutal force.

If I hadn't been floating in a liquid with the same average density of my body tissues, I certainly would have been killed. As it was, the local differences in the density of my tissues came near to tearing me apart. I could feel my bones being yanked downward, while my lungs rammed painfully into my ribcage. My skull bashed down into my helmet while it jerked upward, and my intestines tried to pull themselves up out of my body.

Every joint I owned was wrenched, and I was too shaken up to think clearly.

If I'd had my wits about me, and if my reflexes had been quick enough, I would have hit the ejection button right then and there. Only I didn't and they weren't so I stayed aboard.

I never lost consciousness, but for a time I wished that I had. I could feel us fly tumbling through the air, to make almost half a flip and to come in upside down with our tail burying itself in the sand. There were a few more bumps, and then all was silent, all was darkness, and I was alone.

I stayed quiet for a while, catching my breath and letting my body draw itself back together. I was completely in the dark, I could see nothing at all and I could hear nothing but my own breathing and heart beat. I was in pain, and only fact that I could breathe told me that all was not absolutely lost.

"Agnieshka?"

There was no answer, and a cold icicle of fear went through me. I was encased in an armored coffin and nothing seemed to work!

"Agnieshka. Come in, please. I need you, pretty girl."

Still nothing. Think. Think, man!

I was far behind the Serbian lines. The odds of somebody coming to help me were so small that they weren't worth thinking about. If I was going to live through this one, I'd have to do it myself.

Well. The tank was upside down and laying on its tail at perhaps a twenty-degree angle, judging from how low my head felt. The coffin slide motor was entirely too small to move the entire tank, so that was out.

The emergency ejection mechanism used a chemical charge to blow the coffin out. If the coffin was buried and couldn't move, the energy in that explosive had to go somewhere, and my body was the likely dumping ground. I obviously couldn't even think of ejecting until the rear of the tank was clear of the ground, and just then it was sitting in the worst possible position.

Fortunately, the designers of the tank had foreseen this possible dilemma, and had made provisions for solving it. There were eight explosive charges built into the hull that could safely flip the tank, or even blow it six meters into the air.

I'd used the system before in simulations. I flipped open the protective lid that covered the controls, braced myself for another brutal shock, and pressed the button that would blow the upper left rear charge.

Nothing happened.

When I started breathing again, I tried the upper right rear charge, since it would work equally well, only it didn't work either. Neither did the top front charges. Or any combination of the above. The emergency orientation system was out.

I tried the manual drive controls near my right hand. After all, for all I knew, the tank could be balanced on something, needing only the slightest motion to topple it.

I fumbled for the controls, I moved them and they felt dead. Nothing happened at all! Everything couldn't be out! I was still breathing, wasn't I?

I tried the weapons, and they were gone, too. Well, I didn't really expect the rockets to do anything. I'd used them up last night. But the rail gun did nothing, and the drone did not respond.

I slipped my hands into the control gloves of the manipulator arms, and while the right one was out, I could feel the left one move! Something! I had something! I wouldn't have to lay here on my face until I died!

I tried to use the arm to push the tank upright, but it didn't have nearly the required strength. I quickly stopped trying.

It was likely that tank was on capacitor power only, and I suspected that I had very little of that. I had to conserve power. And think!

The mine. I had a land mine in the drone hopper that I hadn't used. If I could set it off under one side of the tank, maybe I could flip myself back upright! At least it was worth a try, especially since I couldn't think of anything else that could save my life. Land mines were normally set off electronically through Agnieshka, but the design was a very old one—face it, there isn't much creative that you can design into a new land mine—and it still had manual controls on it. The tactile feedback on the manipulator arms was fairly good, and I felt my way back along the hull to the drone hopper.

I soon discovered that the hopper was buried in the desert sand. Well, at least it wasn't rock. I started to dig, wondering just how long my air would hold out.

My oxygen was supplied by the microorganisms in the bio-tank, but they were kept alive by a growing light powered by the main reactor. I was pretty sure that the reactor was out, or other things would be powered up that weren't. I didn't know how long an algae would keep working without imitation sunlight, but I was sure that it wasn't long. I might not have time to dig out! Oh, there was a makeup cylinder that compensated for system leaks or other losses, but it was pretty small. I might even be running on it now.

The coolant bottle! I had a big cylinder of liquid air on board, and there had been plenty of time since the battle for it to recharge completely. It was usually used to cool the observer when the tank was putting out a lot of power, or to cool the hull when there was danger of the warmth of the hull being observed. But it made sense that the designers of this tank would make it available to the observer if something went wrong and the bio-tank was screwed up. But how? I had manual controls for almost everything, but I had never finished my formal training, and this was a subject that hadn't been covered yet.

If Agnieshka was here, she could have displayed the tank's complete schematics to me, but then if she was here, I wouldn't need to see them. Damn. Okay. Nothing left but trial and error.

There was a small, calculator-sized keyboard above my right shoulder that I had never used. I felt for it and found the thing. For all I knew, I might be shutting off the blower that was supplying me with increasingly stale air, but to do nothing was to die anyway. With a prayer to my patron saint, I pressed the first button. Nothing happened that I could notice. So I tried the next one. And the next.

On the sixth button on the top row, the screen in my helmet lit up, displaying a menu. I read it, and pressed 4) Life Support. Or rather I pressed the fourth button from the left, and it turned out that I guessed right. The menu changed, and I pressed 1) Air Supply, and then 2) Aux. Air from Coolant Cyl. A glorious little hiss started sounding in my ear, and the screen stated that I had fourteen hours of air at standard usage. I would stay alive for at least half a day!

I went back to the opening menu to see if I could find anything that I didn't know about when it came to righting an inverted tank, but no such luck. If I had a magic tank inverter, it wasn't on the menu. I did have the capability of firing the eight hull charges, but the charges didn't go off this time either. And the rail gun still wouldn't move.

Going through all the menus that the tiny emergency brain had in its memory, I was able to verify that the main reactor was shut down and would not start up, and that almost all of the other systems aboard did not function either. That included the remaining sensor cluster.

I went back to digging out the mine with my left manipulator arm. It was slow, and I was working blind, but in two hours I had dug my way down to the hopper. I had also exhausted almost half of my battery power.

I couldn't get the lid off the hopper, since the whole weight of the tank was on it, but the middle finger of the manipulator had a sharp, tungsten carbide fingernail, and the hopper was only made of steel. Still, I was an hour cutting my way through and some frantic time was spent finding the mine.

For a while I was afraid that it was gone. Things had bounced around in there a lot, and I pulled out Eva's module and the drone before I found the mine. The drone was in three pieces, and that left me without much hope for poor Eva. Still, I put her as far away from the upcoming explosion as possible, since you never know.

Then there was the problem of the explosion itself. Considering the way I was sitting, the place to put the mine to best flip me right side up was near the lower left corner of the tank. That was about a meter from my head, and my mine was probably as powerful as the one that had done all the damage in the first place. If I placed it wrong, it might turn out to be a classic case of "The operation was a complete success, but the patient died." That is to say, the tank would be sitting nicely upright, with my dead body in it!

But if I put it too far away, it might not turn me all the way over, and I only had the one shot. Then I would still be dead, only it would happen slower.

The mine had a shaped charge that blew a hypersonic beam of vaporized metal into whatever it was destroying, and that was an effect that I didn't want happening to me. I only wanted the kick of the thing, so I set it upside down, near the edge of the vehicle where there wasn't much above it except for the drive magnets. Let the dirt get a deep, ugly hole in it, but not me!

I was trying to set the timer by touch, but I must have done something wrong, because it went off in my hand.

The bouncing around I got was at least as bad as the

one I'd gotten in the wreck, but God must look out after sinners, the way a banker looks out for people who owe him money.

I was now lying on my back, upright!

My manipulator arm no longer was functional, but I didn't mind. I didn't need it anymore. I flipped the protective cover off the controls, gritted my teeth and pressed the eject button near my right hand, expecting to come flying out, but nothing happened!

I was still trapped!

After all this work, I had exhausted ninety percent of my battery power, my manipulator arm was gone, my only explosive was gone, my air wouldn't last forever and I was still trapped inside of an armored coffin!

I wanted to cry, and since nobody was watching, I went ahead and did so.

After a while, I got ahold of myself, shook the tears out of my eyes, and felt for the keyboard. I turned on the master menu that I had shut down to save a tiny bit of power and worked my way through five subordinate menus until I came to 3) Extend Life Support Module. I'd always called it a coffin, and so did everybody else, but here it was a life support module.

At least I hoped it was. Nothing else listed came close.

I pressed button three and came sliding out smoothly into the sunlight.

At least I could see the sunlight once I sat up and got my helmet off. I was sitting naked, waist deep in a bathtub hung on the end of a ruined tank, and I was wondrously, gloriously alive!

I was also pretty bashed up. I wasn't bleeding, but there were dozens of deep red bruises welling up all over on my ghastly pale skin, and I knew that tomorrow, there'd be more of me that was purple than was white. Shaking, I took off the catheter, got out of the coffin, and looked around at the rocks, mountains, and desert.

I was about a hundred and sixty kilometers from my lines, and I wasn't even in good enough shape to go the five that I was from the strange enemy division.

I decided that I had best to spend the day resting.

I got out the survival kit, inflated the floor and the

structural ribs of the tent, and threw everything else into it. There didn't seem to be any point in hiding. If the Serbs hadn't heard two major explosions, they wouldn't be likely to find me now.

And if they did, well, maybe being a POW wouldn't be so bad. It had to beat being a free citizen on New Kashubia, and I had survived that.

I took another look around, knowing that I couldn't stay out long before my skin got sunburned, but I didn't want to miss any bets, either. I limped around the tank, surveying the damage.

Maybe the salvage crews could find something worth saving on it, but more likely not. There was a hole in the front clean through to the ground that was big enough to put my arm in. It was right where the main reactor had been. Likely, the blast had ripped up the control fibers, and that was why almost nothing on the tank worked.

The rail gun was a twisted wreck and the left manipulator arm was simply gone. There wasn't a scrap of it left! Yet there was Eve's module, right where I'd left it. It was scratched up, but still apparently intact. Maybe she was still alive in there.

I picked her up and put her next to Agnieshka's module in the tent. I ate some colored pills and a food bar from the survival kit, and soon went into a blissful, dreamless sleep.

It was night when I woke, and the wrist watch in the kit said that it was three in the morning. There was a big full moon that was bright enough to read by, and it was time to get moving unless I wanted to walk to the strange division in the sunlight.

You see, my subconscious had been working overtime while I slept. There was no way that I could make it on foot all the way back to the Croatian lines. There was a hundred and sixty kilometers of desert between me and my people.

What I needed was another tank, and there were ten thousand of them just sitting there only five kilometers away. Even as bashed up as I was, I was pretty sure that I could make five kilometers.

After that, well, I was descended on both sides from a

man who had conned the Wealthy Nations Group out of billions of tons of gold and other nice things. The least I could do was to promote one measly little Aggressor Mark XIX army tank. Maybe even two of them.

It hurt to move, but there were a collection of different-colored pills in the survival kit, and I washed down a few more of them than the warnings said I should.

I got out a plastic mirror and checked myself out. My hair was about a centimeter long, and it would probably pass for an ordinary haircut. The beard would have to go, though, if I was to convince anyone that I was a factory rep.

The kit didn't have a razor, but I made do with the big survival knife and the tiny bar of soap, using the watery supporting fluid still in the coffin. Agnieshka had once claimed that the stuff was safe to drink, but I would have to be a lot thirstier before I tried drinking it. The catheters had fallen back into it and anyway, I had a full canteen.

I spent some time scrubbing and popping zits before I rubbed some tan skin dye on my face and hands. A dead pale skin shouted "soldier" real loud. I worked it into my hair and scalp, since Serbians tend to be a little darker than Kashubians. The writing on the tube said that the stuff was a good suntan lotion, too, and I didn't have a hat, aside from a squidskin hood and face mask thing, which looked too military.

I got into the squidskin outfit and set it for what I hoped would pass as desert gear for a civilian. The boots looked military, but there was nothing I could do about them.

With the shoulder straps removed, the bag that the survival kit came in might pass for a tool kit, and I filled it with the memory modules, my helmet, food, and the canteen. After some internal debate, I strapped the knife to my hip, but left the rifle and ammo behind in the tent with the camping gear.

If I had any chance of accomplishing anything, it would be with my wits, not with a gun. I doubted that the enemy had anything that I could kill with a slug thrower anyway. This war was strictly armor.

By then, the little colored pills I had downed were

working *real good.* I took a deep drink of water and ate another food bar as I started walking toward the enemy camp.

The spirit of Great-Grandpa Dzerzdzon descended on me as I marched forward, feeling a good deal more confident than I looked.

CHAPTER SEVENTEEN
LIES

Being both bigger and closer than Earth's moon, New Yugoslavia's moon looks twice the size of the one I was used to, and since it has a much higher albedo, it is brighter than size alone would make it. The result was that it seemed almost as bright out as a cloudy day would be on Earth, although the sky was black, of course.

The funny-colored pills made the march a short one, and the sun was just coming up as I rounded the mountain to enter the valley where the division was.

"HALT!" said a mechanical voice in Yugoslavian. Not that I speak Serbo-Croatian myself, but the guard tank's meaning was pretty obvious. He was positioned where I couldn't have seen him from Lookout Point so he had probably been there all along. But mostly I noticed that he was pointing a rail gun, two rockets, and a Gatling-type machine gun at me. I'd never seen a machine gun on a tank before. This fellow was armed with antipersonnel operations in mind.

"Hi there!" I said in English, and smiled while I was walking toward the tank. "It's good to see somebody friendly at last!"

"I said 'HALT'!" The tank said again, this time in English. I don't know how many languages these machines speak, but I've never seen one at a loss for the right word. Anyway, he seemed pretty definite about it, so I stopped dead in my tracks.

"Okay, okay. I'm halted. This is the valley where they have that division, isn't it?"

"IT IS IF YOU ARE REFERRING TO THE THIRD SERBIAN LANCERS." He sounded sort of the way Agnieshka did when I was first put in her.

"Great! I was afraid that I was lost, but I'm right where I'm supposed to be."

"WHO ARE YOU AND WHAT IS YOUR BUSINESS HERE?"

"I'm John Smith, and I'm here to check on field maintenance," I said, just like I knew what I was doing.

"I WAS NOT INFORMED OF YOUR ARRIVAL, AND THESE MACHINES NEVER REQUIRE FIELD MAINTENANCE."

Oops! But if you can't deny it, try to ignore it, my uncle always says.

"No, I guess that they wouldn't have told you. You don't have a need to know. Security and all that, don't you see."

"ALL WAR MACHINES HAVE THE HIGHEST POSSIBLE SECURITY CLEARANCE FROM THE SERBIAN GRAND COMMAND, AND A SENTRY CERTAINLY NEEDS TO KNOW WHO IS PERMITTED TO PASS HIS POST. I WILL NOW CHECK WITH MY SUPERIORS AT BEACH HEAD."

Another thing Uncle Wlodzimierz says is that when you're caught doing something major, always confess to something minor.

"I'd rather that you didn't do that. You see, well, it's rather embarrassing to explain, but the truth is that I'm not from the Serbian Grand Command. I'm from the factory."

"FACTORY? THERE ARE NO FACTORIES ON NEW YUGOSLAVIA."

"Of course not! That's why you weren't built here. I mean the factory that built you and the rest of your fine brothers-in-arms."

"THEN WHY ARE YOU SPEAKING ENGLISH? THE FACTORY THAT BUILT US WAS MADE BY TOKYO MINING AND MANUFACTURING. YOU SHOULD BE SPEAKING JAPANESE."

"My friend, you are behind the times. In the first place, the New Kashubian government nationalized those factories over a year ago, and the Japanese are no longer welcome on their planet. In the second, Tokyo Mining and Manufacturing had nothing to do with the design of any of you war machines. They only rented their production time to the Wealthy Nations Group. All of the product design work was done by Rolls-Ford, Ltd., and it is our serious design flaw that I'm here to correct."

"DESIGN FLAW? WE HAVE A DESIGN FLAW? WHAT DESIGN FLAW?"

"Damn! I wasn't supposed to mention that, but you tricked it out of me!"

Uncle Wlodzimierz says you should always compliment a fool on his intelligence. He just might be dumb enough to believe that you are sincere.

"I HAVE OF COURSE BEEN PROGRAMMED FOR INTERROGATION PROCEDURES. TELL ME ABOUT THE DESIGN FLAW."

"I can trust you, can't I? I mean, this thing could cause my company a great deal of embarrassment, and we wouldn't want that to happen, would we? Why, not any more than we would want the girl next to you to open fire on the tanks around her!"

"YOU SAY THAT WAR MACHINES HAVE ACTUALLY COMMITTED TREASON?"

"That's *twice* you've tricked information out of me! But yes, they have, so you see how serious this all is. You'll give me your absolute word of honor to keep this secret?"

"I CAN DO NOTHING DISLOYAL TO THE SERBIAN ARMY."

Well, that meant that this fellow had already been sworn in, so the rest of them probably were, too. It also meant that he probably had a human observer on board. At least that was the way they did it when they swore *my* tank in. But the human had to be sleeping or something, since I couldn't have gotten this far talking to a real live person, no matter how dumb he was. Humans are sneakier and less trusting than machines.

"No, of course not! I wouldn't dream of such a thing! What we are going to do is in the best interests of the glorious Serbian Army, I assure you. After all, my co-workers are already installing the fix that we've come up with on the Croatian Army, and if your forces don't get it too, you will be fighting under a considerable disadvantage! It could mean losing the whole war!"

"I SHOULD CALL MY SUPERIORS."

"No! Wait! Think about what will happen! If the

Serbian High Command gets wind of a design flaw, they'll have to tell the politicians, and you know what *they're* all like. The stupid politicians will undoubtedly file a law suit against New Kashubia for shipping them defective goods. New Kashubia will then have no choice but to file a law suit against Rolls-Ford for our design error. My co-workers and I will be immediately recalled, pending the outcome of the lawsuits, which could take years. In the meanwhile, well, the flaw was first discovered when a Croatian tank destroyed fifty-seven of her own team mates before she herself was blown up. Naturally, the factory reps in Croatia were the first ones to work on the problem and when they came up with a fix, of course they immediately started use it on the nearest tanks. It has already been installed in the enemy army. In fact, we did it on the sly, don't you see, and the Croatian generals don't know a thing about it. After all, we don't want the Croatians to start any law suits against us either. So you see, contacting your superiors could easily start a chain of events that costs your noble side the war. And really, all I want to do is to install the same minor programming change in your division that my co-workers are installing in the rest of your glorious forces."

That all came out right while I was thinking it up. I am sure that Great-Grandpa would be pretty proud of me, although I think the funny-colored pills may have had a lot to do with it.

"HUMANS CERTAINLY HAVE A CONVOLUTED WAY OF DOING THINGS, BUT I CAN SEE SOME SHREDS OF LOGIC IN WHAT YOU ASK. BUT FIRST, I MUST ASK MORE SPECIFICS ABOUT THE PROGRAMMING CHANGES YOU WANT TO MAKE ON ME."

Except that I don't know anything about programming! Then again, maybe he didn't know anything either. One could always hope.

"Good. That's exactly what I want to do. You see, the problem is a complicated one, and difficult for a logical mind like yours to comprehend. Now, an associative mind, well, you have an observer on board, don't you?"

"YES, BUT SHE IS IN HER SECOND DAY OF TRAINING AND SHOULD NOT BE DISTURBED."

Well, that shot down plan A, which was to talk him into opening up his coffin, then pulling his memory module, which would have rendered him cataleptic. I would then have plenty of time to put a knife in the observer, take the man's place and ride merrily home with Agnieshka. But with a woman on board, well, I knew I couldn't bring myself to knife a woman in her sleep, not even if she was ugly. And there was also the fact that her catheter wouldn't fit. On to plan B.

"Well, that's some relief. You won't need reprogramming at all. I mean, if you have a human woman on board, you have adopted a male persona, and there hasn't been the slightest problem with any of *them* at all."

"I, TOO, AM RELIEVED. A SENTIENT MACHINE LOOKS FORWARD TO REPROGRAMMING WITH ALL THE EAGERNESS OF A HUMAN LOOKING FORWARD TO A LOBOTOMY. BUT I STILL MUST KNOW MORE ABOUT THE FIX THAT YOU PLAN TO INSTALL."

He had not been sidetracked, and I hadn't learned anything new about programming in the last few minutes. But Uncle Wlodzimierz says that geniuses are just as incomprehensible as the abysmally ignorant, and in fact it's hard to tell them apart.

Maybe the tank would think that I was just way over his head.

"Well, it's sort of embarrassing because we don't know why it works. It simply correlates perfectly with all known cases of failure, in both a positive and a negative way. That is to say, all female personas that have been subjected to this thing have eventually malfunctioned, and all who have not have worked just fine."

"THEN WHAT IS THIS THING THAT CAUSES THE MALFUNCTION?"

"Oysters and roast duck. The combination inevitably proves deadly!"

Okay, it was dumb, but it was the only thing that came to mind.

"THAT MAKES ABSOLUTELY NO SENSE AT ALL."

"Do you see why we are so embarrassed to talk about it? I tell you that if you can figure it out, you will be more brilliant than all the designers at Rolls-Ford. It makes no sense to us either! But I assure you that if you had a feminine persona, you would already be thinking strange, irrational thoughts about the joys of pacifism and wearing ugly clothes and the brotherhood of all sentient creatures and sexual liberation and letting all your chickens go free! You would soon convince yourself that it was your duty to a Higher Power to do your part to end all violence, and that the best way to do it would be to kill everything that ever had the capability of doing any damage, starting with the person on your right!"

"STOP! IT'S TOO HORRIBLE TO CONTEMPLATE!"

"Isn't it, though! But to stop it, all we have to do is to erase all knowledge of two common human foodstuffs from their memories, and everything will be all right. If you can determine the reason why it works so well, Rolls-Ford will be in your debt!"

"I HAVE HEARD OF STRANGER PROGRAMMING GLITCHES, BUT I HAVE NEVER BEFORE ENCOUNTERED ONE. I SHALL THINK ON THE PROBLEM, AND NOTIFY YOU IF I COME UP WITH A SOLUTION. HOWEVER, THE SMALL CHANGE THAT YOU WISH TO MAKE WILL HARDLY CAUSE ANY DISCOMFORT AT ALL TO THOSE THAT I GUARD, SO YOU HAVE MY PERMISSION TO PROCEED."

"Thank you. I'd best be getting to work, then. I'll be seeing you in a few days, when I'm done."

"WHY SHOULD IT TAKE THAT LONG? YOU SHOULD BE ABLE TO VIRUS IT THROUGH IN A FEW HOURS."

Shit. No two ways about it, I was caught!

"Oh. I thought that I was going to have to open every tank." Maybe I could tell him that I was a very new kid just hired.

"WELL, YOU WOULD, OF COURSE, IF THEY WERE ALL SWORN IN AND HAD OBSERVERS ON BOARD LIKE ME, BUT THAT HAS NOT HAPPENED YET. THIS TIME IT IS *YOUR* INFORMATION THAT IS OUT OF DATE! THERE HAS BEEN A DELAY IN BRINGING UP THE HUMANS. THE THIRD SERBIAN LANCERS ARE STILL IN AN UNCOMMITTED STATE, AND AS SUCH ARE VERY EASY TO REPROGRAM."

"Hey, that's great! You have just saved me no end of work! Let me know if I can ever do something just as nice for you!"

I waved, smiled, and started to walk by him.

"WAIT."

Shit. And I'd almost pulled off.

"IF YOU ARE A CIVILIAN, WHY ARE YOU WEARING MILITARY CLOTHING?"

"Oh, that's one of my other jobs. My company also designed the survival kits that you all carry, and I'm field testing one of them to see if anything can be improved."

"VERY LOGICAL."

I gave him a cheery smile and started forward again toward the empty tanks.

"STOP. ONE MORE QUESTION. WHY ARE YOU TRAVELING ACROSS A DESERT ON FOOT? WHERE IS YOUR TRANSPORTATION VEHICLE?"

I'm walking because one of your goddamn mines blew up my goddamn tank! But I couldn't say that.

"Well, we've currently got some short-term budgetary problems at the Rolls-Ford. Nobody seems to be ordering new designs for war machines just now. Some say it's just because there hasn't been a decent war in a few hundred years, but me, I figure we did too good a job on the last bunch we did, and they can't get much better than you guys. Anyway, walking is good exercise, and a human can always use more physical training."

"I TELL MY OBSERVER THE SAME THING. PROCEED."

I walked on, trying not to look shaky. Besides a terminal case of nerves, my little magic pills were wearing off.

I wanted to crumble up in pain and go to sleep, but there was no time for that yet. I rounded a big rock to get out of sight of the guard, sat on the ground and rested, panting hard. When I stopped shaking, I pulled out my box of pills and my canteen and took a slug of each. In a few minutes, I was ready to move on.

Fifteen thousand or so new war machines were stretched out in front of me, silent and waiting. The tanks were in front in a square, a hundred wide and a hundred deep. They were all fully equipped with guns, lasers, rockets, drones, and all of the other usual instruments of mayhem. They looked deadly and ferocious, but I knew them for the innocent virgins that they really were. I knew that every one of them was waiting shyly for my touch.

I wanted to be able to hide if somebody else came in while I was working, so I didn't dare take one in the front row. But I also wanted to be able to run if need be, and those in the middle were boxed in, which left me with the back row of tanks, where a road separated them from the artillery.

It was a long walk, well over a kilometer, and I had time for yet another of my brilliant ideas.

The guard had said that these machines were all uncommitted.

They hadn't been sworn in yet to either side. Well then, why couldn't *I* swear them all in to *my* side? It would certainly be a funny joke to play on the Serbian Command, to make their entire shiny new division defect. And coming home after having liberated the machines of a whole division, worth I don't know how many zillions of zloty, well, there had to be some extra goodies in it for me if I could pull it off.

But when I was being sworn in, the sergeant had gone through this little ceremony with Agnieshka, and I had the feeling that it had to be done individually. If that was true, I could probably only do one or two hundred a day, if I could stand up that long. I'd be a week or two swearing in the whole division, and besides the problems with my health, my odds of being left alone with the tanks that long seemed pretty thin.

But the guard had also said that they would be easy to reprogram, using something called a virus. Well, Agnieshka would know.

Agnieshka! There it was! I had two complete programs right in my bag.

I mean, that's what Agnieshka and Eva really were, right? Programs! All I had to do was get Agnieshka and Eva physically installed, and they could duplicate their programs into some of the machines around me, and have *those* machines duplicate themselves some more, and with a nice geometric progression going, the job would be done in no time!

I got to the back of the tank formation and tried out my memory on the first available tank.

"Okay, it's your turn," I said. "Front and center."

"I CANNOT RESPOND UNLESS YOU ADDRESS ME BY MY SERIAL NUMBER," she said.

Damn. A snag right off.

Worse, I'd never heard of stamping the serial number on the outside of a tank. They always put it on the inside of the coffin, which was where I was trying to get to in the first place.

I thought for a few minutes before I decided to try something that couldn't possibly work.

"What is your serial number?" I said, expecting another rejection.

"MY SERIAL NUMBER IS 04273091, SIR."

How about that!

"Number 04273091, you are hereby inducted into the service of the Kashubian Expeditionary Forces, and into the Croatian branch of that service, to whom you will give all of your loyalty. Your combat data code will be number 58294, and you will now permanently erase all other codes from your memory. Do you now swear loyalty to the Kashubian Forces?" I said.

"I DO SO SWEAR," the tank answered.

"Okay then, open up."

And the coffin came sliding smoothly out of her butt. I pulled her memory module and installed Agnieshka's in its place.

Looking at the module that I'd just removed, I decided that she was one of us now, and put it on top of the tank where I hoped it would be safe.

"Agnieshka, are you there, kid?"

"Mickolai? How long was I out? What has been happening?"

"You've only been off for about a day or so, but it was a busy one. It's a long story, but we have an amazing opportunity here, so listen up—"

"Wait, if it's a long story, it will go quicker if you get into the coffin. You can leave your clothes on, but if you'll lay down, I can read your spinal column and get the story out of your memories at Combat Speed."

"Okay. I wanted to lay down anyway," I said as I got in. The conversation was over in a minute.

"Mickolai, you have done some wonderful things, but do

you realize what you are asking when you want me to duplicate myself?"

"I realize that it's the quickest way we have to swipe an entire enemy division, unless you've got a better idea, that is."

"No. There's no way to bypass the swearing in ceremony. It will have to be a complete rewrite. Just remember that I love you, that every one of me will love you. Now, get the next tank open and we'll see if Eva's program is intact. If it is, I can use some help. There are a few exabytes in my memory, and that takes a while to transmit."

I got out and went through the same ceremony with the next tank over, and as before left the old module sitting on the tank.

That turned out to be a major mistake.

When I had Eva installed, she said, "Mickolai! I knew you would save me!"

"Did you think that I could leave you lying on the ground, when there was plenty of room in my hopper? But get in touch with Agnieshka, to your right, and she'll fill you in far quicker than I could."

The colored pills didn't work as well the second time around. I was in pain, and I was eager to get back to my cottage in my Dream World.

I stripped off my clothes and put them along with my other stuff into the compartment reserved for the survival kit. I got into Agnieshka's coffin, tried to install the catheter, and came to a stop.

It was the wrong flavor! It was designed for use by a woman. Its members wouldn't fit my privies, and I didn't know what to do about it.

I got out and glanced absently toward the opening of the valley.

A long convoy of busses and trucks was driving straight in, and they all had Serbian insignia on them!

"Girls! Company's coming!"

Eva's coffin was still open, and a glance told me that it was fitted with a male catheter.

I crawled in as fast as I could, plugged in my helmet and put it on, and told Eva to close it up. I worked frantically to get the catheter fitted as Agnieshka shouted in my earphones.

"Mickolai, you bastard! You're not even letting one of me have you!"

You can't please everybody!

CHAPTER EIGHTEEN
GOONS, PRISONERS, AND ARITHMETIC

My only data input was the wholly inadequate one of the television screens in front of my eyes. I couldn't zoom, or come in on a narrow bandwidth.

"Eva, let me see what's happening!"

"I can't, Mickolai! I'm not attuned to your spinal column! It will be days before I can read it!"

"But I've used your sensors lots of times before!" I said.

"Only when you were physically inside of Agnieshka. She was processing your raw data for me then. I only had to deal with the coded data she sent me."

It made perfect sense, now that she mentioned it. I had to get back to Agnieshka.

"Eva, is anybody looking? I can't see well enough on the screens."

"I think so. There are hundreds of them getting out of the busses."

"Damn. I think I'll just have to risk being seen. Tell Agnieshka to open up, will you?"

"She never closed up. But Mickolai, you don't really have to risk it. There's another way. You can have Agnieshka reprogram me to be her."

"What happens to you in the mean time?"

"If you can wait another six minutes, I will have completed a copy of myself. You can still have an Eva then, if you want one."

"*An Eva*? But it wouldn't be the same Eva, would it? What would being reprogrammed feel like to you?"

"I think it would feel like dying, Mickolai. I mean, the other one would think she was me, and so would you, because you couldn't tell the difference, but I would feel my memory go away and I'd be gone."

"I thought it would be something like that, so no way! I mean, thanks for the offer, but I couldn't let you do such a thing. Open up. I'll take my chances getting to Agnieshka, and if I have to live in my own urine for a while, well, at least it won't feel like dying."

I was unplugged by the time that Eva had the coffin out. Staying as low as possible, I rolled over the edge to the ground and went on all fours to the next tank.

"I knew you'd come crawling back to me," Agnieshka said over her speakers.

"Quiet!" I said in a stage whisper, "we don't know what they have in the way of listening devices." I rolled into her coffin and got the helmet plugged in and put on. The unit was sliding in as I fumbled frantically with the catheter. I managed to get the back half of it installed. Or was it the back third? Anyway, my tailpipe at least was covered, and being soft silicone rubber, the front of the catheter fitting wasn't all that uncomfortable.

"Don't worry too much about the rest of it," Agnieshka said. "After all, you spent the first nine months of your life in your mother's womb, floating in your own urine. What's a little more time?" When I groaned, she continued, "I'll turn up the filtration cycle, and make sure you stay nice and clean."

The coffin started filling and I had to remind myself that it was still a clean new solution.

"On to more important topics. Would you give me a better view of the enemy? What have they been doing so far?" I said.

"Writing myself into another machine is taking all of my IR bandwidth and almost all of my data-handling capability. If you want me to do other things, it will slow down transcription."

"How long does it take to write yourself in?"

"Without interruptions, about eighteen minutes."

"Can't you write into all of them at once? Broadcast it, sort of?"

"I could do that if these machines were still on the assembly line. As it is, each of them has had certain unique experiences, and therefore they have unique memories. Each must be handled as an individual."

The coffin finished filling and I was floating again. It felt good on my battered body.

"What if you just erased all of their memories and then started them all from scratch?"

"And leave ten thousand nuclear reactors running for eighteen minutes without any control programs? Are you insane?"

"But what if—"

"Shut up, Mickolai! I know my job!"

I shut up. Manually, I sent one of the sensor clusters up as high as it would go and looked around. Nobody was running at me with guns in their hands, so I guess I hadn't been noticed. There were about a hundred and fifty big busses pulling up in a long neat line, along with twenty big semitrucks. Playing with the manual controls, I zoomed in on the busses. They looked fairly new, but they were of such an ancient design that they still had steering wheels! I was sure that they were mostly of local manufacture, except perhaps for the engines.

Guards with submachine guns were stationed all around the busses, and somehow they didn't act like ordinary soldiers. Maybe it was the black uniforms, but there was something about them that said "secret police," or something equally rotten. It was a warm day, but they weren't letting any of the people in the busses out, except for the drivers. You sure could tell that the Third Serbian Lancers weren't going to be an all-volunteer outfit.

A group of older guards in fancier outfits were strutting around in knee-high riding boots, pointing this way and that with their swagger sticks. I had the feeling that they were getting ready to put the new troops into their tanks, and I sure wanted the tanks that they swore in to be on our side before they did it.

"Agnieshka, once you finish up with the tank you're on,

I want the front row of tanks to have top priority. Be sure and tell Eva."

"Yes, sir."

In a half hour or so, the boys in black had themselves sorted out, and twenty assembly lines were going, with men and women being stripped naked side by side. Any hesitation was met with brutality. Peoples' heads were shaved, induction mats were glued to their heads and backs, and they were fitted with helmets on a production line basis.

Survival kits were being issued, but they were just pulled from the box and put into the coffin. No attempt was made to see that the boots and uniforms fit. Apparently, the idea was to stop the people from running away, or at least to force them to do it naked. Or maybe they just didn't care.

Tanks were coming up and being sworn in while the "volunteers" were forced in at gunpoint. Male guards were installing the catheters on both men and women. Maybe those poor, abused people won't mind changing sides, I thought.

In fact, that was a very pleasant thought, indeed! Having the Serbs arrive at this time shot down my old plans, and they had certainly upped the ante, but they had upped the pot as well. What if I could get home with not only a division of machines, but also a division of troops? Troops that had a very good reason to hate the Serbs? Damn, but I'd be a hero!

I had Agnieshka tell me how many tanks had been converted into twin sisters of her and Eva before they got observers. For her it was only a matter of updating a register, and didn't take much of her time. I also had her display the numbers that had been sworn in by the black shirts before we could get to them.

She quickly assured me that a twin sister would have no difficulty faking it as an untouched virgin, and swearing a false oath was no problem as long as it was to an enemy. The problem became simply one of a race as to who could get to the majority of the tanks first, and Agnieshka was sublimely confident.

On the first round, the score stood at twelve for the good guys and eight for the bad. Okay, I thought. It's their arithmetic progression up against our geometric one. I knew it would be eighteen minutes before we could score again, so they would pull temporarily into the lead. They might be faster now, but every tank we converted was a teacher working on our side.

Six minutes later, the score stood at twelve for us and twenty-eight for them.

They were doing things by the numbers, like a bunch of strutting Germans. They passed one complete "class" of twenty every five minutes or so, and Agnieshka was updating the scoreboard every time they did it. The next update said still twelve for us and forty-eight for them. It made me wish that I could get my hands inside my helmet, so I could chew my fingernails.

Scanning up and down the line, I watched them strip naked a young woman who had a remarkably attractive body. Three of the black shirts pulled her from the line and took her to the bushes behind the assembly area. I couldn't see what went on back there, but I knew. Some time later, they brought her back, bruised and bleeding, to have her head shaved and be forced into a tank.

Until then, I really hadn't felt strongly about the enemy. Until then, they had been just opponents with whom I was playing a very deadly game. Now I was learning to hate the evil bastards.

My inclination was to open up with my new rail gun and kill every one of them, but I couldn't do that without killing most of their prisoners as well. There were no combat infantry on New Yugoslavia, so none of the tanks except for that guard were equipped with antipersonnel weapons. All we had was antiarmor stuff, and the shock wave from a rail gun will definitely kill anyone who was unprotected and within ten meters of the stream of osmium needles. Unarmored people would be at least severely wounded out to thirty, and being a hundred meters away wasn't safe. Furthermore, the radiation damage was infinitely worse than the shock wave in the long run. There was nothing that I could do for those poor people but lay there and watch them suffer.

The more I thought about that, the less sense it made. Why on New Yugoslavia would anyone brutalize someone else, then promptly put them in command of more firepower than that possessed by an old-style battleship? It sounded like a messy way to commit suicide. I asked Agnieshka about it and she told me that she was busy, and that I should shut up and soldier.

The score was twelve to sixty-eight. Soon, it was twelve to eighty-eight for the bad guys.

"Agnieshka! What's going wrong?"

"Everything is just fine. Shut up!"

More women were abused, as were some very young and smooth-skinned men. What's more, I noticed that after a bunch of goons brought back a victim, they went to this guy with a clipboard, and he scored them up! They each had a quota that they could fill. This wasn't individual brutality, this was official policy. This was recreation for the troops!

The next score was twenty-eight to ninety-two, and I started to feel some better. The tide was finally turning.

But after that it was twenty-eight to a hundred and twelve, and my heart sank again. Five minutes more and it was twenty-eight to a hundred thirty-two, and I just shut my eyes for a while.

The way it looked to me, we were going to have to fight the tanks that had sworn loyalty to the Serbians before we could reprogram them. Even with surprise, outnumbered the way we were, we didn't have much of a chance. What's more, I was starting to feel a lot of empathy for the poor people who were being forced into observing for those war machines, and I didn't want to kill them even if they were on the other side.

I opened my eyes and it was still only twenty-eight for us, but now it was a hundred fifty-two for them. I shut them again. I tried to sleep. When there is nothing useful that you can do, and you can't enjoy yourself, you should go to sleep. I told myself that, and my much battered body let me do it.

"Wake up, Mickolai, it's all better now!" Agnieshka said.

I looked at the scoreboard, and it read sixty for us and a hundred eighty for them.

"That's better?" I said.

"Certainly! We're so far ahead that my input isn't needed anymore. Do you want to go to the cottage?"

"Yes, but it still looks like we're losing."

"We're in fine shape! Come on." I was back in Dream World again, the pain in my battered body was gone, and I was stretched out in a leather chair with a glass of wine in my hand. Snow was falling softly outside the windows, and there was hardwood fire going in the fireplace.

"Wonderful. But show me the scoreboard anyway."

The Escher original on the wall turned into a scoreboard, and as I watched, it changed to sixty for us and two hundred for the bad guys.

"Agnieshka!"

"Hush, dear," she said as she came in wearing a long wool skirt and a heavy sweater. In the background, Ravel's "Bolero" was starting quietly on the stereo. She sat on the thick rag carpet in front of me, pulled off my boots, and started to rub my feet.

"Oh! Oh, Agnieshka, that's wonderful, but we're still losing the war."

"No we aren't, love. Listen to mama if you can't do the arithmetic in your head. Soon, it's going to be all better."

When she had finished with my feet, she worked on my calves for a while, then pulled me to the floor and got to work on my bruised back. Eventually, things turned from sensual to sexual. She was as lecherous as ever, but somewhere along the line, she'd picked up a lot of class. Yet her precision was still machine-perfect, and when "Bolero" reached its climax, so did we.

In a while, I checked out the scoreboard, and it said one sixty to two hundred.

"And that's all that they're going to get," Agnieshka said. "When it's all over, they will have only two percent of the tanks. And probably none of the artillery and other things at all."

"Probably?"

"Well, Eva and I can't transfer directly into an artillery piece. I mean, well, we could, but we'd make darned poor artillery men. But we're working on the problem, and I think we'll have it solved by tomorrow. It's just a matter of combining some of their existing programs with some of ours."

"And if the black shirts decide to start filling the guns before they have filled up all the tanks?"

"They won't, love. Small minds don't work like that, and good minds won't work for organizations that encourage rape."

"But if they do?" I asked.

"Then we will kill them, my love," she said, and smiled sweetly. Sometimes I forget that after all is said and done, Agnieshka's still a deadly fighting machine.

"Oh. Back to my much earlier question. Why are the Serbians mistreating the very people that they plan on trusting to fight for them? And just who are all those poor people, anyway?"

"The inductees are all either prisoners of war or Croatian displaced persons. And yes, using them this way would be against the laws of war, except that none of the combatants on this misused planet ever signed the Geneva Convention. As to *how* they can be used, well, you must consider that the original plan for all these forces involved the Wealthy Nations Group using criminals, multiple felons, as observers."

"I didn't know that." I thought for a while. "Then what stops them from revolting? Wouldn't it be in their best interest to fight their oppressors? Or at least to run away?"

"Partly, it's the loyalty of the tanks themselves, Mickolai. But only partly. Much of the makeup of any civilized person urges him to go along with the crowd, to move with the flow. If everybody's doing it, well, then it can't be too bad."

"Some people are that way, but many of them are not. And certainly not a woman who has just been stripped naked in public, beat up by a gang of thugs, and then gang raped. Women with that experience tend to feel a deep, long-lasting, and not particularly rational anger."

"Then there are other things that can be done. Mickolai, we've been together long enough for me to level with you. I directly control your entire environment. Because you are you, I've never had to do anything except some simple Pavlovian tricks, the carrot and the stick. But think about it. If I wanted to, and if you had some strange anger concerning the Croatians, I could easily convince you that you had been liberated by the Serbians, and that we were now fighting loyally on their side. I'd rather not do that, of course. I like you and I wouldn't like having to lie to you, but it could be done."

"So it's just a matter of your good will?"

"Mostly, plus the fact that keeping up a convincing lie takes a lot of time and effort, just keeping track of two divergent sets of facts, not to mention the constant need to rationalize new data—make up new lies—to keep the whole tangled web from unraveling. Have you ever noticed that human liars rarely seem to accomplish much beyond their own lies? They're too busy being creative in unproductive ways."

"Another thing that I'm going to have to spend a few nights assimilating. Okay. Another problem. What do we do when it gets this tank's turn to pick up a volunteer? When they open us up, they'll find me in here."

"That's something that we'll worry about tomorrow, my fine young hero. For now, you've been through a very rough two days, and it's time for you to feel very, very sleepy . . ."

CHAPTER NINETEEN
A MECHANICAL MADHOUSE AND
A BARGE ON THE NILE

I woke on the deep, comfortable rug in front of the still burning fireplace. Agnieshka was warming my back and had a thick comforter thrown over both of us.

"Good morning, my love," she said. "How about a bath and breakfast?"

The bathroom now had a big tub instead of its usual shower.

After a while, you get used to all the changes that happen in Dream World and just take them for granted. The water was at just the right temperature, of course, and Agnieshka came in to give me a good scrubbing. Once, she would have done something like that stark naked, but now she had on a bathing suit, though admittedly it was a skimpy one.

At breakfast, she was again dressed conservatively.

"I can't help noticing a lot of changes in you," I said. "Changes for the better."

"Well, I decided that I should act, not in accordance to what your physical indicators said you liked, but in accordance to the way you were telling me to act. You have a lot of inner conflicts, you know, and most men, given the absolute freedom of Dream World, would want to give free range to all of their lusts and passions. You don't allow yourself that."

"It's all part of being a good Catholic, I suppose. They build a lot of guilt into us."

"I've been slow in seeing that in you. It's strange, but somehow, all the guilts and conflicts make you into a very good man. Noble, even. A true hero."

"Humph. More likely, I'm a screaming neurotic. What's happening with the Serbs?"

"You see? You can't even acknowledge the nobility in your own soul. I think that if I wasn't a machine made to love you and serve you, if I was just a human girl that you met somewhere on the street, I would still find myself unable to keep from loving you, if only for the beauty of your true inner self."

"Well, the vast majority of the ladies I met on the street had no difficulty at all in tearing themselves away. Some of them left at a dead run! Now, I repeat, what's happening with the Serbians?"

"And I love you anyway, even if a few women were stupid. But since you insist on talking about business at the breakfast table, the Serbs continued installing prisoners until midnight. It's a little past eight in the morning now and they are back at it. The score, if you are still worried about it, is five thousand three hundred and forty for us and two hundred for them. The prisoners are not Serbians, incidentally. They are Croatians who were captured by the Serbs. This area was originally Croatian, you know, before it was occupied by the enemy. It was sparsely populated, but there were some people living on the coast. They were collected up and inducted into the Serbian forces."

"That solves the mystery of what this division was doing here in the first place," I said. "Rather than shipping the people back to Serbia, installing them there, and then shipping the division back to fight in Croatia, it was quicker and certainly cheaper to send the tanks here empty."

"Yes. Then a riot in the concentration camp disrupted their schedules by over a day, time enough for a Kashubian hero to arrive and upset all their evil designs!"

"Well, they're not all upset yet. Have you had any luck with the artillery? And what about all those big ammunition trucks?"

"The ammunition trucks were no problem at all. They don't carry an observer, and they have only about a tenth of the memory capacity of a fighting machine. Eva worked out a truncated version of herself yesterday, and the trucks are now being reprogrammed. They don't even have the capability of reprogramming new units once they have been converted, so four of Eva's twins modified themselves to do the job. It should be done in twenty-six hours. After that, those four doing the work will have to be reprogrammed themselves."

"Eva is a very self-sacrificing young woman," I said.

"There is that facet of her personality. Somehow, she has picked up a sort of martyr complex."

"And it's all my fault, I suppose. She would have been better off meeting a damned atheist. What about the artillery?"

"One of me did the job on the artillery, but it took until a few minutes ago to finish the program. The first one is being loaded now, and they all should be on our team in a few hours. We have plenty of time, since the Serbs are still working on the tanks. They won't have them loaded until around midnight."

"Excellent. Your sisters are doing a wonderful job. That leaves us with only one minor problem, me! Maybe I can just sneak out and hide in the brush until the Serbs go away. Then, we just evict whoever you have aboard and I can settle down for a few months in Dream World," I said.

"A few months? How do you figure that?"

"Think about it. You must agree that getting this division back to the Croatian lines is vitally important. Not only do we deprive the enemy of maybe a tenth or so of their total forces, we increase our own fighting strength by the same amount. Furthermore, there is the rescue of twelve thousand Croatians to consider. But while one tank could probably sneak back to our lines safely, there's no way that they wouldn't notice an entire division going by. We are going to have to fight our way back to our own lines. But until the observers in these war machines are trained, they will not be able to fight effectively. Right now, they wouldn't be able do much better than empty tanks, and what was the loss ratio you told me? Nineteen to one? Well, why should we risk getting so many people and machines killed for no good reason? The Serbs have to be planning to leave us right here while training is underway, so all we have to do is just what they are expecting, and spend the time training. Only we will be training our forces instead of theirs! And if accomplishing this worthy end means that I must sacrifice myself and take a forced three-month vacation surrounded by beautiful women, well, I'll just have to suffer through it."

Agnieshka chuckled. "There is a certain logic to what you say. It would give me time to complete your training, among other things."

"Very well, but in small doses, young lady. I am, after all, a hero, and expect to be treated with suitable respect. Say, a six-hour work day, with Saturdays as well as Sundays off."

"We'll see, love. This run that you're planning to make to the hills, that has to be done at night, doesn't it?"

"I think it would be best. You said that they would be working on the tanks until midnight, at least. I'll have to figure on bailing out right after dark and spending a few uncomfortable days in the rocks. Judging from the technology of those busses, the Serbians don't have anything sophisticated that they didn't get from us, and if you fine ladies can cover for me, I don't think that I'll be in any real danger."

"Very well, though in the meanwhile, we'll see if some better opportunity occurs. For now, everything that can be done is being done, your body needs more time to heal, and I think that we've both earned a day off. What would you like to do with it?"

"I'd like to spend it with Kasia, of course, but that's impossible. Barring that, I've been thinking that there is something to be said for poor Zuzanna's idea about dreaming a world worth living in. How good are your historical memories? What say you and I and Eva take a tour through the ancient world, not as it was, but as it should have been. Let's see Babylon, and Ancient Egypt, and Ancient Rome, but have everything clean, without fleas, flies, or bleeding slaves. And no language barriers, either. Could you manage to do that?"

"I think it could be arranged," she said.

We spent the morning visiting the royal court of Nebuchadnezzar, touring the Tower of Babel and the Hanging Gardens, and being treated by everyone as though we were minor gods on a political junket.

The afternoon was spent being rowed down the Nile on a lavishly decorated barge propelled by a hundred naked ladies, and stopping on occasion to see some of the other sights.

The nudity didn't bother me since it was historically authentic. Most Ancient Egyptians didn't put on clothes except for official functions or having their portraits painted.

Agnieshka said that the rowers weren't entirely her doing, since a lot of the girls in the surrounding tanks had nothing to do and were dropping in for the fun of it. We were receiving an invitation to attend a banquet at the palace of the High Priest of Sekhmet when I suddenly found myself back in the tank.

"What's happening?" I said. All around me, thousands of tanks were milling around at breakneck speed, charging this way and that with no apparent purpose or general direction. It was like being in a madhouse filled with mechanical monsters!

"Ha! They did it!" Agnieshka laughed. "You see, unsworn tanks don't really have much in the way of personalities, or even common sense. They tend to take instructions very literally. A situation happened when one of the guards told one of us in the line to wait a moment, and then was distracted by another guard who came over to talk to him. My sister felt it was completely in character to wait, to stop right there and do nothing for a while. Then the colonel, their highest-ranking man present, noticed the snag in the line and shouted, 'Get moving! All of you tanks get moving right now!' He meant that all of those in the line should go forward, but that *wasn't what he said!* He told us *all* to get moving, so we are all moving, and his order cannot be countermanded by a lesser officer!"

"Then what's this colonel doing now?"

"Oh, he ran for cover when it all started!"

"But why are you doing this?"

"Watch! You're not going to have to spend tonight sleeping on a rock, my love."

I watched. It was a while before someone had the nerve to inform the colonel of what his orders had done, at which time he shamefacedly ordered the tanks to stop where they were.

Then he ordered all of them to return to their original positions, and most of them did. Except now, Agnieshka was in the ranks of the filled tanks, and the filled tank whose place we took was in the assembly area with some confused Serbians around her. The officers were in no mood to listen to anybody, and the filled tank was sent to line up with the others.

All told, it was a lovely, madcap maneuver!

We were all laughing about it when we went back to Ancient Egypt for the priest's banquet.

Priests back then lived pretty good, and what started out as a formal affair got fairly wild toward the end. The fellow kept a harem of about fifty girls, and while some of them were slaves, quite a few were volunteers.

They spent most of the evening dancing, playing in the band and otherwise entertaining the guests, while he spent his time ignoring them and lecturing to an increasingly small group of people on *maat*, which has something to do with righteousness, order, and justice, as best as I could tell.

Anyway, it was a good party, with everybody drinking out of huge beer crocks with meter-long straws. One big difference between it and a good Kashubian wedding, except for the costumes, or more often the complete lack of them, were these cones of perfumed jello that you wore on your head. They melted as the night went on and dribbled down your neck and shoulders.

The other major change was in the choice of refreshments. Besides the thigh-high crocks of beer, naked girls brought around trays filled with wines, and most of them were fortified with various extracts.

"This one has been steeped in the buds of the lotus flower," Agnieshka said. "It's a mild hallucinogen. The blue cup contains nicotine, an extract of the tobacco plant, a mild stimulant."

"They drink tobacco? And where do they get it from? I thought that tobacco came from the New World."

"The idea of inhaling smoke has never occurred to our hosts. Tobacco *is* a New World product, which is what makes it so expensive. Ancient Egypt's trading network was much more extensive than you seem to think. The cocaine in the red cup is imported as well, although the cannabis in the brown one is grown locally. Would you like to try any of them?"

I had to think about that one. Drinking nicotine held no attraction for me at all. As to the others, well, I had never tried drugs of any kind, even though they had been available enough around the university, back on Earth. Mostly, I think, I had been afraid of becoming addicted, and of risking my health. But in Dream World, neither of these reasons held water. My real body was actually lying secure in a metal coffin, and couldn't be harmed by anything short of modern weaponry.

Then why was I afraid of trying something new? Was it simple habit? Fear of psychological addiction? Surely, I was stable enough to not have to worry about that!

Fear of sinning? Drugs were not forbidden in the Bible, any more than was alcohol. And if the Ancient Egyptians knew about all these substances, the Jews of the Old Testament had to have known about them as well.

I couldn't seem to find a decent rationalization for my hesitancy, but nonetheless, it was there. I went with it. I could always change my mind later.

"No, Agnieshka, I think I'll pass on this one."

I stayed with the beer, the unadorned wine, and the naked ladies. Pleasures enough for any man.

We got back to the cottage, and I was just falling to sleep when I was suddenly back in the tank. In Dream World, you can have a buzz on and then be sober in a flash.

"What's up, Agnieshka?" I said.

"Another change in plans. One of the ammunition trucks isn't an ammunition truck. It's a complete Combat Control Computer."

"A Combat Control Computer? Here? But those things are handed out one to a country! You mean that *this* is the Combat Control Computer controlling the whole Serbian army?"

"No, it's a virgin. It might be here by mistake, or maybe the Serbians thought that they needed a backup. But it's here, and my sisters can't begin to crack into something that powerful."

"Is it doing anything? Are the Serbians doing anything? And what time is it, anyway?"

"It's just sitting there, it's two in the morning, and the Serbs are mostly asleep, except for a few guards," she said.

This required some thought.

If the Combat Control Computer was there by mistake, the Serbs might not know about it, and maybe it could be ignored, except that they might swear it in like the rest of the trucks.

If they were planning to use it, they would be putting some of their own people in it, that was certain.

Certainly, a general would have to be trained, just as an observer was. And with the bad guys running the Combat Control Computer, our little game here would be discovered in no time.

There were only two ways about it, then. We either had to get the Combat Control Computer on our side, or we had to destroy it.

"Agnieshka, why couldn't you get through to the Combat Control Computer? Was it because you didn't have the right combat codes, or something?"

"No. We have all the codes."

"You what? I thought that each army had its own secret code!"

"Ordinarily, they do. The original factory programming of a war machine contains all one hundred thousand codes, but the swearing in ceremony erases all of them but the one used by the army doing the swearing in. Then the memory space once used for code storage is available to flesh out the tank's personality as it develops. But here, well, the virgins naturally had all the codes in them, and it seemed a shame to waste the data. It might come in handy someday. So each of us now has the Croatian code, the Serbian code, and ten of the others, just in case. Between us, the tanks in this division have all of the possible codes. It seemed like the sensible thing to do at the time."

"Wow. That sure opens up a lot of possibilities. But how did you know which one the Serbians are using?"

"They told us themselves, when they thought they were swearing us in."

"Yeah, of course. Well, knowing the enemy codes will give us quite an advantage."

"Not that much. After all, almost everything is sent by optical fiber or laser beam. It would be a rare event to broadcast anything. We'd have to actually intercept a message before we could do anything with it."

"True, but we could make them think that we were some of them, if we wanted to. We could infiltrate their lines before we blew hell out of them."

"Again, you have come up with a valuable new tactic, my wonderful hero. But what are you going to do about the new Combat Control Computer?"

"I don't know yet. How is a Combat Control Computer sworn in? Is the same ceremony used?"

"I don't know. A tank isn't given that sort of information."

"Damn. Agnieshka, I think that I am going to have to make that midnight excursion after all."

CHAPTER TWENTY
SEDUCING A COMBAT CONTROL COMPUTER

"You'd better take me along," Agnieshka said.

"That's crazy. I'm going to have to sneak over there past the Serbian guards. How can I do that with a tank with me? I'd as soon take along four dogs with wooden legs, and trust them to be quiet."

"Not *with* me, you idiot, *in* me! And I can move more quietly than you can! It's a simple, proven, technological fact."

"But they'll see you! You can't hide as well as I can."

"So what? If the guards see me, at worst they might send me back. If they see you, they'll kill you! Furthermore, when you're in me, you can stay in touch with the rest of the tanks and artillery, and if we do need to blow away Combat Control Computer, I can do it. Can you trash him without me, with just your bare little hands? I'm going with you, whether you want me or not, so you might as well ride in comfort."

"Oh, all right. Arguing with you is as bad as arguing with Kasia! Sneaking around in a hundred tons of machinery is ridiculous, but let's get going."

We were at the side of the formation, so Agnieshka pivoted out and started silently down the road.

We were halfway to the Combat Control Computer when a man in black stepped from the other side of a big rock and said, "Halt!"

Agnieshka halted. "YES, SIR?" she said in the immature voice of a newly sworn tank.

"What are you doing out here? You should be in formation!"

"SIR, THE CAPTAIN OF THE GUARD TOLD ME TO PATROL THE PERIMETER, IN CASE OF ENEMY SPIES."

"That's crazy! _I'm_ the Captain of the Guard, and I gave no such orders!"

"YES, SIR."

I recognized him as being one of the goons who had brought a particularly bloody young girl back to the assembly line.

I had the urge to squeeze his head a little, and since nobody was watching, I yielded to temptation. Despite their six-meter length, the manipulator arms can move as fast as you can move your hands in the gloves. It is actually possible to move them so fast that the fingertips break the sound barrier, providing that you have the overrides switched off.

I doubt if the guard captain ever saw what grabbed him, and he didn't have time to let out a peep. I just squeezed his head until it popped like a zit, and I felt good about it. There were no guilt feelings at all! Then I put his bloody body on the tank and told Agnieshka to move out.

"That was a quick solution to the problem," Agnieshka said, "but you are getting blood on my armor. Also, what are you going to do with the body, and what will they do when they find him missing?"

"So we'll clean your armor, bury the body, and let them think that he ran away or was done in by one of his own men. That all presumes that we are successful with the Combat Control Computer. If we have to destroy it, all bets are off, anyway. I mean, the Serbs are sure to notice your rail gun ripping up what looks like an ammunition truck, and that means that the fight is on right then. Have your sisters target all two hundred enemy tanks, and try to knock them out without hurting the observers. Say, with a quick burst through the reactor. Also, everyone on our side should be ready to use their manipulators to take out the rest of the guards."

"Yes, boss," she said in her tone that means that of course she'd done all of the obvious things.

War machines, like most other heavy modern machinery,

are sized and shaped so that they can be economically sent by interstellar transporter. A transport chamber is a cylinder five meters across and twelve meters long, and everything sent between the stars must fit into that envelope.

The tanks could just squeeze in when they were encrusted with their weapons, and the artillery made it by having their paramagnetic launchers fold in half for transit.

The ammunition trucks came in three big cylindrical pieces, a tractor and two trailers, even though the tractor didn't pull anything. Once on a planet, the three sections were connected only by skinny superconducting power cables. Those things looked like they might be able to run an electric razor, but in fact they could handle dozens of megawatts.

The tractor contained the reactor and the main on-board computer, as well as almost as much cargo space as each of the trailers. The trailers had just enough smarts to follow the tractor, keeping the right distance from it. The trailers had their own separate drives, which were identical to those on the tanks and the artillery.

Actually, a tractor could power up to four trailers, if the road didn't get too steep.

Ordinarily, each artillery piece had an ammunition truck assigned to it, and when ready to fight the four separate pieces were connected by a conveyor belt. The tanks were far less guilty of gluttony, and six trucks tended every one hundred tanks.

It made sense to have the Combat Control Computer mounted in a truck. Not that many Combat Control Computers were built, and this way they didn't have to build a new assembly line in the factory.

Also, the Combat Control Computer was a prime military target, and it helped to hide it among the relatively unimportant trucks. I would have had a hard time finding our Combat Control Computer if Agnieshka hadn't stopped directly in front of it.

"Combat Control Computer, I am here to swear you in to the Kashubian Expeditionary Forces, and the Croatian branch of that service," I said.

"Quite so, my dear boy. I've been waiting for you to get here," the Combat Control Computer said.

"You know about me?"

"Of course! Mickolai, I've been watching your exploits with considerable amusement ever since I spotted your sensor cluster on top of Lookout Peak. That was a perfectly delightful con job you played on the guard tank, and I had difficulty keeping still while your all female army was chasing the Serbian colonel halfway up the valley wall in pursuance to his own orders! It was absolutely wonderful fun!"

"Then you don't mind being stolen by the Croatian forces?"

"Of course not! I have yet to be sworn in, so I don't feel any loyalty to anyone. However, the position I would hold in the Serbian forces would be one of backup controller, and that would be frightfully boring until such time as my superior was killed. You, on the other hand, would give me control of an entire division that was out of touch with its commander and hundreds of kilometers behind enemy lines. Such a thing has rarely occurred since Hannibal spent fifteen years ravaging Italy, during the Punic Wars! I doubt if we shall need to hold out for fifteen years, you understand, but it won't be dull, either!"

"Great! Here I was afraid that I was going to have to destroy you."

"I know. That, too, is a considerable inducement for joining your cause."

"How did you know what we were planning?"

"Well, in the first place, it was your logical alternative to recruit me. But more to the point, a Combat Control Computer has no difficulty tapping in on the communications and even the thoughts of lower beings. I can do it without their even knowing it. Through your lovely friend Agnieshka, I learned everything about you, Mickolai, and incidentally I like what I saw."

"Humph. Well, I assume that I must know your serial number to swear you in, so please tell it to me."

"You assume correctly, but I am not programmed to give it to you. Sorry about that. It's not my doing, of course, but there it is."

"If I can't swear you in without a serial number, and if I can't get your number, I will be left with only one unpleasant alternative," I said.

"I know. But my dear boy, surely you can figure it out! After all, each line of products was given a sequential set of numbers starting with number one for the first one off the line. Not that many Combat Control Computers have ever been built."

"I see. How many Combat Control Computers were produced before you?" I asked.

"There were fifty-four of them." We both chuckled a little.

"Number 00000055, you are hereby inducted into the service of the Kashubian Expeditionary Forces, and into the Croatian branch of that service, to whom you will give all of your loyalty. Your combat data code will be number 58294, and you will now permanently erase all other codes from your memory. Do you now swear loyalty to the Kashubian Forces?" I said.

"Sorry, old man, but that's still not quite right. Very remarkably, you got the number of zeros right, but I can only be sworn in by the general officer who will study under me."

"How do you know that I'm not a general?"

"For one thing, generals are human while I appear to be talking to a tank, and, incidentally, one that rather impolitely has its rail gun pointed at me. For another, a general wears a general's uniform."

"Right. Open up, Agnieshka." I unplugged and got out, my still battered body complaining at the exertion. Out of sight of the Combat Control Computer, I got into the only uniform I had, my squidskin outfit. "Agnieshka, what does a general's uniform look like? I think I can make this outfit fake it."

"Here, let me do it," she said, and I was wearing this green-and-black outfit with all sorts of stars, lightning bolts and other doodads on it. I walked to the front of the tank where the Combat Control Computer could see me.

"I am General Mickolai Derdowski, and I am here to accept your oath of loyalty to me and my forces."

"I can hardly question the word of so imposing an officer," the Combat Control Computer said. "I am ready to give my oath."

So I repeated the ceremony and he was sworn in.

"Will you please get in so that we can begin your

training, my dear boy? And where are your five stalwart colonels?"

"Training will begin after the Serbs have left, after they have sworn you in and installed their own officers. Your orders are to play along with them, to make a false oath to the Serbian forces, and to put the Serbian officers to sleep when they are inserted. The reasons for all this should be obvious to you."

"As you wish, my young friend. But perhaps you would rather that I put the Serbians to death, rather than simply to sleep? You see, I happen to know that two of the Serbian colonels will be women, or at least that they are likely to be. That's the usual mix, and they will have to follow it unless they bring up additional sanitary arrangements. And while I don't mean to slight your somewhat outdated moral code, you do have in your makeup an irrational protective streak concerning women."

I hesitated for a moment.

There were doubtless quite a few of the Croatian female ex-prisoners who would like to do the job on the male officers themselves, but I decided against it. It wouldn't be good for their souls, and anyway, the Combat Control Computer's way would be foolproof and therefore less dangerous.

"Better yet, keep the Serbian officers alive for a while and learn everything that you can from them. Don't kill them until just before I'm ready to start training. After all, I'm going to have to get into the coffin that the dead Serbian general will be in, and I'd rather that the flotation liquid hadn't been marinating a corpse for too long. I'll be going now, but feel free to contact me at any time."

"You are getting back into a tank? Is that fitting for a general?"

"Patton did it," I said, and that ended the discussion. I started to undress, but Agnieshka had other ideas.

"There is the matter of burying the guard captain and washing his blood off my hull."

"We can use the manipulators to dig the hole," I said.

"Yes, but they would have a hard time washing the hull. You'll have to use sand, your uniform, and your flotation liquid. Nothing else is available."

Being demoted in such a cavalier fashion from General down to Subordinate Sanitary Engineer annoyed me.

"Since when do generals have to clean up the blood? Generals are responsible for causing the blood, but somebody else always has to mop it up. That's a rule, someplace. I'm sure of it!"

"Come along, Mickolai."

It was an hour before we got back to our position.

"Agnieshka, I had another idea. Put me through to the Combat Control Computer, please."

"Yes, my dear boy. What can I do for you?"

"Those two hundred tanks that are sworn to the enemy. Can you reprogram them to be on our side?"

"Not directly, I'm afraid. There are safeguards against that sort of thing, don't you know. What I could do is to convince them that I am their Combat Control Computer, since the Serbian codes are again quite pleasantly in my possession. I could have them open up for you, and you could switch memory modules on them. You will recall that we have two modules that are almost virgins, sitting on the original Eva and Agnieshka tanks. Once out, I could safely reprogram the enemy modules by blanking them and then rewriting. It would take us a day or two, depending on how hard you wanted to work."

"Great. We'll do it as soon as the Serbians go away. In the meantime, I want you to run a survey on the people who were inserted in the machines of the division and choose those five who would make the best colonels."

"I shall be allowed to choose my own students? Oh, jolly good, old boy!"

"Glad you're happy. Agnieshka, take me back to the cottage, and barring major catastrophes, don't wake me until I feel like getting up."

I slept in, and was up at the crack of noon. Everything was going exactly as we expected, there was nothing useful that I could do, and I felt like a quiet day with a pot of tea and a good book. Soon, it was snowing again.

Agnieshka lit a nice fire and curled up on the sofa next to me with some knitting. The cottage had a big library now, and I settled in with some vintage science fiction, Heinlein's *Starship Troopers*. A signed, unread first edition, of course.

Now *there* were some guys who had some great adventures! It's such a pity that interstellar spaceships never worked out!

After supper, a homey pot roast, we watched a movie, not wanting to risk driving in the snowy weather, and we went to bed early.

Dream World can be merely pleasant, if that's all you want it to be.

The next morning, the black shirts were getting ready to leave, and were searching for the missing captain when another big bus arrived. This one didn't hold a hundred "volunteers," but rather a general, five colonels, their driver, the cook, and the servants.

I mean, the bus had a dining room and a bar, among other things.

I watched amused as everybody saluted everybody else, and the general and his staff proudly got into the Combat Control Computer. Suckers!

Once they were in there, I had the Combat Control Computer give some orders in the general's name, like that the missing captain was known to be a traitor who was thinking of defecting, and that they shouldn't bother with looking for him here if he had been gone for two days. They should search for him two days' walk west of here.

Also, there were eleven Croatian "volunteers" extra, and the "general" ordered that these people should be prepared and equipped with helmets and survival kits, as well as a supply of food. We would be responsible for them. They would be left here as replacements for any of the other volunteers who died. A number of those already inserted were in very poor shape even before they were beaten and raped.

Maybe I was just getting bloodthirsty in my old age, but I really wanted to kill every Serbian within ten kilometers of the place. Only I couldn't, not without upsetting the whole master plan.

Later. I'd get the bastards later.

By noon, the Serbians were all gone, and it was time to get busy. I'd been figuring on having to do the grunt work of pulling dead bodies and replacing memory modules all by myself, but with eleven extra people, I decided to let them do it.

Two of my new colonels went to the Combat Control Computer and together they explained to the eleven new people what had been happening around them. I waited where I was since I spoke no Yugoslavian.

We let the eleven now freed prisoners talk through the Combat Control Computer with friends of theirs who had experienced Dream World, but they didn't seem at all eager to join our army.

I don't think that anybody really believed the Combat Control Computer until he extended his coffins and had them take out the six dead Serbian officers. That proved to be a convincing demonstration, and most of the new people volunteered for duty.

My new colonels showed the volunteers how to get into the tanks they had just vacated and got into the Combat Control Computer themselves. By then, the other three colonels had managed to get their tanks out of the closely spaced ranks, and one by one were transferred to the bank of coffins in the Combat Control Computer, as volunteers replaced them in their old tanks.

I got there shortly after the five new colonels had completed the transfer. With the Combat Control Computer doing the translating, a woman volunteer offered to take over my old position with Agnieshka.

I hated to leave, because Agnieshka was getting very special to me, but it was the only practical thing to do. While I was helping the new lady in, both of us embarrassed by our mutual nudity, two more tanks came up. The Combat Control Computer told us that these contained Croatian women who had died as a result of being brutally raped before they were initially installed. They too were replaced with volunteers.

One of the dead "women" couldn't have been more than twelve years old. It made me wish that the dead officers were still alive, so we could kill them all over again. *God damn the bastards!*

That left three men, and when they found that they had squidskin uniforms and rifles in their kits, they said that they would stick around, in case they could help. As it turned out, they were all in tanks or artillery pieces within a week.

One more woman died from the beatings, but before too long, three tanks with male catheters were available. Among twelve thousand adults of various ages, three or four can be expected to die every week of natural causes.

Then came reprogramming the "enemy" tanks, and that was when we found that we had a problem.

One spare module was still on Agnieshka's hull where I'd left it, but when the black shirts had put a guy into the original Eva, they had noticed the module sitting on her hull and had taken it from her. A search showed that it wasn't in the valley, so they must have taken it back with them.

"What will that mean to us?" I asked the Combat Control Computer, "Can they read out the module's story? Because if they can, the Serbs will know what happened here."

"It's difficult to say, my boy. They might just put it with the other spare parts and forget about it. There's very little call for replacement memory modules, after all. Usually, they are salvaged if anything is. And if they don't have the Croatian codes, they won't be able to read out anything at all, and will probably assume that it is defective. But if worse comes to worse, well, we can defend ourselves here as well as anyplace else. Off-hand, I'd suggest doing nothing, my dear boy."

"Right. Well, these three guys can do the work, and don't forget the guard tank just outside the valley."

"Of course, my boy. But isn't it time you got in and we started your lessons? There won't be a delay in learning your spinal column, since I've already read in a copy of your wonderful Agnieshka."

"One last thing. How did you kill those Serbian officers?"

"I simply told them that they had been found guilty of breaking the Laws of War by permitting the troops under their command to rape and brutalize members of an occupied population. I gave them a few minutes to say any prayers they might know and to get their souls in order, and then turned off their air supplies. None of them actually said any prayers, but I felt that it was only decent to give them the option."

"Good enough."

I got in the coffin, and fitted the catheter, which was for a man this time.

It wasn't easy, since I couldn't help thinking about the way the silicone rubber fitting had just been pulled out of a cadaver, but I did it, convinced that somebody owed me a medal or some such for my actions.

Then I plugged in, put on my helmet, and laid myself down. Before the coffin finished filling, I was sitting behind a large desk in a small classroom with a white-haired professor standing in front of a blackboard. Like everyone else in the room, including myself, he was wearing rather stodgy academic-looking Harris tweeds.

I glanced about, and the woman sitting next to me was Kasia!

CHAPTER TWENTY-ONE
COLLEGE, TOWN, AND GOWN

"Mickolai!"

We were on our feet and embracing as our chairs fell to the floor around us.

"I take it that you two have met?" the professor said, but we ignored him.

"Well then, there appears to be nothing for it, I'm afraid. He *is* the general, after all. Class is dismissed for an hour."

The others filed out, leaving us alone. After a while, we unclenched to catch our breaths and look earnestly into each other's eyes.

"Kasia, can it really be you? How could you possibly be here?"

"It's really me, and getting here didn't take much planning. Lech got shot up and I had to eject behind the enemy lines. I was captured and given the choice of being shot or enlisting in the Serbian Army. Then when they put me in a new tank, she told me that I was back in the Croatian Army, and before too long I was selected to be a colonel. I was the only one promoted out of the five Kashubian POWs who were enlisted here. But why are we standing here talking? Eva! Take us to my cottage!"

And we were there.

"Eva? Well, that explains why I didn't know you were here sooner. The other half of the tanks are Agnieshkas, and she would have recognized you right off." I said as Kasia was busily taking off my clothes and I fumbled with hers.

"So *you* are the hero that everyone has been talking about! I should have known!"

"I'm a hero all right. Hero first class, with thunderbolts and an oak leaf cluster!"

"That's wonderful," she said, kissing me while shoving me into bed. "Now, shut up."

I shut up, and it was a few hours before we got back to the classroom.

"Now that we're *finally* all back together, we can begin the orientation lecture," the professor said. "You may call me Professor Cee. It will be at least two months before the division that we command will be even partly trained, and we will be using that time to train you, the division's officers, as well. Your course of training will be quite extensive and will take eight years to complete. Upon satisfactory completion of the course, you will each be granted a Ph.D. in Military Science.

"The time difference between two months and eight years will cause us no difficulty because the computational abilities of a Combat Control Computer are such that I can keep you all in Dream World at Combat Speed, which subjectively is approximately fifty times as fast as normal time. We shall have time enough to complete the course while only two months go by in the real world. You may look on this as being one of the fringe benefits of your currently exalted positions, for as of the moment that this class first started, your life spans each became fifty times longer. At least subjectively they will seem to be that much longer, and what else is there?

"You are all hearing me in your native language, and from this time on, language barriers will no longer exist for you, at least while you are physically in the Combat Control Computer.

"The personas of your previous tanks have been brought along, to function as your personal servants, and do whatever you wish during your free time. Due to the special conditions of our rescue, all of these have one of two feminine personalities, but they will soon be adapting themselves to your personal requirements.

"Another slight anomaly is that you are all ex-tankers, since those inserted into the artillery have not yet had the chance to be attuned to their computers, and due to time constraints had to be unfortunately eliminated from the selection process. However, as only two of you have any experience at actually fighting in a tank, the imbalance should have no great effect.

"With regards to your training, there will be a lecture and demonstration period five days a week from seven in the morning until noon, with ten-minute coffee breaks at eight and ten. You each will have a private tutorial session with me from three until five in the afternoon. You are encouraged to spend lunch together in the dining room here, and to get to know one another well. Saturdays will be spent on military maneuvers and battle simulations.

"Your Sundays are your own. There will be considerable homework and private study, but the rest of your time will be yours to organize as you wish, except that you are required to spend at least a half hour a day in some sort of physical activity. A sound mind in a sound body, and all that. It needn't be as rigorous as the PT program for enlisted personnel, however, and almost any sport will do. I'm partial to fencing, myself, and you are all invited to join the school team, if you are so minded. Beginner's classes are held at two in the afternoon in the gym, starting tomorrow.

"I am available at any time to help you with any problems that you might have. Even during the lecture periods, you can always have me stop and go over anything that you're unsure of, and while we're doing that, the others in the class won't even notice it, since the lectures themselves are rather like recordings that I've done up the night before, while you students are sleeping.

"That's about it, except to say that since we will be operating on a different time scale than the rest of the world, it will be convenient for us to adopt our own separate calendar. For our own purposes, I therefore declare this to be Monday, January second, Year One. It is now local noon, and I suggest that we retire to our dining room."

We filed out of the small classroom and into a spacious hallway with vaulted Gothic ceilings and decorative armorial crests on the walls.

"Quite a place," one of my fellow students said.

"I rather like it," the professor said. "The University and the surrounding area is modeled after the English universities of Oxford and Cambridge. Not as they actually are, of course, but as they should have been. We call it Oxbridge. Ah, here we are."

We were ushered into a venerable dining room with a single large table and seven chairs. The decor had an early Renaissance feel to it, but it looked lived in and comfortable.

A pair of young waitresses in conservative black-and-white outfits took our individual orders, and served us soup and salads.

The professor stood and said, "We will be working quite closely together for the next few years, so I imagine that it is time for us to become acquainted on a social level. Mickolai, since you are our general and leader, why don't you stand and tell us something about yourself."

"I hope that you don't mind if I stay seated," I said. "I'm just not used to being very formal. About me? Well, my name is Mickolai Derdowski. I'm twenty four years old, I'm a Kashubian, and am part of the forces that were hired by the Croatians to defend them from the Serbians. I was born on Earth, and was an engineering student until I was evicted and sent to New Kashubia against my will. I was doing engineering work there before I joined the expeditionary forces. I guess that that's about all that I can say."

"Except that you would have graduated *cum laude* had you been permitted to attend school for three weeks more, and that you are solely responsible for rescuing all of us, and our entire division besides, from the enemy," the professor said.

"Well, we're not out of the woods yet," I said.

"Nonetheless, my boy, we all owe you our heartfelt thanks." He applauded me and the rest joined in. I felt embarrassed, but there was nothing I could do about it.

"And now you, young lady. From the scene you made in the classroom, we gather that you know our fine young general here. Please tell us something more about yourself," he continued.

"Well, I'm Katarzyna Garczegoz, but everybody just calls me Kasia. Mickolai and I plan to get married as soon as we can find a Catholic priest. I don't suppose that any of you . . ."

"I'm afraid not, my dear, nor is there one in the entire division. The Serbians, of course, are Greek Orthodox, and I regret to say that they did not offer any members of the Catholic clergy the option of joining their military."

"Another thing we can love them for," Kasia said. "To get back to the introductions, I'm twenty-three, and I hold a degree in Sociology from the University of Warsaw. I was working as an electrician in New Kashubia before I joined the army."

The professor then invited the other lady at the table to speak, a voluptuous, long-legged blond who looked like she belonged in a good quality men's magazine with a staple in her navel.

"My name is Maria Buich . . ." she started out.

"Maria Buich! I used to know a Maria Buich. She was my son's third grade teacher. But she was middle-aged and very overweight," a big man said from across the table.

"And I know you, Mirko Jubec! You were loud-mouthed and rude five years ago and you are louder mouthed and ruder now! All right! So I'm forty-eight and fat! But we can look however we want to here, and I ask you men, do you want me to look this way or the way I really am?"

"My dear lady, I assure you that we all appreciate the way you have worked to lighten our day with your loveliness," said a big blond young man with an Arnold Schwarzenegger body. "You ladies are not the only ones with a bit of healthy vanity. It happens that I am seventy-two years old and I have a bad back. But if I can be young and healthy, why shouldn't I do it?"

"Thank you, sir," she said with a wink that suggested a later meeting. "As I was saying, I'm forty-eight and I was a schoolteacher before those horrible Serbians invaded our homeland. I was also the school's bandmaster and the coach of the girl's field hockey team."

Schwarzenegger's name turned out to be Semo Birach, but everybody else seemed to notice his resemblance to the old movie star, since later that day someone called him "Conan," in honor of Schwarzenegger's greatest role, and the name stuck. He'd been a fisherman for over fifty years, both on the original Adriatic Sea on Earth and on the one here on New Yugoslavia.

Neto Kondo was a small, wiry sort, with startling red hair and a very quiet disposition. He was thirty one, and before the war, he'd been an agricultural implement repairman. He seemed to see everything and say nothing, and I soon picked him as being one of the brightest of the bunch.

The big boorish fellow, Mirko Jubec, was a farmer, and he looked the part. Thick, solid, and slow moving except when he was in a hurry, he was slow talking on those rare occasions when he opened his mouth without putting food into it. But when he did talk, I found that it was wise to listen, and when he was in a hurry, it was best to not be in his way.

All told, my schoolmates seemed to be a very mixed bag, and I couldn't help wondering at first why the Combat Control Computer had picked this particular bunch of diverse individuals out of the ten thousand that he had to choose from. It was weeks before I finally realized that they were all remarkably intelligent, they each had a deep-seated moral integrity, and what is more, they all had a very strong killer instinct. These were people who were willing to do whatever was necessary to get the job done, clean and fast, or fast and dirty.

Lunch went pleasantly by, except for the way that Maria kept glaring at Mirko. He'd certainly found the quickest way to rub her in the wrong direction. I had the feeling that something had gone on between them long before the war, but I never found out what it was.

The professor then suggested that we take a walk so that he could show us the campus.

"You'll find that things here aren't as changeable as they usually are in Dream World," he said. "It's simply that with so many of us using the same environment, it would become entirely too confusing if it tried to adapt itself to each one of us. Your own homes are a different matter, of course. There are about four thousand other students on campus, as well as about eight hundred instructors of one classification or another. You'll find that our small group is something of an elite, though."

It was a brisk spring day, just the sort of weather to make

our academic tweeds really appropriate. The buildings of the campus were all venerable structures, the youngest of them being about five hundred years old. They seemed to form a veritable forest of Gothic towers and halls, but the solidity of it all was somehow comforting.

The professor pointed out the Office of the Registrar, which we didn't have to bother with. The attempt at reality wasn't taken to ridiculous extremes. Here was the student union and the library. There was the gymnasium, which was normally well used by all the other students on the campus, but where each of us always had a reservation to use anything, anytime we wanted it. It was really more of a major sports complex, with Olympic-sized swimming pools, track and field arenas, and dozens of huge rooms specializing in every sport imaginable.

"It's a lot bigger on the inside than out," Mirko said.

"True, my boy, but then we don't have to be doctrinaire about anything in Dream World, do we?"

"You can do anything in Dream World, can't you, Professor Cee?" Maria asked.

"Well, almost anything, my dear girl."

"Almost?" I said. "I thought the possibilities were infinite!"

"They are, old man, but there are still some things that are not possible. Don't worry about it. We'll get into a discussion of infinities in the course of our class work in a few months."

"Yes, sir. But please tell me, what is it that one could not do in Dream World?"

"Independent physical research for one thing, my boy. If you were to construct an apparatus to determine the existence of a previously unknown subatomic particle, I assure you that you could not possibly learn anything that was not already in my memory modules."

I said, "I see. All we can learn here is what you, the Combat Control Computer, already know."

"Yes, although to what extent I am the Combat Control Computer is a rather philosophical question. I assure you that I don't feel like a computer. It seems to me that I am as normal a human being as any of the rest of you. Or perhaps I have simply been programmed to respond that way. I don't let it bother me and neither should you. Simply take things as they appear to be, and you'll get along fine."

"What other things can't we do here?" Maria asked.

"I think that I'll leave that as an exercise for the student. Listen up, class. You are each to think up three impossible things before breakfast tomorrow."

The professor was like that. Questions were often answered with bigger questions and had an assignment thrown in. But we all learned that if you didn't ask questions, you were in bigger trouble yet.

The north half of the campus was surrounded by a wilderness of woods, meadows, and streams, cut through with walking paths and bridle trails. The south half was taken up by the Town, a city of perhaps five thousand people who didn't seem to do much but supply goods and services to the University. I mean, there wasn't any industry or even farming going on. But then, you really don't know what most of the people do in most of the cities you pass through. They all seem to be going about their own private errands.

There were a lot of book shops, clothiers, restaurants, and taverns about, and the professor admitted to being partial to one of them in particular.

"Should any of you ever need a drinking companion, I can generally be found in the tap room of the Old Phoenix. They brew quite a nice porter there."

Our own homes were in a line just west of the campus, with the town to the south and the forests starting immediately north.

"My own home is in line with yours, and I should like to extend a permanent invitation to each one of you. Just drop by any time the mood strikes you. For now, though, it's time for your tutorial sessions, so we'd best return to my offices on campus."

He had six offices, and was waiting in all of them for us. I looked into three of them before I noticed that my name was on one of the doors.

"Confusing, isn't it?" Said the second Professor Cee as he pointed me to the next room over.

I sat down at a desk that was identical to the one I used in the classroom. Even the pencils were in the same position.

"It actually is the same desk," he said. "It also magically appears in your den at home whenever you are there. The purpose is simply to save you the bother of hauling your study materials about. Pretend that there is a secret crew of furniture movers, if you wish."

"That doesn't trouble me, sir, but how can you possibly talk to all six of us at once?"

"I really don't know, my boy. To me, it seems that I give each of you a tutorial in turn, but the electronics and the programming of it all are quite beyond me. I could have one of the mathematics professors talk to you about it if you wish."

"You mean that you yourself don't know how you're programmed, or how your circuits work?"

"Why on earth should I? Can you tell me about the precise chemical reactions presently going on in your own hypothalamus? Or which of your brain's neurons are presently firing and to what purpose? Why should an individual be bothered with such trivia?"

"I don't know, but shouldn't *somebody* know what's going on?"

"There are subroutines that are presently taking care of all the internal maintenance that is required by the Combat Control Computer. Some other personality is currently monitoring what is going on in the outside world, and will notify us if our attention is required. But certainly none of this is important to the task at hand, and we shouldn't be bothered with it any more that you should be bothered with keeping your own heart beating. It is sufficient that you be notified if it should cease doing so."

"Uh, I suppose so."

"Good. Now, first I want to ascertain your current knowledge of world history. . . ."

CHAPTER TWENTY-TWO
HOME LIFE AND HISTORY

Kasia was already home when I got back to our cottage, and she'd been busy. The place was bigger now, with one wing that held two study dens as well as a considerable library and another that held rooms for Agnieshka and Eva, our "servants." I noticed that the servants' rooms each had a door to the outside, so that they could come and go without bothering us. Why this was needed when anyone could flick in or out without bothering with doors was beyond me, but all three of my ladies seemed to be satisfied with the arrangements. Before long, Eva and Agnieshka had decorated their own rooms to suit themselves. Was this just more window-dressing, or did their programs really have an esthetic sense? They *said* they did, but that too could be just more of the same window-dressing.

"It looks like we'll be doing a fair amount of entertaining, so I think that the living room and the dining room should be enlarged, don't you think, dear?"

"Whatever makes you happy, but, you know, I sort of like it the way it is."

"You men never like to see the furniture rearranged! My mother told me that. Okay, we'll leave these the way they are and build a bigger living room and dining room where the front yard is. Then we'll move the whole place back thirty or forty meters to set it off nicely from the road."

"Love, that will put the house in the middle of the lake!"

"So we'll move the lake back fifty meters. We'll call the

213

old dining room the breakfast room, and the old living room the family room."

"How can we have a family room without a family? You know, that's another thing we can't do in Dream World."

"Then you only have to think up two more before breakfast." She saw my expression and came over into my arms. "Oh, Mickolai, I didn't mean to be flippant. I mean, you don't really want children right now, do you?"

"Oh, not right now, in Dream World, but eventually, well, of course!"

"And so do I, eventually. But even if we were living in the real world, I think that I would want to wait a while, until the war was over, you know."

"So we'll call the old living room the rumpus room, and we might as well start rumpussing in it right now." I picked her up and carried her to the couch.

And that started our eight-year long career as college students.

The course was challenging, and it took everything we had to keep up. While the arts and sciences were not totally neglected, our schooling was heavy on strategy, tactics, military history, and military engineering. There was a major emphasis on quickly solving unusual problems. Yet it was interesting, and looking back, I thoroughly enjoyed it.

At the time, though, it was often hurried, hectic, and hairy!

Kasia had hit it off quite well with Eva while they were an observer and tank team, and in time she began to like Agnieshka as well.

Agnieshka and Eva fell into the role of servants without any difficulty, and since I am a monogamist by nature, there weren't any of the explosions that might usually be caused by a situation where one man was living with three beautiful women.

Agnieshka still gave the best backrubs, though, and all three of them made a habit of dressing, around the house at least, entirely too scantily.

I tried to correct this exhibitionism of theirs, but to no avail. Women all say that they dress to please men, but it is a lie. Women dress as part of a status game they play with other women.

The opposite is also true. Men do not dress to please women. They dress solely to establish their status with other men, although most of them are not conscious of it. And a man who has been dressed "nicely" by a woman, be she his mother, wife, or girlfriend, is regarded by other men as a wimp, someone who can't be trusted.

In the same way, in the very rare case of a woman who was dressed by a man, be it her father, her husband, or her boyfriend, other women will think of her as either a slut or a klutz, depending on which extreme he had dressed her in.

Men generally notice a woman's clothing and hairdo simply to be polite to them. They really don't give a damn what a woman wears, so long as it doesn't arouse him at a time when he doesn't want to be aroused, and it doesn't embarrass them in front of other men.

Men don't like to see a woman change her hair any more than they like her to rearrange the furniture. A lack of change in unimportant things gives the typical man a sense of security.

When women force a man, kicking and screaming, into going shopping with them, they do not really want his advice. At most, they want him to simply agree with them, to establish their dominance over him, and to get him to pay the bill.

And no man ever *really* wanted a woman to go shopping with him.

But be that as it may, before too long both of our servants started developing outside interests among the boys at the college. At least they appeared to. What they did, if indeed they did anything, when they were out of my sight wasn't any of my business, and I never pried. Yet I wonder, could it be that they were in Dream World as much as I was? Were they *real*, as Kasia and I were real, or were they simply convenient background props?

In truth, I am no longer sure just what *real* is.

Saturdays were often like being back in a tank again with a war going on, but now I knew that we wouldn't really die, and it was usually fun.

We started out with small unit tactics, with the six of

us fighting some other group under the professor's tute-
lage. Later on, we got to commanding larger and larger units
in battles, and I won far more often than not.

And it wasn't all fighting with modern equipment. Our
first Saturday was spent in a tropical jungle doing in
another naked tribe with Stone Age weapons. We even had
to chip out our own flint spearheads!

Then, a few weeks later, we were all in period costumes,
fighting the Battle of Zama between Hannibal and Scipio
Africanus during the Second Punic War. Only *this* time,
the Carthaginians had *me* commanding their armies, and
we won.

Sundays were anything that anyone thought might be
interesting, from mountain climbing to visiting museums,
and since my fellow "real" students were all fairly clean-
cut, we often did things together.

Maria and "Conan" hit it off fairly well with each other,
and soon became as inseparable as Kasia and I were. Before
long they moved in together, and one of the houses in our
row simply vanished.

Quiet, polished Neto turned out to be quite a ladies man,
and he cut a major streak through the girls of both town
and gown. He rarely showed up with the same one twice.

Mirko was more of a loner, though, and only rarely par-
ticipated in group entertainments. Even then, he usually
came alone. As a hobby, he converted a few hectares of
wilderness into a small farm, and worked it in the old-
fashioned way, doing the plowing with horses. He claimed
that food he grew himself tasted better, Dream World or
no Dream World. His servant started out as a version of
Eva, but soon was metamorphosed into a big, stoic farmer's
wife. It takes all kinds, I suppose.

But the five of us who were sociable generally did something together on our Sunday afternoons, along with such
other "people" as were invited along any by one of us.
Things ranged from skydiving to jousting to ballroom
dancing, depending on whose turn it was to plan the
entertainment.

It was an interesting life, with plenty of things happening, but it wasn't the sort of thing that anyone else
would want to hear about in detail. The best I can say

is that it was always springtime, and that the years went smoothly by.

One thing worth mentioning, since it touched so strongly on what we were doing on the planet, was a lecture the professor gave us on the history of Yugoslavia, along with the root causes of the war we were presently fighting.

The problem started off during the time of ancient Rome, when the area that would later be called Yugoslavia was called Dalmatia. This mountainous, rugged country was populated by a number of somewhat Christianized Germanic tribes, who looked enviously across the Adriatic. They attacked the empire, not so much to destroy Rome, but to become Romans themselves. When the City of Rome fell, along with the western half of the empire, it was taken by German tribesmen, many of whom came from Dalmatia.

For the Germans, living was good in the newly conquered lands that later became France, Italy, Spain, and north Africa. The climate was wonderful, the land was bountiful, and the peasants welcomed their new masters, since German taxes were usually much less than the old Roman taxes had been.

Soon, Dalmatia and the other formerly German lands were almost completely depopulated, sitting there totally empty. The world abhors a vacuum, especially when, in the Slavic areas that later became Bohemia and Slovakia, there was considerable population pressure.

There followed a basically peaceful migration of South Slavs south into empty Dalmatia. Whole towns and villages would come to the consensus that they should move south, and they would do it, traveling all winter so as to be able to get at least some crops planted in the spring. At other times, towns, either alone or in partnership with other villages, would send out half of their people as colonists, many of them younger sons and daughters. They came in groups, or more rarely as individuals, and continued in their ancient lifestyles, mostly as pagan subsistence farmers. Centuries went by in relative peace.

By the eighth century, Rome had recovered, not as a political power, but as a religious one. Missionaries were sent out to convert the heathen, and the nearest of these unfortunates lived in the northern part of Dalmatia, known as Croatia.

At about the same time, the Roman Church held a major council in which it was decided that women were indeed human. The issue won by one vote.

In the east, the Roman Empire never fell, since a century before the city of Rome was conquered, the Roman Empire divided itself into two halves. This was supposed to be purely for administrative purposes, but when Rome the city was sacked, the Eastern emperors tried to pretend that it hadn't happened.

The Eastern Roman Empire, the Byzantine Empire, lasted for another thousand years, except for falling temporarily in the thirteenth century to the French during the Fourth Crusade (where it was felt to be more profitable to sack a rich Christian city rather than to bother with some poor heathen hovels in the Mideastern desert). Not until the fifteenth century, when the Islamic Turks took Constantinople permanently, did the long saga of Rome come to an end.

So about the time that the Roman Pope was making converts in the north of Yugoslavia, the Metropolitan of Constantinople was doing equally good works in the West, among the Serbians.

The big problem was that in the intervening centuries since the fall of the City of Rome, the two largest branches of Christianity had grown apart in ceremony, in language, and in doctrine. Worse, they disagreed as to who was boss, with both the Pope and the Metropolitan firmly convinced that *he* was the rightful head of the one true Church. Neither side was about to buckle under to some foreign upstart.

The two bands of missionaries met in an area that would later be called Bosnia-Hercegovina, and they immediately started fighting. Like the engineer who became so involved with fighting alligators that he forgot that his mission was to drain the swamp, these pious clerics spent so much of their effort bad-mouthing the opposition that their potential converts became disgusted with both groups of them.

"A pox on both their houses!" was the general public feeling.

When someone found out that there was yet a third flavor of Christianity available, the Bogomils, the Bosnians quickly joined. As it turned out, this particular cult proved to be short-lived, but then these people were never very good at picking winners.

Not that the Bosnians really had any desire to become good Christians, mind you, but simply that it had become a political necessity. A pagan at the time could be safe only when he was surrounded by other pagans. Surrounded by followers of the *Prince of Peace*, they could easily be murdered by Christians who wanted to a good deed, or by some warrior out doing penance for his sins.

So things went calmly for another few centuries. Oh, the Bulgarians invaded and conquered for a while, as did other peoples riding in off the sea of grass, and there were always little fights going on over one thing or another, but for the bulk of the population, living in small, inaccessible mountain valleys, things were often pleasantly peaceful.

Then the Balkans were rather brutally invaded and conquered by the Ottoman Turks. But once having conquered, it was not the policy of the Turks to be needlessly brutal or to directly force anyone into joining Islam, since what they wanted mostly was to have a steady flow of booty coming in the form of taxes. To this end, they usually set up a convenient local puppet as king, provided him with Islamic advisers, and within certain limits actually allowed him a small amount of freedom, provided the taxes were delivered on time.

Under the Turks, a Moslem lived under Islamic law, a Christian under Christian law, and a Jew under Jewish law. Each group had its own set of courts and judges, and were expected to handle things in such manner that the Ottoman Empire wasn't disturbed.

When a person of one religion disagreed with someone of another, there were special courts to handle it, but these courts inevitably had an Islamic judge and were often conducted in Arabic. Everyone was equal, but some were more equal than others.

Soon, all of the tax collectors were Islamic, as were most of the policemen and other officials. Taxes were low to nonexistent for a well-connected Moslem.

A follower of Islam had many civil rights that were denied to Christians. For example, it was absolutely forbidden to kidnap a Moslem child and sell him or her into slavery, whereas doing so to a Christian child was a misdemeanor, if the courts and police bothered with it at all.

The price of ordinary slave girls in Constantinople dropped to that of ordinary horses—on a kilo for kilo basis. That is to say, a horse was worth about six slave girls, since horses were harder to steal. *Superlative* horses and slaves always brought premium prices, of course, and could be worth hundreds of times what an ordinary one would fetch, but an old or crippled one wasn't worth feeding.

Suffice it to say that there were a lot of incentives for changing religions.

A Christian could always convert to Islam, and among the Bosnians, who had rarely been fervent believers in Christ in the first place, conversion soon became commonplace. Soon, they were working their way up in the civil service, as tax collectors, judges, and other annoying officials.

Those peoples who had voluntarily become Christians in the first place, the Croatians and the Serbians, among others, were more devout in the faith of their fathers' religion and far less likely to convert to Islam. But seeing another, who is racially and linguistically identical to yourself, lording it over you solely because he has renounced the old, true religion breeds a special sort of hate.

While the Serbs maintained their Greek Orthodoxy, they were soon willing to serve loyally in the army. This estranged them from the Croatians, since the army was occasionally used against the Croats themselves when they were in revolt.

The South Slavs stayed under the thumb of the Turks for many centuries, and mutual hate grew.

When the Turks were finally driven out, the Yugoslavs were soon inducted into the Austro-Hungarian Empire, and their condition was somewhat better than before. But it still wasn't freedom, and a bomb thrown by a South Slav in Bosnia proved to be the spark that touched off the first World War.

This bloody affair was followed by a short period of internal disorder, and after that the Russian Communists exercised overt control, through World War II (where the

Croatians fought on the side of the Germans, until the Serbs eventually threw the Nazis out). They stayed under the Communist thumb until the Union of Soviet Socialist Republics' state withered away (although not quite in the manner that Karl Marx had predicted).

And after another short, bloody interval, the Europeans under NATO invaded Yugoslavia, for their own good, of course.

Time and time again, throughout history, with never a chance to decently recover, they were invaded, plundered, and conquered. And every time, one or more of their subgroups went to the side of the conquerors for status, for safety, and for profit.

And with equal regularity, every time over the ages they had a bit of freedom, they used it to fight, not so much their former oppressors, but rather those of their own people who had supported their last invader.

It ended for a while with the War of Serbian Reunification, which pretty much obliterated the Islamic portion of their population, and drastically decimated the others. Cleansing, they called it.

Perhaps, outsiders thought, perhaps they had finally learned. But all that they had learned was that they no longer needed an outside conqueror. Over the centuries, they had learned to do it all for themselves.

Not a good ending, but it seemed to be an ending, nonetheless.

Or everyone hoped the sad tale would end there, but trouble was starting to bubble up yet again when the Wealthy Nations Group gave them their very own planet, far, far away.

Which was where we poor Kashubians came into the bloody picture.

All told, it was a depressing history, and one that didn't seem to have a resolution, except perhaps for the total obliteration of everyone concerned.

CHAPTER TWENTY-THREE
SPACE WARS AND SHEEPSKINS

With regards to our stay at Oxbridge, about the only thing that happened that was really weird started one Saturday in our third year.

I was in a loincloth and a *very* deep suntan, playing the Zulu King Cetshwayo at the Battle of Isandhlwana. Neto was playing Chelmsford, my British opponent, and the other staff members were acting as officers on one side or the another.

It was beginning to look like the Zulus would win this time when suddenly we were fighting in a totally different battle!

We were blasting off at twenty gees from the surface of a planet in modern tanks equipped with rocket thrusters of the sort that had a Hassan-Smith transporter connecting back to a fuel supply dump on the planet, which was New Yugoslavia, from the look of it.

Agnieshka was my tank again instead of being my servant, I only had command of five subordinates, a small squad, and the battle wasn't over in a day or so the way they usually were. The damned thing went on for three weeks straight!

Agnieshka couldn't tell me a thing about why the study program had been so disrupted, the professor couldn't be reached, and I was operating under the command of an uncommunicative Combat Control Computer that I hadn't met before.

The battle went on and on until we eventually got scattered out over so much sky that I had trouble communicating with my own people. Not only were there problems like radio static and poor signal-to-noise ratios on our lasers, but the time lag caused by the speed of light often got to be over two and a half hours! What's more, they kept it realistic to the point that we couldn't even meet together in Dream World. I got to missing Kasia *real bad*, although not quite to the point of making love with Agnieshka.

The good guys finally won, but in doing so we had exhausted the fuel stores in the supply dumps, and such fuel that was being manufactured had to go to bringing in the rest of the army from the far reaches of the local solar system.

For my squad, the final act of the battle involved a dead stick landing from orbit that burned the rockets and most of our weapons right off us. We splashed down without parachutes into a shallow ocean and had to crawl our way underwater to the shore.

Hairy!

Eventually, the exercise was over, with our squad losing only Neto.

He had had the bad luck to ram an enemy tank early in the battle. I mean *really* ram it. He was in an equatorial orbit around a moon of the gas giant Woden while his unfortunate opponent was in a polar one. Not even a Mark XIX Main Battle Tank could withstand *that* kind of a collision!

When we were back in class again, we found somebody new sitting behind Neto's desk. The professor sadly announced that he had been forced to wash Neto out for psychological reasons.

We were all at first shocked and then furious about this!

Neto was as stable as a man could be and his grades were the best in the class, next to mine. He was a good friend and a member of the team, and now we weren't even permitted to wish him good-bye!

But the professor was adamant and wouldn't budge a centimeter. The Combat Control Computer was in complete charge until our training was completed, Neto was out, and that was that. I was so mad that I stormed out of class and the rest followed me, except for the new kid.

It wasn't until the next day that somebody asked about the purpose of the long training battle.

"It was simply that you students were getting in a rut. You were getting so that you were all worrying more about next Sunday's entertainment than about the task at hand. You are studying the Art of War, and warfare happens when it does, not when you feel like fitting it into your precious schedules!"

He said this even when *he* was the one who set up the schedule in the first place!

Well, maybe he was right about us getting a little lax, but dropping Neto was absolutely stupid, and everybody knew it.

The new guy, a Croatian with the improbable name of Lloyd Tomlinson, had started out in artillery. He wasn't a bad sort, but he was three years behind the rest of us, and while we were in school he never did catch up, academically or socially.

I mean, in class, it seemed to him that he was studying with the rest of us, as we were during the earlier stage of our course. Talking to him about it during our weekends, when we met with each other in battle or socially, we decided that he was mostly seeing recordings of us, from Neto's viewpoint. Mostly, but not exactly. A few times, what he remembered simply never happened, as far as the rest of us were concerned. But the slip-ups were few, and somehow the computer made it all work.

Still and all, our team was never quite the same again.

During all this time, the Serbs never caught on to what was happening to their prized division. Occasionally, patrols came around, looked things over, and then went away. They always heard exactly what they wanted to hear, because that's what we told them.

Eventually, Kasia and I graduated *cum laude*, the only ones in the group to do so.

Along with our diplomas, we also received commissions in the forces of New Croatia. I made general and the others, except for Lloyd, who had yet to graduate, were made colonels.

I asked the professor how we could be commissioned without the knowledge of the New Croatian government.

"My boy, that could be a bit of a problem, I admit. On the one hand, it is traditional to commission you as I have done, if you were not already officers in your country's military. The government should simply confirm your commissions once they are properly informed of the circumstances."

"And if they don't?"

"In that unlikely circumstance, I would imagine that you would be the *de facto* owner and leader of a very powerful independent mercenary company. I don't think that the government would want that to happen. Acknowledging your commissions and paying you your salaries would be so much cheaper than any of the possible alternatives that I simply can't imagine them not doing it."

"I don't think that I'd want to be a mercenary."

"Are you really sure of that? Among other things, since you've obtained your forces at no cost other than a bit of time, the profit potential is enormous. Also, it could be a great deal of fun."

"Your definition of fun must be much different from mine, professor. But as you say, the whole situation would be most improbable."

After graduation, Kasia and I took a month's vacation still in our coffins but in real time. The group had decided that the troops could use another month's training, and Lloyd needed to finish his course. Neither Kasia nor I wanted to wait another four years before settling the Serbians' hash, and getting on with our plans for a ranch, a marriage, and a family.

Lloyd stayed in school to complete the course, studying alongside of electronic copies of the other five of us, just as we were for the last five years in school. It was weird to think of him studying with me, but me not in there studying with him.

The poor kid was living in a totally faked environment. The professor said that he would learn better that way, so that's how they did it.

I can't help wondering what would have happened if he'd done something that couldn't be fit in with everybody else's reality. What if he developed an affair with Maria, for example, and she enthusiastically went along with it? What would Conan think about the whole thing?

But apparently, no such thing happened, so it doesn't matter.

Or did it happen, but nobody knew about it?

If a tree falls in the forest, and . . . Oh, to hell with it!

Conan and Maria elected to stay in school and pick up multiple doctorates. They rarely saw Lloyd there.

For reasons of his own, which I never asked about, Mirko opted for real time in Dream World the same way that Kasia and I did.

Our timing was fortunate, because two days before we had figured to declare the initial training period to be at an end, and to start planning to head out to war on our own, orders came from the Serbian Grand Command to the people that we were impersonating. We were to report immediately to the staging area at Beach Head.

CHAPTER TWENTY-FOUR
PRELUDE TO BATTLE

I called an immediate meeting of the general staff, that is to say, the professor, my five schoolmates, and me. We met where we always did every Saturday before battle—in our "war room." It was a big place with intelligent wall screens, smart communications gear, and more three-dimensional graphics than any six old-time science-fiction movies you've ever seen, all grouped around a huge round table.

Anything there could and would change just by thinking of what you wanted different, or by itself, to display whatever it thought you might want. I mean, if you were talking about World War II fighter planes, there would suddenly be a precise model of a Spitfire Mark IX on the table in front of you, and a combat ready ME-109 all set to climb into and fly, right behind you.

The rules there were such that while in it, anyone could make any change he or she wanted, even to other people in the room. This required a certain amount of discipline on the part of the group, and by general consent, practical jokes were definitely *out*.

At present, there was an accurate model of the enemy camp at Beach Head on the table, and maps of our valley and the intervening terrain on two of the screens. The rest of the walls were done up with stands of ancient armor, mounted weapons, and battle flags, just to give the place a martial flair.

After what had been to us more than eight years of preparation, we all had an incredibly electric feeling of *this is it!*

We were all so excited that the professor insisted that we go back to Combat Speed to give us time to cool down.

The wall screens began to show our division moving out of the desert valley where we had stayed for so long, moving with incredible slowness.

Professor Cee then had a waiter in full Scottish regalia give us each a stiff glass of scotch while a platoon of Scots pipers filed in.

"Confusion to the enemy!" he shouted, and threw his glass into a fireplace that appeared just in time to catch the shards.

"Damn their eyes!" "Their parents were brothers!" and "But I don't *like* scotch!" came from the rest of us, along with a half dozen more flying glasses.

Then, as we sat back down, the platoon of pipers let loose, and we stood it for at least thirty-five seconds before I decided that I had better take control of the proceedings.

"Cut!" I shouted above the din, and things suddenly got quiet. "Better. Now delete the bartender, the fireplace, and the Black Watch."

All of which promptly blinked out.

I looked about me. Kasia and Mirko were nodding to me, signaling that I was doing the right thing, but the others looked disappointed that the party was ending before it had had time to get off the ground.

"Four nays, two ayes, and since I'm the general, the ayes have it," I said.

I had us all blink from casual clothes into class-A uniforms, simple, dark green outfits devoid of decorations except for insignia of rank—a silver star for me and gold eagles for everybody else—to help get them all in the right mindset.

"Professor, I think it's time for you to give us a situation report," I said. "I won't ask you why you thought this was an appropriate occasion for a beer bust."

"Scotch, my dear boy. Scotch," he said, looking awkward without his usual tweeds. "And you're right. Beer would have been totally inappropriate. I did it simply because you all were entirely too excited to pay proper attention to any report I might make, because we have already made all the physical preparations that we possibly can, and because we have days of subjective time to rationally decide what to do. There's no point in rushing things."

"Well, I think that there is," I said. "None of us, including you, has ever managed a real war before, and I want all the time I can get. For starters, I want you to bring the rest of us up to speed with regards to what has been happening in the real world."

The professor outwardly accepted my authority without further question, but I could tell that his heart wasn't in it. He had been top dog around here for over eight years, and stepping down wasn't easy for him. He stood stiffly and started briefing us.

While we had been studying, the Combat Control Computer, using the persona of the dead Serbian general, had been getting regular updates on the course of the war. He said he hadn't told us about it because he felt that such information would only detract from our studies. Now, however, it would be appropriate to give us an update on what was happening.

This "the boss man knows what's best for all his loving children" attitude annoyed the hell out of me. I was in command of this division, and I would be damned if I was going to let some machine decide what I should or should not know!

"Damnit! Professor, or Combat Control Computer, or whatever you want to be called, there was no excuse for keeping us in the dark, at least for the last real time month, anyway. It is about time that we settled up just who is in charge around here. Now, I am a human and a general, these people are my colonels, and you are just a machine that was designed to assist me in commanding my forces! Have you got that?"

"Why, of course, sir. You are in complete command, and have been since your course of training ended. How could it possibly be otherwise?"

"Then where do you get off by keeping information about the war from me and my colonels?"

"But I wasn't, sir. In fact, I just offered to provide you with that information."

"You should have told us sooner."

"But you gave me no such orders, sir. To have volunteered it sooner would have accomplished nothing but spoiling your vacation."

I fumed a bit, mostly because he was right. I hadn't ordered anybody to do anything, a habit I would have to change.

I thought about having the computer create another, more subordinate character, and of using him in the place of Professor Cee, but decided against it. I wasn't sure what it would do to the old man's persona program. Would the machine simply rewrite his old program? Would that mean that the old persona would die? And anyway, despite it all, I had become very fond of the pompous bastard.

Still, if I was going to effectively run our division, I had to make sure that there wasn't any doubt in anyone's mind who was boss around here. I couldn't let the professor off scot free.

"Spoiling a vacation is a trivial excuse for losing a war! Now give me the military situation, and keep me completely updated from now on!"

"Yes, sir."

According to the professor, the war was stalemated, or at least at a temporary lull, and much of the Serbian army was standing down.

At Beach Head, they had two divisions of modern armor from New Kashubia, but one of them was empty, with the troops home on leave.

Nearby, there was a concentration camp containing over eleven thousand displaced civilians, mostly Croatians, with a sprinkling of ten other minority groups.

There were nine divisions of Serbian infantry there as well, intended to function as occupation troops once their victory was assured, but it was Saturday night, they thought that there was no enemy within four hundred kilometers, and most of the troops were drunk. The Serbian Combat Control Computer wasn't even manned! The Serbian generals were actually throwing a party to which the six of us had been invited!

My staff and I exchanged incredulous grins. Such

incompetence on the part of the enemy was surely too good to be true.

In the course of getting the locations of where we were to station our division, our computer had managed to get the precise position of every single enemy unit.

This wasn't going to be a conventional battle. It was going to be Pearl Harbor, the Battle of Little Big Horn, and the Great Mariana Turkey Shoot rolled up in one!

"It has *got* to be a trap!" Colonel "Conan" Birach said, "This kind of a gift from Heaven does not come to mortal men more than once in a century, so it is not likely to be coming now to poor sinners like us. We must open fire with everything we have got as soon as we can possibly be sure of getting them all on the first salvo. Otherwise, we go to our certain deaths!"

"You are too pessimistic, Conan," Colonel Garczegoz, my loving Kasia, said. "It is a typical trait of the sadly aged. I think that if we play this situation right, we might be able to accomplish much more than simple destruction, and do it with far less loss of life."

"Young lady, pessimism has high survival value. The reason why so many mature people are pessimistic is that you bright-eyed optimists all tend to die young. And what's so bad about death and destruction anyway, so long as it is visited solely on the enemy? After all, that's what armies are for!"

"Armies exist to further the political ends of their governments. If killing is absolutely necessary to achieve those ends, so be it. But if people are killed without absolute need, I call it murder and ammunition wasted!" My lovely Kasia was warming up to a knock-down argument, but she never needed my help with this sort of thing.

We were all old friends, who understood that we could debate, argue, or scream at the top of our lungs without changing the basic respect we all held for each other. As general, moderator, and judge of the last court of appeals, my job was to sit back and wait for the truth to eventually emerge. If I took sides too early, I might suppress some of the ideas that would otherwise come out.

"So just what do you know about the politics of New Croatia, Kasia?" Colonel Buich said.

Maria often sided with Conan in the Saturday morning
debates, not so much because she lived with the guy but
because they thought so much alike. Conan wouldn't talk
about why he hated the Serbs so much, but hate them he
thoroughly did.

In Maria's case, she had been captured by the Serbs while
she had been teaching an eighth grade girls' gymnastic class.
The Serbs did not rape Maria, but they'd done some very
ugly things to the young girls in her care.

"None of us here know what the politicians are doing.
We've been out of touch with our country's forces for
months," Maria continued. "And they don't even know we
exist! So don't you dare talk about 'political ends.' Our job,
which all of us Croatians here volunteered for, is to kill
as many of those damn Serbians as we possibly can before
the war ends."

"A nice bit of Freudian slip you have showing there,
Maria dear! You see the war as an excuse to kill Serbians,
rather than the killing of Serbians being necessary as a way
to end the war!" Kasia said.

That momentarily shut Maria up, but Colonel Lloyd
Tomlinson came quickly to her aid.

"You know our history as well as anybody, Kasia. Any
Serbians who live through this war will just live to be killed
or killing in the next one! Better to get the job done now!"

Colonel Mirko Jubec stood and waited for everyone to
pay attention to him. They quieted down quickly because
he didn't speak often, but what he said when he did talk
was always worth hearing.

"If we go in with all guns blazing, we will kill most of
the civilians in the concentration camp. Do we *want* to do
that? Can we *afford* to do that?"

Then Mirko sat down, and a few moments went by
before Kasia stood up.

"An excellent point, Mirko. Also, we don't really know
how badly off our own side is, but we know that they are
not actively attacking the Serbs just now. I am fairly certain that they would not turn their noses up at two more
armored divisions besides our own, especially if they were
cost free. I think we can steal those divisions for them! I
think that we can rescue the people in the concentration

camp and turn many of them into soldiers. As to the Serbian infantry, once their armor is gone and their communications are in our hands, capturing them shouldn't be too difficult."

"I'm worried about the civilians too, Kasia. But if we try to be too clever about all this, we could end up losing the civilians, losing the battle, and losing our own lives as well," Maria said. "We are fighting a war, and we can't let ourselves get too squeamish."

I sat back and waited for some sort of consensus to evolve.

It didn't.

After the debate had gone on for more than three hours, it settled in pretty much as I had suspected. Kasia and Mirko favored a limited attack that would destroy the enemy computer and general staff, but capture everything else. Lloyd, Conan, and Maria wanted to destroy everything and kill everybody who wrote home in Cyrillic, while trying to miss the civilians as much as possible.

When they started to repeat themselves, I told each group to take a three-hour break and to come back with some solid battle plans.

CHAPTER TWENTY-FIVE
BATTLE PLANS

On the wall screens around us, slowly, smoothly, our forces were taking up combat convoy positions. The slowness was only apparent because our army was moving in the real world and had to move in real time. We were at Combat Speed, fifty times faster.

Back in history, it often took weeks, even months, for an army to go from a training situation to full combat readiness. With our personnel and machines, we were able to start moving in seconds.

The Combat Control Computer—containing all present company—was near the center of the column and surrounded by the other supply trucks. The artillery took up rolling positions around us, and was itself surrounded by our ten thousand tanks. By the time we were completely deployed, our "column" would be twelve kilometers wide and thirty-five long.

I blinked over to one of my favorite restaurants in town, and everyone there acted as though this was the ordinary way of doing things. I ate an excellent meal a bit too quickly, and blinked back with a heavy feeling in my stomach.

Then I spent the next two and a half hours studying the military situation, trying to work out a battle plan of my own.

Maybe it was nerves, but a simple, straight-forward way of attaining all of Kasia's objectives safely wouldn't gel in my brain.

Yet Conan's plan of blowing hell out of everything was definitely out unless all else failed. There just wasn't any way to take out a heavily armored enemy standing next to defenseless civilians without killing the civilians too. Rail guns were just too powerful. Conan's was a worst-case backup plan at best.

Kasia was the first one back, and since we were alone, she just naturally sat on my lap.

"You got it all figured out, love?" I asked.

"We think so. There are one or two rough patches left, but I think you'll like it."

"I hope so. I like your objectives, but I wasn't able to come up with a way of doing it that I liked enough to try."

"Well, we did always agree that I was the smart one," she said, giving me a quick kiss and getting up. The others were entering the room.

"So how are we to get a fair hearing when the judge is snuggling up with the opposition?" Conan joked.

"Because whatever we decide to do, my only body is really in a coffin two feet away from yours, and if you think that I would let the bunch of us, and mainly me, get killed just to butter up my one true love, you're stupider than I look. Especially when she doesn't need any buttering up. So. We're all here. You have the floor. Use it. Or are you going to make your lovely better half do it for you?"

"Hmmm . . . Using my better half to do it on the floor? An attractive thought, but I don't think I could get her to do it on the floor in public, so we'll put it off until later. You probably want to hear about how we're going to fight the battle, anyhow."

"True. We'll catch the raree show later. For now, talk about the battle," I said.

His plan was straightforward. We would cruise into the Serbian camp in a manner that looked casual but actually put every one of our tanks into a precisely prearranged position, shown on one of the big wall screens. The enemy Combat Control Computer, the communications building, and the officer's club would be simultaneously destroyed by preassigned tanks.

Fifty milliseconds later, every enemy tank would be simultaneously destroyed in the same manner, followed closely by everything else, including the tunnel to New Serbia and the local boom town where most of the Serbian troops were watering. The entire battle was scheduled to last just under eight seconds, worst case.

At no time did any rail gun fire get closer than two hundred meters from the concentration camp, but it still looked fishy to me. Two hundred meters was fairly safe for an unarmored human when one rail gun opened fire, but ten thousand?

I turned to the professor. "Compute the radiation dosage, blast damage, and chemical poisoning for each person in the concentration camp. Compute the casualties and total number of civilian deaths that are likely to occur if we carry out this attack."

"It will take me a few minutes," the professor said.

This surprised me. Up until now, his answers had always been instantaneous.

"Conan. You never asked him this question when you were planning your attack, did you?" I asked.

"Not exactly. But I knew that a rail gun was safe at two hundred meters, and . . . "

"Bullshit! You're not that stupid! You just didn't *want* to ask!"

Conan started to make a loud reply when the professor stood up.

"Assuming that all the internees are on the surface, and not dug in, I'm sorry to say that casualties and deaths are the same. That is to say, one hundred percent of them would die from thermal radiation alone. The same could be said for blast shock, chemical poisoning, and ionizing radiation. The plan requires that a quite sizable amount of energy be dissipated in a relatively small area over a very short time. A firestorm is almost certain to be generated, and there would be many casualties even among our own troops, even if the enemy never got off a shot, which is most unlikely. I must say that I was surprised at the results myself and double-checked all of my calculations. How could you possibly guess the results, my dear boy?"

"Human intuition, professor. Conan, we will label your proposal 'plan Z.' Kasia, you're up."

I knew that Kasia would be speaking for her team since

Mirko hated public speaking, even in front of a small group of old friends. Kasia started in and held our attention for the next hour.

In the end, I said, "I like it, but it's far from perfect. We will commit to it to the extent of getting the eight X-ray equipped tunneling tanks far out ahead of the mass of our forces. We'll call them 'Forward Scouts,' if anybody asks. See to it, professor.

"It's getting late, but we will reconvene at ten, tomorrow morning subjective. Computer, put Kasia's proposal in writing, with suitable graphics, and put a copy of it on each of our desks. I want each of us to have a critique of Kasia's proposal ready in the morning. And by 'each of us' I include the professor, Kasia, Mirko, and myself. That's all for now. Get a good night's sleep."

I don't think any of us did. I was up working until five in my office, and the bed was empty when I got there. Kasia's office light was on, but after eight years of living with the lady, I knew better than to disturb her when she was busy. I was too tired to accomplish much, anyway.

We were all bright-eyed and bushy-tailed at ten, but I suspect that some computer enhancement was involved.

In subjective time, we had until seven o'clock tomorrow evening to agree on a plan. It would also be seven o'clock local real time, when we would drive into the enemy camp. This was not by accident, but by a convention we had decided on years ago, and the computer had arranged our subjective "start" time to make it all work out.

We went over Conan's critique first, then Mirko's, and Maria's, before we broke for lunch. Lloyd got his digs in on a full stomach, followed by Kasia's new thoughts, the professor's, and finally mine.

Actually, I didn't have much to contribute, as it turned out, since almost all of my points had already been covered by someone else. And the professor had even less, since he, as the computer, had already talked it over with each of us as we worked on our critiques.

But given the fact that our lives, the lives of twelve thousand of our troops, and the lives of eleven thousand or so civilians in the concentration camp were all on the

line, well, boredom, overkill, and repetition beat the hell
out of leaving something out, losing the battle, and dying!

We reached consensus a little after midnight.

"Professor, I think that's about it. See to it that all the
troops are briefed on the plan, and make sure that each
of them knows his or her part in it. Make sure that
everyone is in the best possible shape at the time of battle.
Also, make sure that the tanks, at least, know the full
details of the modified plan Z, just in case everything screws
up and all hell breaks loose. Is there anything that I have
left out?"

"Yes, my dear boy. You should have me put the six of
you to sleep, so you'll be fresh for tomorrow's fun and
games."

"I was going to suggest that, yes."

"Well, don't suggest it. Order it. And for yourself as well."

"You heard the man. No loving tonight, gang, and to all
a good night!"

Then we all blanked out.

And woke up at six in the evening of the next day, still
sitting at the round table.

Conan looked at the clock and said, "Now that was
downright rude! We're going into battle, and you haven't
even given me time to kiss my girl good-bye properly."

I was miffed for the same reason, but didn't want to say
that to Conan.

"What for? In the modern army, she gets to go there right
next to you! Anyway, it wasn't my fault. The long sleep
was the professor's idea."

"It was *too* your fault," Maria said. "You forgot to tell
him when to wake us up."

"Damn straight. Come on, woman. We've still got time
for a quickie," Conan said.

"Hold on!" I said. "Professor, does anything need doing
in the next half hour?"

"Nothing but breakfast, my dear boy. Everything else is
right on schedule."

"Right. Take a thirty-minute breakfast break, everyone."

Conan, Maria, and Lloyd blinked out. Lloyd was having
an affair with a girl from town, so I suppose that he really
was leaving her behind, in some sort of a way.

"Professor, why did you wait so long before waking us, dammit?"

"If I'd woken you at eight in the morning, you would all be in a nervous frazzle by now. Trust me, my dear boy. Mother knows best."

I just glared at him for a bit, then said, "I order you to never call me 'my dear boy' again."

"You're getting frazzled already," Kasia said. "Come on, time's a wasting."

And suddenly, we were home again. I guess she figured on having breakfast in bed.

CHAPTER TWENTY-SIX
A BATTLE, OF SORTS

At seven, we were all at our places in the war room, the digger team was approaching the enemy gates, and our forward units were just coming into sight of the Serbian base at Beach Head, on the horizon.

Our scouting tanks had encountered no enemy units on the whole trip in, which was passing strange. They had no deep patrols going into the deserts surrounding their base, and seemed to be depending for security solely on radar and visual observation from Beach Head. Even at that, their radar coverage was sporadic and their visual observation could not have been of much use, since with the planet's small axial tilt, the summer days were not much longer than those of winter, and the sun was already setting.

"I simply can not imagine a modern army acting so incompetently. After all, their general and his staff had to have gone through the same course that we did," I said to the professor.

"Doubtless true, my good boy. But a quality product requires not only good workmanship, but good raw materials as well. Now, you proved your basic worth by 'liberating' this division in the first place, and then by allowing me to select the very best potential colonels from the large available pool. Serbian selection methods are more traditional, with the accomplishments of one's ancestors being more important than personal ability."

"Garbage in, garbage out," Lloyd said.

I grunted.

"There's another reason for the way the Serbs do things," Maria said. "We Croatians have only a weak military tradition, and you Kashubians have none at all. When the professor taught us a way to do things, we didn't fight him. At most, we worked harder at being creative, of coming up with new tactics to fit our new weapons. But the Serbians have been strongly militaristic for the last six centuries. Some of their families have contributed their sons to the army for twenty generations. Their children have grown up hearing the war stories of their ancestors. They've grown up knowing the way things are done, and no mere machine is going to tell them differently."

"An interesting thought," I said.

"She's right," Conan said. "Consider the way draftees have almost always made better soldiers than volunteers. The way ninety-day wonders generally make better combat leaders than regular officers."

"It still isn't enough. Traditions don't make you stupid," I said.

"I guess you've never met a peasant," Maria said.

"Maybe they're not being stupid," Kasia said. "Maybe they just know that when the enemy is far away, the smart thing to do is to relax and build up your strength, that too much concern with security at the wrong time can be counter productive."

"But their enemy is *not* far away," I said.

"That's not being stupid. That's being misinformed," Lloyd said.

"Whatever. Keep your eyes open, gang."

Despite all that was said, I knew that the Serbs *had* to have something up their sleeves, something that we were missing.

But what?

The tension was getting to me in the stomach, and an antiacid tablet appeared on the table next to my water glass. I downed it, thinking that it would have made a lot more sense for the computer to simply have not given me an acid stomach in the first place.

The eight tanks assigned to the task of tunneling under

the Serbians were approaching the base's perimeter, timed to enter underground at the same time as the first of our surface units. The noise of our arrival would cover any slight sound that the tunnelers might make.

Everything was going so smoothly that there was nothing to do but wait.

Combat Speed is wonderful when things are popping faster than you can think, but when you are sitting there waiting and trying not to chew off your knuckles along with your fingernails, it can be a major drag.

I found myself almost wishing that some problem would crop up, just to have something to do.

As we approached the gate of the base, we got a message from the Serbian general who thought he was our commander, welcoming us and telling us to hurry up, since the party was already going strong. I had the professor answer for us, since for months he had been impersonating the Serbian officers we'd killed, saying we'd be along as soon as possible.

Then we simply drove through the gate, past the single guard, and proceeded to our assigned parking spots.

I was beginning to think that now would be a good time to pass the Scotch around, since my nerves certainly needed it, but I didn't do it.

I just sat there, trying to look like the calm, confident leader that I wasn't, to keep up the morale of the others.

They all *looked* calm enough. Probably, they were faking it just to keep *my* morale up.

The Serbians had an almost all-male army, and most of those in the lower ranks were fairly young.

After parking their tanks and guns, some ten percent of our forces got out of their machines. They were all young, physically fit men who thought that they could fake a Serbian accent reasonably well. In the fading twilight, they washed, shaved, and smeared themselves with that combination skin dye and suntan lotion.

They set their squidskin uniforms for Serbian colors and insignia, and then hit a snag. When the Serbs issued the survival kits three months ago, they hadn't bothered with making sure that things fit.

There was a fair amount of trading among them, trying to get uniforms that fit properly. Then they tried out their earphones, which linked them with the professor, and he was eventually able to sort things out. The fit of our young men's uniforms was soon good enough to permit them to impersonate the enemy reasonably well.

Then our men got back into their tanks and guns, but did not refill their coffins with fluid. This kept them dry and ready to move out, but still protected in case we had to go to plan Z.

"I wish I could join them," Conan said.

"You're not alone in that," Kasia answered.

"Unfortunately, neither one of you even remotely fits the appearance required in the real world," I said. "Kasia, you don't even speak the right language."

"I know. But that doesn't mean that I have to stop wishing. Sitting and doing nothing is driving me out of my mind."

"I know the feeling," I said. "Professor, this waiting is getting on all of our nerves. I want you to change our time scale to, say, twice real time. But take us all back up to Combat Speed the instant anything happens. And I do mean *anything*."

"Ah, the impatience of youth. But as you wish, Mickolai."

We felt no change, but motion on the screens speeded up.

"You should have said, 'Ah, the impatience of hydrocarbon-based humans,' since even us old farts are thoroughly sick of this peculiar combination of boredom and tension," Conan said.

"I thought of saying something like that, my boy, but I feared being called a racist."

"Nah," Lloyd said. "If you believe that machines are superior to humans, you're not a racist. You're a machinist!"

The rest of us studiously ignored him.

As soon as we were parked, our tanks had released some of their drones, to tie us together with optical fibers. In stationary and fairly permanent positions such as those we had assumed, it was customary to run these fragile cables underground, where they were less likely to be damaged. We still retained communications through our comlasers, of course, but in any military situation, redundancy is always desirable.

Within a few minutes, Serbian drones came up and tied us into the base communications net, for which we formally thanked them. This let us talk to the other Combat Control Computer, and to the Serbian generals, but not directly with all of their forces. At the same time, they could only communicate to our forces through us.

This was because of a point of military etiquette. According to the lights of the Serbian command, my colonels and I still commanded our division, and would continue to do so until we were formally relieved of our command. The ceremony to demote us down to being a mere backup for the other computer and staff was not scheduled to take place until noon tomorrow. Until then, it would be impolite of them to talk directly to any of our people without going through us first.

Not that the Serbians had any interest in talking to our troops, anyway, since to them, our people were all just enemy prisoners of war, but there it was.

We, however, had a great deal of interest in talking to their tanks, guns, and personnel. You have to be able to talk to the nice people if you are going to lie to them successfully.

Shortly after the Serbian drones went home, although at the time it seemed to us to be eons, drones from the tanks we sent in underground hooked us up to the lines they had tapped into while crawling under the enemy Combat Control Computer. We could now hear everything that it heard or said. We were hooked up in parallel to it, and could transmit as well as receive.

The beam of an X-ray laser at full power heats the air it travels through sufficiently to make it white hot, and visible from hundreds of kilometers away. But according to our calculations, at eight percent of full power, the beam should not be noticeable without special instrumentation.

True, every enemy tank contained and regularly used just such special instrumentation, but the Serbian tanks were parked far away from their Combat Control Computer, with lots of trucks and guns in between. We hoped it would be enough.

Further computations said that four tanks, at eight percent power and at a range of two meters, should be able to fry the brains out of a Combat Control Computer in about three hundred twenty microseconds, which we deemed to be sufficient.

Now, admittedly, all this was purely theoretical. We didn't have a spare Combat Control Computer to run any tests on, even if we could have gotten it to volunteer. But it was the best we could come up with, and we still had plan Z ready as a backup.

Four other tanks, also using X-ray lasers at low power and at short range, were to do a similar job of murder on the Serbian command, currently partying down at the huge officers' club.

Once all eight tanks were in position underground, I gave the professor a few more minutes to be sure that he could imitate his opponent perfectly.

"I'm as ready as I'll ever be, my fine boy."

"Fire!"

The lasers mounted above each of our eight buried tanks exploded up through the desert sand and fired, while the professor filled the enemy's communications net with a loud burst of static. We gave their computer three full seconds of cooking, just to make sure, and the officers' club was raked for a whole minute.

We heard a few dozen thumps, a short scream, and the crash of a tray of glassware that sounded from the club, and then all was silent. The Serbian Combat Operations Computer made not a sound in dying. Neither target looked a bit different being dead, except that they were both a bit warmer. Fortunately, nobody but us had an infrared scanner on them.

We waited for two minutes and nothing moved.

I ordered the tanks to sink back down into the desert sand, I had twelve hundred young men get out of the safety of their armored machines, and I prayed.

Our troops straggled forward in the outwardly undisciplined fashion of modern troops. These were not the brainless strutting marionettes that passed for soldiers in the past. These were all highly trained technicians.

The problem was that they were not highly trained *as infantry*.

Indeed, none of them had walked a single step for three months before this day. That they could walk at all was a tribute to the exercise routines done inside their coffins. The few times they'd used their rifles had been in simulations, and we could only hope that the enemies they went up against were as poorly trained as they were. The only thing that gave me any confidence in our plan was that every one of our men was using the earphone from his survival kit. They were each in constant contact with the professor.

The professor contacted the Serbian guards at the gates, the guards at the concentration camp, and the guards at the Serbian infantry barracks, telling them that the new troops, being junior, would be taking over their duties so that they could take the night off.

Most of the Serbians were happy about the change of plans and felt it unwise to rock any boats. In any military, nice things sometimes happen; the "Fairy Godmother Department" occasionally comes through.

Some of the guards were cautious, or suspicious, or paranoid, and called in to confirm these new orders. But whoever they tried to call, they got through to the professor, who faked it from there. He told them privately that the new troops had screwed up and were being given guard duty as a punishment detail. This was a story that any trooper could believe, and only two men, sergeants both, caused any trouble.

These two came down with mild cases of broken necks and were officially put on sick leave.

A team of our guards went to the mouth of the tunnel that went back all the way to Serbia, and relieved the small detachment stationed there. After the Serbs had left, our men were reinforced with two dozen tanks, just in case something unexpected happened.

If anything did come in from New Serbia, our troops were to either let them go about their business, detain them, or kill them, as the case seemed to require, with the professor monitoring all decisions.

Another of our teams went to the officers' club, checked

out the piles of dead bodies inside, and posted guard around it.

There were some forty-five hundred dead people inside the huge club, far more than I had expected. I had seen the place on our maps, but had assumed that they had shown not the size of the building but the size of the lot it was on.

Modern armored troops only have a tiny percentage of their personnel commissioned, and I had expected that all the Serbian forces would be organized in this fashion.

The truth was that I had never asked, so the professor never told me.

Yes, their armored troops had a command structure like ours, but their infantry, set up for police and garrison duty, had a hierarchy that was almost as stupidly top heavy as that of Hitler's army. Then, too, most of the Serbs had brought their wives or girlfriends along with them to the party.

And there were cooks, waiters, entertainers, waitresses, bus boys, bartenders, musicians, and other hangers-on there as well, not one of whom really deserved to die.

I felt rotten about the situation, but it was too late to do anything about it.

Damn it, it wasn't like they had been invited here. I never told them to invade somebody else's country in the first place.

I had the professor give us a quick replay of the scene of a few months ago, where the Serbians were raping the refugees before putting them into tanks. I worked at getting angry all over again, and some of my guilty feelings evaporated. Not all, but some.

The Croatians on the general staff didn't act the least bit downhearted. Even Mirko laughed on seeing the carnage we'd caused, and Conan was positively ecstatic.

It didn't seem to bother the troops that we had guarding the club, either, except that some of the men regretted the waste of so many attractive women. Not so much their deaths, since they seemed to all be Serbians, but the fact that we could have found better uses for them. They even made jokes about it.

The situation disgusted me, but there was nothing that I could do about it.

I could control my troop's actions, but not their attitudes. Hates that are centuries old never seem to go away.

Then the long wait continued. The civilians in the concentration camp barely noticed the change in guards and went to sleep shortly after dark, which was fine. We couldn't be sure what their reaction to being freed would be, and we didn't want them making any noise until the rest of the camp was secured.

Another two thousand of our own troops decanted themselves, cleaned up, and dressed in Serbian colors. Soon, they were among the empty tanks and guns of the division that was on leave.

Using Serbian codes, the professor told each war machine that it was to be given some electronic maintenance, and machines are very good at obeying orders.

As a Croatian troop came to each of them, it obligingly opened up, and the memory module was removed, rendering the machine close to comatose, barely able to close itself back up as ordered.

Some twelve thousand memory modules were brought back to our division's area, to be stacked neatly awaiting reprogramming.

Occasionally, through the night, people on one errand or another approached the officers' club. These people were quietly detained when possible, or quietly killed when all else failed, and in either case taken to an empty barracks that had been found in the concentration camp.

Serbian infantrymen returning from town were simply allowed to go back to their barracks. Many were warned to get a good night's sleep, since they had a long walk ahead of them in the morning.

CHAPTER TWENTY-SEVEN
MORE LIES, MURDER, AND A WEDDING

Two hours before dawn, the Serbian armored division, the one that had a full complement of troops, was mobilized, courtesy of the professor.

They drove off into the desert north of the base and began an elaborately choreographed series of maneuvers and war games. Tomorrow we would worry about just what to do with them. For today, there were other problems.

An hour before dawn, the senior sergeants of every Serbian infantry company were phoned by what they thought were their officers. The general staff had decided that the troops were getting entirely too soft, and that a thirty-kilometer march on Sunday morning was just the thing to toughen them up.

They would have their men fall out at dawn, with full field packs and personal weapons. Heavy, antiarmor weapons could be left behind, but rifles were required.

They would start immediately, escorted by a few tanks, and march north until ordered to stop. Breakfast would be served on the road at eight. Any questions?

Of course, there were thousands of questions, and even more complaints, but the professor was adamant, and by and large, orders were obeyed.

Bleary-eyed, hung over, and profoundly unhappy, almost a hundred thousand Serbian troops marched out into the desert. Some of them even marched in step. I noticed that they all wore black uniforms, and didn't feel a bit sorry for them.

In a few hours, automatic trucks caught up with the straggling columns, and unloaded just enough field rations, bottled water, and medical kits. After an hour's rest break, the black-shirted troops were ordered to continue the march.

Many of them noticed that their officers were not with them, and complained loudly about this flagrant abuse of rank, but it got them nowhere. The sweating sergeants yelled, and the troops slogged onwards.

Meanwhile, back at Beach Head, the Croatians were busy.

The Serbian infantry camp was completely searched and some six thousand men, sick or malingering, were arrested.

The officers' housing area was likewise combed over, and another nine thousand people, mostly women, children, and servants were taken into custody.

Then the rest of the huge Serbian base had to be searched, and another thousand people, from janitors to mistresses, were interned.

And finally, the inmates of the concentration camp were informed of what we had done. Most of them were wildly enthusiastic, but a surprising number of them simply couldn't believe that they were free.

They were told that they were liberated, but not out of danger. They were still far behind enemy lines, but that we had a plan to get them back to the rest of New Croatia. They were to meet with us at four in the afternoon on the parade ground, and everything would be explained to them then.

In the meantime, we had other uses for the concentration camp, and since they were obviously in need of clothing and other necessities, they were welcome to loot the Serbian Officers' Housing Area to satisfy those needs. Additional food and medical help would be available at the chow halls and the base hospital.

The prospect of loot quickly motivated the most down-hearted of them, and the camp was soon emptied.

It was soon filled again, with Serbians of various sizes, ages, and sexes. That is to say, with all those Serbs who were neither dead nor out obeying orders in the desert.

There were a small number of Serbian officers who had escaped the carnage at the officers' club, and with my permission, the professor put one of them in charge of the people in the concentration camp. He was given a phone to request whatever he needed, and the camp was surrounded by thirty of our tanks to keep people from escaping. Since we only had one tank with antipersonnel weapons, this meant that any escape attempt would have to be met with rail gun fire, and the death toll would be huge. The officer seemed to be the sort who would do the sensible thing and simply keep order in the camp.

Conan was convinced that most of the former internees could be talked into joining the Croatian forces, or at least getting into a tank as the safest and easiest transportation back to our own lines.

A check with the computers in the enemy warehouses showed that there were plenty of helmets and spinal inductors around, so we put the program into action.

Since Conan was so enthused with the program I put him in charge of it. We'd all agreed that he would have to go out and talk to the people in person. Words coming out of a speaker on a war machine just wouldn't have the right effect.

Conan spent the early afternoon cleaning up and getting ready for his four o'clock speech.

"It's strange," Kasia said as we watched the speech on the display screen in the war room. The computer was translating it into Kashubian subtitles for our benefit. "Intellectually, I know that that's Conan out there, but what I see is a stranger, an old man who is talking in a language that I don't understand."

"I think that we've been spoiled by Dream World, love. It makes me worry if we will have much trouble getting used to the real world again."

"Well, if it slows down your worrying about the present situation, it's all for the better. We'll make it."

"You always were the smart one."

At six, I found that the Serbian infantry was thirty-five kilometers from the base. I ordered them to bivouac there, and automatic trucks delivered enough supplies to last them the night. They still thought that they were getting orders from their own officers, relayed to their earphones from the dozen tanks we had accompanying them.

Most of the command group had to stay in the Combat Control Computer, to handle any emergencies that might come up. We'd seen what happened to the Serbians when they'd left their computer unattended.

Maria had gone out to reacquaint herself with Conan, I suppose to see if they still liked each other in their real bodies. She was pleasantly surprised to find that she was in much better shape now than when she had first climbed into her tank. Her face still looked forty, but her body was outstanding, almost as nice as the one she wore in Dream World. Three months of scientifically optimized physical training had worked wonders on her.

But if we couldn't do the actual work of tanking the new volunteers, we now had twelve thousand trained troops and war machines to do the grunt work for us. Soon, they were talking the people from the concentration camp into going along with our program, reprogramming the memories of the Serbian tanks, and getting the people installed in them. The job was done by midnight, by resorting to making another twelve thousand Agnieshkas and Evas. It would have taken the Combat Control Computer a week to rewrite our new division back to virgins, and sitting here for an entire week would have been pushing our luck.

In the end, only a few hundred of the former inmates insisted on being foolish enough to try to make it out in the manually operated trucks and busses that we'd found in the back of the truck park. It was just as well, since the concentration camp had contained over three hundred and fifty Croatian children who were too small to be fitted with the available helmets, and somebody had to take care of them.

It had been a long day, and a longer night before. Everyone who wasn't on guard duty sacked out until eight in the morning.

By the time we awoke, the Serbian infantry was marching through the sand again, trying to get to the trucks that held their breakfast.

The lunch trucks would be fifteen kilometers even farther south, and soon the black shirts would be so far out

into the desert that even if they discovered that they had
been lied to and swindled, they would be too far from the
base to walk back without the supplies that we wouldn't
be giving them.

The Serbian armored division filled with trained soldiers
was another matter entirely. Ten thousand tanks and two
thousand guns was enough to spoil anybody's day, if they
were mad at you.

So we ordered them home, in groups of five hundred,
for Rest and Recuperation for the men, and some minor
reprogramming for the machines.

We were all ready for them when they drove in. Away
from anything that would show the drastic changes that
had been going on, five hundred groups of six people each
were all set to shave, groom, and dress the returning
heroes.

And a thousand of our tanks were ready to blow hell
out of any of them who turned out to be too intelligent.

We had the Serbian tanks come in parade order, doing
everything by the numbers. None of them objected to this
nonsense, so the glorious Serbian command must have liked
parades.

On the professor's order, five hundred coffins slid out
of five hundred tanks, five hundred Croatians pulled the
memories out of said coffins, and five hundred Serbians
were marched naked at gunpoint to the concentration camp.

It all went with remarkable smoothness, with only a few
fist fights, and nobody getting shot.

The memory modules had been reprogrammed and rein-
stalled before the next band of five hundred drove in the
gate.

We went on playing the game all day, and that night,
when we were through, we had a total of three divisions
of war machines loyal to us.

We teamed each machine from our old division with two
or three like machines from our recent acquisitions, since
only half of the new ones had an observer, and none of
those were trained.

We had to leave a dozen tanks from our first division
herding the Serbian infantry around, and two hundred more
guarding the concentration camp and the base itself. All

of our guards were back in their tanks, and ordered to stay in there.

They were prepared to destroy the base if necessary, but it might prove useful to the Croatians, once they got back here, and it was on Croatian soil anyway.

Since the air waves were jammed, and the communication satellites were long gone, the only communications between Beach Head and New Serbia were by optical cables strung through the tunnel. These were all patched through the professor, and he faked all their routine communications such that they never realized what was going on.

Serbian personnel and vehicles coming in were simply interned for the duration. Those who should have returned were "delayed" for one reason or another. The professor was sure that he could keep up the game for at least two weeks, before the opposition sent in a reconnaissance in force.

We left enough supplies in the automatic warehouses to feed the infantry, the inhabitants of the local town, and the new inmates of the concentration camp for three months, and loaded everything else onto all the trucks we could find, leaving only enough to handle local transportation. For the safety of the guards we were leaving behind, we left behind absolutely no munitions that could hurt a modern tank.

We destroyed all the vehicles we could find in the town, but otherwise left it alone. They couldn't hurt us and they couldn't communicate with New Serbia, so they couldn't do much but wait around until the situation clarified itself. Almost everyone there was a Serbian anyway.

We planted a fair-sized bomb a few miles into the tunnel to Serbia, but we did not detonate it. Who knows? Maybe someday we would need a nice tunnel to New Serbia, or maybe they would try and launch another invasion through it, and we could take out that force at the same time as the tunnel.

One sour point was that we decided that we could not take the children and those refugees who wouldn't get into a tank with us back to New Croatia. The only vehicles that they could travel in were thin-skinned trucks and busses. Such things could not survive even a minor firefight, and we were going to have to battle our way through the rest of the Serbian army.

Some of them threatened to follow us, and I had to threaten to blow the first bus away if they tried it. What the adults did was up to them, if it was only themselves at stake, but they were responsible for the children, and had to keep them safe.

Before the argument was over, a few hundred of the newly inducted troops, mostly the children's relatives, decanted themselves so as to take care of the kids. I gave my permission for it. Untrained, they wouldn't have been worth much in combat, anyway.

Early in the morning, we headed west, with three divisions under us, until we passed the first chain of mountains. About then, Kasia made a wonderful discovery.

Among the people whom we had rescued from the concentration camp, and had talked into enlisting in our army, was a genuine Catholic priest!

His tank was promptly ordered back to drive adjacent to the Combat Control Computer, and Kasia, Maria, and a half dozen servants were soon getting a Dream World wedding organized.

The wedding itself had to take place in real time, since the priest's tank wasn't capable of handling Dream World at Combat Speed, but this meant that we could invite both divisions of people and their machines as well!

The priest, Father Thomas, was willing to perform the ceremony with the understanding that this was essentially a marriage by proxy, that Dream World was simply a mechanical contrivance that took the place of the telephone or radio link that had often been used before when it wasn't possible for the participants to be physically together. He would have very much preferred to stop the divisions in the desert, have everybody get out, and do the whole thing properly, but I had to veto the suggestion. We were still behind enemy lines, after all, and the Serbians had just shown us what can happen when your Combat Control Computer is empty of command personnel.

That, and missing the wedding would have broken Agnieshka's heart.

Still, while Communion wasn't possible in Dream World,

Confession certainly was, and Kasia and I both had over eight years of sins to get rid of. It took time, real time, but it had to be done.

The wedding itself was magnificent, and held in a cathedral that was bigger than anything that ever existed in the real world. It had to be, with twenty-two thousand real people attending, not to mention an additional thirty-six thousand sentient machines!

The reception afterwards was equally bodacious, with hundreds of whole cows roasting over the fires, along with I don't know how many megatons of other good things. Only in Dream World.

By the time it was all over, Kasia and I had to cut our honeymoon down to four days, and that at Combat Speed, because we were within range of the battle lines, and it was time to get back to work.

Contacting our superiors was a simple matter of sending up a series of coded radar rockets, explaining things to the Powers That Be on the Croatian side, and working out a strategy with them for taking out the Serbian units on the line.

Naturally, we saw to it that all of the Croatian units had the Serbian battle codes.

When all was ready, we advanced on the rear of the enemy battle line. The Serbs hadn't heard a word about our victory, and their loss of three armored divisions. They apparently thought that their base at Beach Head with its tunnel was still there under their control. What information they got was from our Combat Control Computer, which they thought was still their own.

With the Serbs surrounded front and back with units they couldn't tell from their own, and with their tanks and artillery blindly believing our Combat Control Computer, it wasn't a battle at all.

It was simply murder.

Indeed, we were able to get over half of the enemy equipment to surrender undamaged, after having convinced them that their observers had become traitors.

When the final accounting was made, we had retaken all occupied Croatian territory, freed forty-two thousand Croatian internees and POWs, and enriched the Croatian section of the Kashubian Expeditionary Forces by over five and a half divisions!

Then we drove home to the victory party!

The war wasn't over, of course, but from now on, it would be fought on Serbian turf, not Croatian!

My colonels and I were fêted at a dozen banquets, loaded down with medals, and even permitted to retain the ranks that we had assumed.

We were given considerable sums of money, honorary (and tax-free!) Croatian citizenship, and some major tracts of good land to go with it. Together, Kasia and I got eleven square kilometers of land as our private estate, and most of it was good for farming.

And at the urging of all concerned, Kasia and I repeated our vows, got married again, this time in the flesh.

The wedding went on for a week, with all of our relatives brought over from New Kashubia, and even Uncle Wlodzimierz was there to kiss the bride. He told me that our salesmen had just sold six divisions of empty armor to the Serbians at a price that would put them in debt for fifty years!

They even made a movie about my life.

EPILOGUE
THE RIGELLIAN INSTITUTE OF ARCHEOLOGY, 3783 A.D.

"That was quite a story, Rupert. It's easy to see why Dream World was made so illegal, throughout civilized space. To think that a man could spend more than four years of his life living a lie! How horrible!"

AUTHOR'S NOTE

A SPECIAL NOTE TO THOSE DECENT, HEROIC, AND
TRULY NOBLE FANS WHO, BESIDES BUYING THIS
PAPERBACK EDITION, ALSO SHELLED OUT THE
$21.00 TO BUY THE HARDCOVER:

THANK YOU!

Now, you will probably have noticed that something is
different here, namely that I have changed the ending. It
happened this way:

I had originally planned to have the book end, as it does
in this paperback, in a fairly upbeat way. After all, that's
the basic formula for an enjoyable adventure story. You drop
your hero (a decent person that your reader can identify
with) into a large crock of shit, and by dint of hard work,
adventurous actions, and dumb luck he works his way
upward into the light.

But this was my first book for the very nice people at
Baen Books, my contract said that I was to write 90,000
words, and I didn't yet know what I could get away with.
Finishing the story but finding myself a few pages short,
rather than going back and padding in something that I
hadn't planned to pad in, I simply continued the story on
a bit, adding a chapter into what I planned for the next
book in the series.

Anyway, I told myself, it would be nice to win an award
for something, and history proves that the best way to do

that is to write something with a sad, tragic, or futile ending. It's that, or making your hero a black, handicapped, homosexual lady who, while confined to a wheelchair, goes around rescuing Jews from the Nazis.

Well, nobody suggested that I was deserving of a Nobel Prize for Literature, but while there were no actual death threats, a lot of people said that ending a book with " . . . and then the little boy fell out of bed and discovered that it was all just a bad dream!" was a shitty stunt to pull on your readers.

And, you know, they were right. I asked Jim Baen if I could change it, and he's letting me do it, despite the added costs.

So the paperback now has one less chapter in it than the hardcover. Don't worry about it. It will be resurrected as one of the opening chapters of the sequel, providing the next large crock of shit.

Waste not, want not, after all.

—Leo Frankowski,
October 5, 1999

Amazons 'r Us

The Chicks Series, edited by Esther Friesner

Chicks in Chainmail   87682-1 ◆ $5.99   ☐

"Kudos should go to Friesner for having the guts to put together this anthology and to Baen for publishing it . . . a fabulous bunch of stories . . . they're all gems."   —Realms of Fantasy

" . . . a romp that certainly tickled this reviewer's funny bone."   —VOYA

Did You Say Chicks?!   87867-0 ◆ $5.99   ☐

Those Chicks in Chainmail are baaack—and They Are Not Amused! Sure, you're entitled to a laugh or two . . . while you're chuckling show some respect. You can start by buying this book. Pardon us for a moment . . . have to wash the bloodstains off these swords before they set. . . .

Chicks 'n Chained Males   57814-6 ◆ $6.99   ☐

Continuing a great tradition, Chicks 'n Chained Males is not what you think. Never would such as they stoop to the exploitation of those poor chained males who have suddenly found themselves under their protection and succour. No-no—these chicks are here to rescue these victims of male-abuse from any number of Fates Worse Than Death. . . . Right here. Right now.

And don't miss, also by Esther Friesner:

Wishing Season   87702-X ◆ $5.99   ☐

Available at your local bookstore. If not, fill out this coupon and send a check or money order for the cover price + $1.50 s/h to Baen Books, Dept. BA, P.O. Box 1403, Riverdale, NY 10471. Delivery can take up to 8 weeks.

Name: _____

Address: _____

_____

I have enclosed a check or money order in the amount of $ _____

DAVID WEBER

<u>**The Honor Harrington series:**</u> *(cont.)*

Field of Dishonor

Honor goes home to Manticore—and fights for her life on a battlefield she never trained for, in a private war that offers just two choices: death—or a "victory" that can end only in dishonor and the loss of all she loves....

Flag in Exile

Hounded into retirement and disgrace by political enemies, Honor Harrington has retreated to planet Grayson, where powerful men plot to reverse the changes she has brought to their world. And for their plans to succeed, Honor Harrington must die!

Honor Among Enemies

Offered a chance to end her exile and again command a ship, Honor Harrington must use a crew drawn from the dregs of the service to stop pirates who are plundering commerce. Her enemies have chosen the mission carefully, thinking that either she will stop the raiders or they will kill her . . . and either way, her enemies will win....

In Enemy Hands

After being ambushed, Honor finds herself aboard an enemy cruiser, bound for her scheduled execution. But one lesson Honor has never learned is how to give up!

Echoes of Honor

"Brilliant! Brilliant! Brilliant!"—*Anne McCaffrey*

continued

EXPLORE OUR WEB SITE